SIMON & SCHUSTER CHILDREN'S PUBLISHING

ADVANCE REVIEWER COPY

TITLE: I Will Find You Again

AUTHOR: Sarah Lyu

IMPRINT: Simon & Schuster Books for Young Readers

ON-SALE DATE: 3/14/23

ISBN: 978-1-5344-6515-2

FORMAT: hardcover

PRICE: $19.99 US/$24.99 Can.

AGES: 14 up

PAGES: 304

ALSO BY SARAH LYU

The Best Lies

SIMON & SCHUSTER BFYR

NEW YORK • LONDON • TORONTO • SYDNEY • NEW DELHI

An imprint of Simon & Schuster Children's Publishing Division
1230 Avenue of the Americas, New York, New York 10020

Interior design by Hilary Zarycky
The text for this book was set in TK.
Manufactured in the United States of America
First Edition
2 4 6 8 10 9 7 5 3 1
CIP data for this book is available from the Library of Congress.
ISBN 9781534465152
ISBN 9781534465176 (ebook)

For Gene, who showed up every day and always stayed until the end of visiting hours

PART I

1.

I'd give anything to be the girl people see when they look at me: Chase Ohara, student council president, captain of the best cross-country team in the state, and clear favorite of her teachers. Expected valedictorian, voted most likely to succeed. A future with her last name etched in gold atop skyscrapers, multimillion-dollar bonuses, Congress or the Supreme Court perhaps. Or insider trading scandals if she goes astray.

They look at me like I have this—*this power*. Like I'm in control.

What they don't know: It's 2 AM on the fifth night in a row that I haven't been able to sleep and the world feels like it's spinning away from me. I get up from bed and the ground sways.

I think about that Chase, the one people think they know. I used to feel like her, or more like her. Like I could do anything, be anything. Like life was laid out for the taking and all I had to do was reach.

Now I reach for the Altoids tin in my bag, shake it. I'm low, but not desperately so. I pop it open and drop a small pink pill onto my tongue, swallow it dry.

At my desk I wait for it to take effect, hoping for the rush, that small burst of electricity. For it to lend me its strength as I stare past my laptop screen to the printout pinned to my wall. "It's not the end of the world," my mom had told me when she found out, but she didn't know what she was talking about. "We won't tell your dad."

I told him myself on our next weekend together. Dad remained silent, but his expression said it all, and in that instant, I knew I wasn't the girl people see when they looked at me, the one who could do anything, be anything. Or at least I wasn't that person to my father—not anymore.

I slip out quietly to avoid waking Mom and my little sister, Aidan, and hit the pavement for a run. All the houses are shuttered and dark, the streetlights alone guiding me under the black sky. I like the solitude, no music, just the strike of my heel against concrete. I run three miles before my mind calms to a soft hum and it's just me and the night, the early November air cold against my skin. I'm not Chase Ohara, future power broker, but just me, a girl alone, as lost as everyone else.

But then I turn onto a bigger street and see a large grocery truck make a tight corner ahead. An image flickers into mind. It only lasts half a second, but it's mesmerizing—I can see myself taking a single misstep, my foot striking the edge of the curb at just the wrong angle.

I trip.

Fall in front of the truck.

And I'm no longer Chase Ohara, expected valedictorian, voted most likely to succeed. No longer obsessed with SATs, grades, Stanford.

That glittering future with my name atop skyscrapers, gone. This pain inside me, gone.

I let the truck fly past me, feel a blast of cold air in its wake, and I'm left unsteady on my feet. I try to push on, shake the image from my mind and force my legs to move, but at the end of mile six, my chest seizes. Hands on thighs, I can't drink in enough air to keep the bile from burning its way up.

Coughing, I collapse to the curb less than two miles from my house, head hung heavy between my knees. I walk the rest of the way back, panting the whole time.

Sometimes, I think there isn't enough air in this town. Not enough air in the world for a girl like me.

2.

A call comes later that night after I finish two essays, a Calc problem set, and a Physics lab report before finally dozing off at my desk, and I lift my head to see Jo Vestiano's name lighting up my screen with a picture of the three of us—me, Lia, and Jo, Lia's mom—all grinning, a snapshot from better days. "Listen, I'm sorry to call so late." It's almost four in the morning. "Have you heard from Lia?"

"No," I say, suddenly wide awake. "Why?"

"She's missing," she says, her voice cracking.

"What do you mean?" My breath catches.

"It's been almost three days. We don't know where she is. She's not answering her phone—she's just, she's gone." Jo's crying now, sniffing and trying to hide it. "I know the two of you . . ." She doesn't finish, leaves our breakup unsaid. I think of Hunter and wonder when she found out, if Jo called her right away. If she knows where Lia is. *Almost three days*. I have to be one of the last people to know. I try to remember if I saw her Thursday or Friday at school, but I come up empty.

Before Lia and I were together, we were best friends, a friendship that stretched back to the age of six, when my parents moved into the house across the street from hers. Back in May when she ended things, she set all that history on fire. It's been six months of being left out in the cold, watching my life through frosted windows.

"Has anyone been out to Montauk?" I ask finally.

"What?" she says. "Yes. We checked the boat. She's not there."

"Oh."

"Did she say something? About Montauk?"

"No," I say, shaking my head even though Jo can't see me. "I just thought—"

Her voice softens. "I know, hon." For a moment, she sounds like she does on TV, the way she calls everyone "hon" as she shares a family recipe or judges amateur chefs. But this isn't TV. We aren't twelve anymore, hiding behind the set, ready to surprise Jo with Christmas cookies for her holiday special. Lia is missing. Gone. "It's one of the first places we checked."

"Okay," I say weakly. After she hangs up, I open my texts, tap on Lia's name, and see a single message from three days ago.

Lia: Meet me in Montauk.

It's a refrain from our favorite movie, *Eternal Sunshine of the Spotless Mind*, a story about exes who decide to erase each other from their memories only to find one another and fall in love again. We loved that it was set in Long Island. We loved that it was about mistakes and second chances, forgiveness and hope.

Meet me in Montauk.

That was our Bat-Signal, our 911 text. *Save me*, it meant. From schoolwork, from annoying parents, from a certain sadness we shared. Those four words used to mean we'd drop everything and take the LIRR out to Montauk, walk along the water or take her family's boat out, even in bitter winter, stay until we felt better. Montauk was our place, once upon a time. It was where we fell in love. It was where I sometimes went even after Lia left me to relive memories that littered the beach: our first kiss, our first *I love you*, whispered like a thrilling confession even though we were all but certain of our shared feelings.

Our last kiss.

I remember the waves lapping at our ankles, the soft May breeze. Her hand in my hair, steadying me, lips a little cold, nose and ears pink from the sun and wind. And then she pulled away: "I can't do this anymore."

After that, we spent the months before senior year on opposite sides of the country—her remaining in Meadowlark, me at a summer program at Stanford. I'd spent that summer miserable, barely sleeping, not making friends, a zombie in classes. When I returned, Lia had become a complete stranger.

But I hadn't known that then. All I wanted was to go back to the way we were. As soon as I landed in JFK, I sent up a rescue flare in the form of a desperate text.

Me: Meet me in Montauk.

She never responded. Not to that or any other text, not to the calls or voice mails, the e-mails begging to talk. Then I saw her at school. Saw *them*. Lia and Hunter van Leeuwen, a senior transplant rumored to have been kicked out of Phillips Exeter, their hands loosely linked, all smiles and happiness. Our eyes met when Lia spotted me. Her expression hardened, I flinched. That was the day I deleted all our texts, all my hopeful, pathetic messages and over a year of our ten-year history, the year when we were in love.

When she reached out two nights ago, I thought it was a mistake. Then I thought, what's the point? It'd been too long. She waited too long.

But now Jo Vestiano's voice rings in my head: *Have you heard from Lia? She's missing.*

I close the AP Physics textbook on my desk and stick it in my backpack. Standing up, I glance at the printout on the wall, the SAT scores that, if left unimproved, would mean Stanford was out of reach. Stanford, where my dad had gotten into but couldn't afford to go, where I'm expected to attend, the next step on my way to a future with my last name atop skyscrapers, multimillion-dollar bonuses, Congress, the Supreme Court. Money and power, a life that mattered.

Meet me in Montauk.

I lace up again and head for the LIRR. They've already been there, Lia's mom said. I don't know what I think I'll find, but I know I have to go.

3.

Sophomore year, we went out to Montauk even though it was the last weekend before finals. Spring was slipping into summer, but the air still held a chill most days, especially along the water.

"Let's go," Lia said. "We'll get marshmallows and make s'mores on the boat."

"Can't. Pre-calc final on Monday."

"We'll study. Promise."

"I don't know," I said, but I was already caving.

"I'm sad." Lia had just come off a bad relationship with some girl named Jana, a music prodigy who bragged about taking private lessons with a Juilliard professor. "Come on."

I almost never said no to Lia. To save time, she drove and I studied. At the marina, we untied her family's two-bed yacht, *The Gnocchi*, and eased out into the water.

"Do you want to talk about it?" I asked as she lit a can of Sterno and tore open a bag of marshmallows. Lia loved her family's boat, and while she was allowed to take it out, she was most definitely not supposed to light open flames on it, not that rules ever stopped her.

After a pause, she said, "Did you know my parents basically

had a heart attack when you guys moved in across the street?"

"What?" Talking to Lia was like that sometimes, conversational whiplash.

"They were hoping you guys were Korean so you could educate me in the ways of my lost culture, et cetera." The Vestianos had adopted Lia when she was one year old and kept her enrolled in Korean language and history lessons until the age of fourteen, when she rioted. They took her to Seoul every other year where Jo would shoot a culinary special that put their mother-daughter relationship under the spotlight. Lia hated it. Hated the way strangers asked her to explain her Italian last name and white parents, the way her mom highlighted her "cultural heritage." In middle school, sick of having to justify her existence, she came up with a line she'd recite to anyone who asked: "I'm ethnically Korean, culturally Italian." It was her shield, a way to stop the questions, even though sometimes they'd continue.

"You know how White Meadowlark is. When you moved in, they were sure you and your sister were going to save me years of therapy just by existing in proximity. So they were devastated at your lack of Korean-ness," Lia said, rolling her eyes. "Absolutely devastated."

"Sorry to disappoint," I said, smiling. Equal parts Japanese, Vietnamese, Chinese, and Taiwanese, my sister and I must have seemed everything *but* Korean to the Vestianos. "Bad luck."

Lia laughed, spearing a marshmallow with takeout chopsticks because we'd forgotten skewers. "Bad luck," she agreed, then grew quiet before adding, "No, Chase."

"Hm?" I shielded the can of flames from the wind with my palms.

"Not bad luck." Our eyes met. "You're the best thing that's ever happened to me. Don't argue."

My lips parted in surprise but I didn't say anything.

"Good," she said with a smile. "So it's settled. Chase Ohara: officially the best thing that's ever happened to Lia Vestiano."

"Ha, ha," I said, but I was secretly pleased. "You're such a dork."

"Lia Vestiano: major dork," she said. "Has a ring to it."

"Ugh, stop it."

"Okay, okay, but seriously, you're the best," she said. "Love you." In that moment, she looked different somehow, her black hair dancing in the salt air, her smile so full of warmth, eyes intense, and a shiver slipped down my spine.

Lia always knew she liked girls. I'd kissed a boy or three at school dances and birthday parties growing up, but nothing more.

That day, shying away from her glance, I wondered.

4.

I peer into the Vestianos' boat. It's been months since we've been out here. No, correction, it's been months since *I've* been here. I think about Lia and Hunter and I have to close my eyes, shake my head. This was Lia's favorite place in the world. Of course they've been here, together.

Meet me in Montauk, she'd sent. Where else could she mean? The lobster shack by the LIRR station, the restaurant by the marina? Or Kirk Park Beach, where we once carved our initials on the large piece of driftwood that served as a makeshift bench? No, it has to be the boat. Where we roasted marshmallows and made s'mores. But there's no one here.

Pressing my forehead into the glass, I search for signs of life but find nothing. I try the door. Locked.

Over three hours on the train and a short car ride to the marina, only to find absolutely nothing. I turn, slump against the door. When I look up, I see a woman standing alone maybe fifteen feet away, cigarette in hand. She notices me—we're the only ones out here on this dreary, cold October day. I recognize her, a waitress at the bar and grill near the marina. Suddenly, I'm nervous. It's been so long and now

I'm trespassing. I should've told Jo about the text but she said they'd already searched the boat. I shouldn't have come here like this. But finally, the woman stamps out her cigarette before heading back to the restaurant without a word, and I'm all alone again.

Meet me in Montauk.

I stare at the words for a moment before placing my phone facedown. I squeeze my eyes shut. A headache works its way up from the base of my skull, pulsing as it travels to the back of my right eye, where it settles, tormenting me with white-hot flashes of pain. My adrenaline is running out and I'm crashing. As I make my way back to the train station, part of me wonders if this is some kind of stunt. If Lia's not really missing, if she's just being an asshole and hiding out somewhere, making her parents worry.

Maybe she's with Hunter. If so, they could be anywhere. Hunter is a member of *the* van Leeuwen family, of the Dutch-French pharmaceutical giant Lemoine–van Leeuwen, and in possession of one of the largest fortunes in the world. They undoubtedly own private jets, fancy homes in every major city—whole islands even. If Lia wanted, she had her pick of places to run away to. They could be halfway around the world getting sushi in Osaka, or spending the night in Paris. Or maybe they're simply at the van Leeuwen beach house in West Hampton, laughing at all of us running around trying to find her.

My head throbs and I feel weak from the pain, the nights of no sleep, the hours of studying. A Physics test midweek, the SATs scheduled for December. My final chance. I take another pink pill from my Altoids tin, press it against my tongue, and close my eyes to wait for relief, but it barely comes. Instead of focus, I just feel restless.

Stupid, so stupid. Shouldn't have come out here. I knew I wouldn't find her but I still held out hope. She'd texted me, maybe she still wanted me. Maybe it could be just like it was, as if a single text could erase the last six months. She's with Hunter now, and I am an idiot.

But then I think about Lia. She wouldn't do that, couldn't be that cruel. The Lia I knew was kind, would rescue every stray she encountered, taking home two injured baby squirrels once.

Still, maybe she *is* hiding out with Hunter. Maybe she just felt overwhelmed the way we both did sometimes. Maybe she just needed to be alone.

On the train back home, I exist in that state of limbo between awake and asleep, a state of survival for me. The human body can't survive without *some* sleep. I've been getting little sips here and there, a few minutes in the car before class starts, a few minutes at lunch, but it isn't enough.

I need more. Sometimes it feels like I always need more.

5.

Hunter van Leeuwen. On Monday I wait for her outside of first-period Physics, the one class I share with both her and Lia and the part of the day I always dread the most. She knows something and I'm sure of it as soon as our eyes meet.

"Hey," I say, nervous. "I need to talk to you."

She stops but doesn't say anything. Hunter is White and tall, almost six feet, with piercing green eyes and beautiful dark hair streaked with electric blue. Her very presence intimidates, and she knows it. "Well?"

"Lia," I say, recovering. "She's missing."

Hunter frowns. "I know."

"Where is she?" I ask with a little more confidence. She's hiding something, I can feel it.

"If I knew, then she wouldn't be *missing*, would she?" she says.

People walk past us into class, a few giving us odd looks. Hunter and I, we don't speak, we never acknowledge each other in the hall. We had an unspoken agreement and now I'm breaking it.

"When was the last time you saw her?" I push on.

"Thursday." The day I got her text. "Then she didn't show at school on Friday."

"I just want to know she's okay," I say. "That's all."

Hunter's grip tightens around her backpack strap, hand forming a fist. "Why do you even care?"

"Of course I care."

"I thought you told her she wasn't your problem anymore."

It stuns me. And hurts. So she knows everything. Or this, at least. Lia's told her about it, about me and the shitty things I've said. Me at my lowest points.

You don't know, I want to shout after her. *You don't know anything about me. About us.*

She thinks she can just swoop in after everything Lia and I have been through and take her away from me.

But that's not true, I have to remind myself. No one took Lia from me. I did it all to myself. I screwed everything up, pushed Lia away, and now it's too late.

Hunter just scoffs at my blank expression and turns a shoulder to go.

"Wait," I say, even though I'm not sure what I want to say.

She stiffens, glances back at me.

"You really don't know where she is?"

She looks a little surprised at the desperation in my voice and she seems to consider me, like she's weighing me against everything Lia's told her. Then her surprise shifts into contempt. "Listen, she really isn't your problem anymore."

"I—"

"Look, she's probably spending a few days in the city. You know how much she hates it here," she says, but it sounds like she's just brushing me off.

"But—"

She cuts me off. "Don't worry about Lia," she says, this time with force. Then she turns to go, letting her words hang in the air, a judgment. Hunter's saying I don't have the right to worry about Lia. That I forfeited that right when I all but dared her to leave me back in May, when I gave up on us. I can't help but think that maybe she's right.

6.

One thing Hunter's not wrong about is how much Lia hated it here. She used to ditch Meadowlark for the city whenever everything felt like too much and she didn't want to go all the way out to Montauk. It was a habit that started after she met Jana, skipping school to go meet her in Williamsburg or the Lower East Side, but it was something she continued even after they broke up.

"Come on," she'd say to me, and we'd take the LIRR to Penn Station, take the 1 uptown for dinner at Peacefood or walk down to the West Village for pastries and gelato.

One weekend the summer before junior year—the summer I fell in love with her—we got fired from our jobs at Long Island College Prep, a local tutoring agency, for calling in sick to spend a weekend in the city just the two of us.

"Where do you wanna go?" she asked. "See a show?" She waved her mother's credit card and I shook my head in exasperation.

"Ooh, I know, dinner at Petal?"

"Come on," I said. Petal was a hot new restaurant and reservations were supposed to be impossible.

"My mom knows one of the owners." Of course she did.

"But then you'd have to call her and tell her where you are."

"True. So scratch that." She sighed. "What about your dad's place?"

After the divorce, he'd moved out of Long Island and bought a loft in Tribeca. Because of work, he was reliably gone from Monday to Thursday of each week, but it was the weekend. I shook my head. "He's probably home."

Lia paused to think for a moment, tapping her bottom lip softly. "I know! Come on, let's go."

"Where are we going?"

"You'll see."

"*Lia.*"

"*Chase.*" She returned my mock withering look. "Trust me, it's a surprise. A good one." We were almost there when I realized exactly where we were headed.

I followed Lia through Chelsea Market to the back of the building, and she punched in a code that gave us access to the second floor where Jo Vestiano shared production offices and a studio test kitchen with a few other shows, most notably *Chopped*. We hadn't been back there in months, when Jo shot last year's holiday special. That was the deal Lia had struck with her mom—she'd appear with her once a year, usually for the December special where they'd bake cookies and decorate a gingerbread house.

We snuck in, Lia taking my hand to lead me through an office surprisingly busy for a Saturday. She punched in another code for her mom's offices and inside, we were finally alone. Jo's office looked out to the Highline, an elevated railroad track that had been remade into a sky garden walkway, with a glimpse of the Hudson beyond.

"What are we doing here?" I asked, plopping next to her on one of the big leather couches that lived by the floor-to-ceiling windows. We lay side by side on the deep cushions, our bare arms brushing.

She shrugged. "I've never been here after hours."

"What now?"

"Be patient."

We napped for a couple hours before sneaking back out to an entirely empty production studio.

"I'm hungry," Lia said, wandering into her mom's test kitchen. "Let's make dinner."

I laughed, thinking she was joking.

She laughed too. "I'm serious! Let's do one of those challenges."

"What?"

"Like on *Chopped*." Jo's test kitchen wasn't built like the *Chopped* set that had four of everything—stoves, ovens, prep areas. The format of her show was mostly casual Italian-inspired recipes and guest chefs who'd cook with her. "It'll be fun." She began to rifle through the pantry and fridge.

"I don't know," I said. "I don't think we should be messing with your mom's stuff."

"It's fine, look at all the food she has! Plus, it's not like she can't just send a PA out to buy eggs." She began setting things on the counter—pancetta, fettuccini, heavy cream, tomatoes. "What should be our mystery ingredient? Canned whole chicken? Century eggs?"

"Does your mom even have those?"

"No," she laughed. "What about anchovies and olives?"

I made a face. "You know I hate both of those things."

"How else would it be a challenge?" she asked.

"Fine, but then we have to use Gorgonzola and mortadella."

"Ew, no!" she shrieked. "I refuse to eat moldy cheese and what's basically bologna. Ew," she repeated for emphasis.

"All cheese is moldy cheese—you just can't see it!"

"Okay, fine," she said. "But it's your fault if we get sick."

"Oh, we're definitely gonna get sick," I said, bumping her shoulder. We didn't get sick but the meal we came up with was too gross and we had to throw it all out.

"Inedible," she pronounced. "I don't know how those judges eat that crap."

"Maybe it's not made by people who don't know how to cook?"

"Hey, just because I *don't* cook doesn't mean I *can't*." She proceeded to make us fettuccini carbonara, expertly chopping bacon and onions and smoothly separating yolks from whites like she'd been doing it all her life, even though she'd never, ever shown any interest.

"When did you learn to cook?" I asked, watching her in amazement.

"When your mom's Jo Vestiano, you pick up a few things here and there."

I rolled my eyes but I ate every last bite when she finished. "Do you think you could do this?" I asked.

"What, professionally, like my mom?" she asked. "No way."

"Why not?" It would've been natural for her to just step into her mom's shoes, like she'd been groomed her whole life. It would've been easy, a whole successful career—no, *empire*—for the taking.

"Come on," she said. "You know me. I'd hate it."

"What part?" I wanted to know.

"Smiling for the camera, pretending I cared. Coming up with recipes."

"Your mom doesn't write all her recipes," I said. None of them did, Jo told us. It was impossible to come up with all of it. If you were one of the top celebrity chefs like Jo, then you had a small team developing and testing them for you. By the third year on TV, she'd run out of family recipes from her nonna to share but they still kept coming, especially around the holidays or special events. "Nonna, God rest her soul, has been cooking up a storm in heaven," she once joked after a few too many glasses of wine.

"I don't want to be like Jo," Lia said. Calling her mom by her first name was something Lia was trying out but didn't want to talk about. "She's so fake."

I shrugged. "They're all like that. It's not fake, it's just business."

"That's why I don't want to do it," she said.

"What do you want to do?"

"When I grow up?" she asked with a raised eyebrow. "What are we, in kindergarten?"

I laughed. "Come on." We were across from each other, me sitting on a barstool and her standing by the stove, elbows on the counter, leaning toward me.

"I don't know. What do you want?" she asked, coming around the kitchen island to move closer to me until we shared the same corner, her face inches from mine. "What is it that you want, Chase?" she asked again, long hair cascading over a shoulder, eyes intense, and my breath caught.

"I don't know," I whispered. She leaned in, and I shifted closer, sitting on the very edge of the barstool until I was balancing on two legs.

Until I wasn't balancing on anything and we were a heap on the floor, first in complete shock and then laughing uncontrollably because I'd lost my balance and fell on top of her when the stool slipped out from under me.

"Get off me, you dork," she said, still laughing breathlessly.

I rolled over onto my back. Our eyes met and we started to laugh again.

"I love you, you know that?" I said quietly after we stopped, almost in a whisper.

She turned to face me and grinned. "I know."

It's crazy, how you can know someone forever and then suddenly see them in a new light. I can't explain what'd shifted. There was no catalyst, no fireworks, no defining moment—we were the same Lia and Chase as always, spending all our time together, going to Montauk some weekends, working as tutors, and now sneaking away to the city together. But when I looked at her, it was just different. I could feel this new—this *possession,* like she was mine. Like I was hers. Like we belonged together and always had.

I began to think I was delusional, that whatever I was feeling was ultimately impossible. While Lia had had plenty of crushes and a couple girlfriends, she'd never expressed any interest in me. It was too much to hope she was having the same exact realization as me at the exact same time, that as I was experiencing all these new feelings for her, she was somehow also falling in love with me too.

7.

At lunch, I skip the cafeteria and head straight for the parking lot where I can be alone in my car. Inside, I pull out my phone and tap on Lia's name.

Me: Where are you?

Me: I went all the way out to Montauk yesterday but you weren't there

Me: Just let me know that you're okay

I wait and wait and wait until lunch period is almost over. No response. I stare at her words—*Meet me in Montauk*—and try to decipher what she could've meant. But then I think about her and Hunter, smiling and holding hands as recently as last week. She looked happy. She didn't look in need of rescuing.

I call her, but it goes to voice mail. Suddenly, it feels like a game that she's playing. A joke, maybe, between the two of them. Maybe it's just jealousy rising in me, but all I picture is Lia telling Hunter about Montauk, *our* place, *our* Bat-Signal, and laughing as she texts me.

Me: Listen, I'm sick of this bs

Me: Don't text me again

She doesn't text back. Instead, someone knocks on my window, scaring the shit out of me. It's Hunter. With me sitting in my car, she looks even taller than usual, looming. For a second, I think Lia's sent her. She saw my messages and dispatched Hunter to tell me to fuck off. But that doesn't seem like the Lia I know.

Then again, maybe the Lia I knew is gone.

"What?" I ask after I lower the window.

Hunter leans forward, heel of her hand against the top of my door, supporting her frame. "Are you genuinely worried about Lia?" she asks, surprising me.

"Yes," I answer immediately.

"Me too," she says. "Come on, let's talk." But the bell rings, cutting us off, and we both look back toward the building. "Find me after school."

"Okay, but I have cross-country." I get out of the car, join her on the walk from the parking lot.

"I'll wait for you at the bus bay," she says, and I nod.

For the rest of the day, all I do is stare and stare at the clock, willing the secondhand to tick faster, but if anything, time seems to slow, taunting me. I can't stop thinking about Hunter and her change of heart. Her coldness this morning followed by her concern at lunch. She must be really worried if she's willing to talk to me.

After school, I catch a glimpse of Hunter on my way to cross-country. I shouldn't but I follow her outside, eyes tracking streaks of bright blue hair against a dark olive field jacket through the crowd in the parking lot as she makes her way to the back of the school. I stay behind and consider skipping cross-country to talk to her. I can feel the early pulses of a headache building anyway and a run will only make it worse. But before I make a decision, I see a car drive into view, a black Lexus with tinted windows. It's familiar, but only vaguely so. Holding back, I lean against the wall around the corner and pretend to look at my phone, stealing a glance or two. From where I'm standing, I can see the driver's window come down, see Hunter lean forward, but I'm too far away to hear what they're saying.

When Hunter pulls back, she looks up and I turn away quickly, clutching my phone to my chest. When I dare to look again, she's gone. I linger, hoping to catch another glimpse of her or the black car. Then I make my way to where she was standing, by the big oak tree behind the building, and cross to the other side of the school, but there's no sign of her. It's strange, following her when I've spent the last few months trying to pretend that she doesn't exist—that Lia doesn't exist. Like the pain inside me doesn't exist. I turn another corner to the front of the school, but I've lost her in the crowd of kids milling around the parking lot, the freshmen and sophomores getting picked up by parents. Finally, I leave when I get a text from Tad London, a teammate, asking me where I am.

As I walk to the gym, the headache grows and makes its way from the right side of my neck, pulsing in waves around my skull until my entire head pounds with pain. It's too bright outside as we stretch before practice, the sunlight burning a thousand needles into my eyes. I squeeze them shut and try to focus on Coach Gimmly.

"A recovery run today, guys," he says before sending us off.

I'm supposed to lead the team but as soon as we start, my field of vision swims and the ground feels uneven.

"You okay, Ohara?" Tad asks, jogging beside me. I look past my shoulder and see a bottleneck, everyone stuck behind me. I know Tad wanted to be captain. He probably still does. The concern on his face masks a curiosity laced with ambition—he's waiting for me to stumble.

"Fine," I say. "I'm fine." I shove the pain deep inside and push on because I have no other choice. By the end of practice, my legs might be shaking and I might be on the edge of vomiting, but I can't show weakness, not now when everything in my life feels tenuous, when all my dreams, once within reach, seem impossible.

After the run, I'm a mess, taking small sips from a cold water bottle to keep the bile down.

"You don't look so good," Tad tells me, that same concerned look on his face.

"I'm fine," I say again. "Just tired." I drop the water bottle into my bag, check my laces.

He hesitates, then says, almost cautiously, "I'm here if you ever want to—"

"Thanks." I sling my backpack over one shoulder and gym bag over the other. I have to get out of here, away from my shitty run and his pitying stares. I have to get better, have to be faster. Once I'm alone in my car, I take out my Altoids tin and slip a pill under my tongue, closing my eyes and waiting for the bitterness to dissolve. Can't let anything get to me, not Tad, not Hunter, not Lia. Not my dad, not the SATs, not the sleepless nights.

Can't show any weakness. Not now, not ever.

8.

Hunter is exactly where she said she'd be, waiting for me at the bus bay, lying on one of the green benches, eyes closed, big headphones on, skin golden in the setting sun, her hair spilling over, swaying in the breeze.

"Hey," I say, but she doesn't hear me. She only opens her eyes when I shake her shoulder.

"Hey, sorry," she says, sitting up. I join her, both of us staring out at the dark magenta sky.

"So. Lia." I check my phone again and see nothing from her.

"I'm worried," she says, and it surprises me, how upset she sounds. "I haven't heard from her since Thursday." The night Lia sent me her last text asking me to come to Montauk. Hunter turns to me, holds my gaze in hers. "We had a fight. It was so stupid." Then she looks away, ashamed.

For a moment, I'm in shock that Hunter would tell me, but more than that, it shatters the idea I had of them for months. The way Lia and Hunter were always smiling and laughing, hands linked or touching, a light palm on the small of the other's back, fingers brushing away stray hairs. They looked happy, they looked perfect. Staring at them was like looking into the sun, all brilliant light and searing pain.

But here it is, evidence that they weren't perfect, and I'm dying to know what the fight was about. If I'm honest, it's not out of some innocent sense of curiosity. I want to know if they were imperfect the way Lia and I were imperfect, if there's a crack in their armor, a way in. But I don't ask because I can't violate the trust Hunter's placed in me with this confession. So I remain quiet, waiting for her next move.

She takes a small breath and tells me anyway. "She was going to get the answers to the Physics test."

"What?" Of all the things I thought Hunter would say, this is beyond anything I could've imagined. "What do you mean, *get the answers*?"

"It was Cole's idea," she says, then adds with less certainty, "I think." Cole Landau, fellow senior and student council member, has a certain reputation. One rumor, the one that he supplies half the school with Adderall, I know is true. The Altoids tin in my backpack is proof of that, though it doesn't contain Adderall but Focentra, the next generation of amphetamines.

Other rumors, like the one where he runs a cheating ring, I knew less about. Last year, he'd approached me but I said no and made a point to keep my distance, cutting him off any time he seemed like he was about to bring it up.

"They'd never done anything like it," Hunter continues. "But Cole's been branching out since last year."

"Branching out," I repeat slowly.

"From the usual."

I understand what Hunter means by *the usual*: trading homework assignments, tips among friends on tests and quizzes, a little light plagiarism.

Cooperative learning.

When you have five or six APs and each teacher acts like theirs is the only class you have, you either crash and burn or you help one another out. One kid does the math homework while another finishes the chem set. First-period Calc kids tell the fifth-period kids what to brush up on during lunch. It meant you could sleep. It was harmless. Mostly.

When we were together, Lia and I did it whenever one of us needed it, though it was almost always Lia who borrowed bio homework or looked at my history essays for inspiration. "Not everyone's a fucking machine like you," she would sometimes say, but it was meant as a compliment. Maybe that's why I never told her when I started going to Cole for Focentra. Maybe I wanted her to think I was a machine, flawless.

"Cole, he's been getting other tests, but not AP Physics, said it would make them a ton of money, selling cheat sheets," Hunter says.

"Money?" I say. "Lia doesn't care about money."

"I don't think it was really about that," she says. "Cole got it into her head that they'd be some kind of revolutionaries. I don't know, I got all of it secondhand. Lia didn't tell me until she'd already made up her mind. We fought about it last Thursday, then she didn't show Friday."

"When did you find out?" I think about the call I got early Sunday morning. Jo Vestiano on the verge of tears: *Have you heard from Lia? She's missing.*

"Saturday," Hunter answers. "I thought maybe she was just mad at me, but—"

She's telling the truth, I know she is. Hunter doesn't know where Lia is either.

"Cole and Lia, were they close?" I ask.

"I guess," she says. "I already asked him, though, and he says he doesn't know where she is either." It suddenly clicks, the black Lexus after school by the oak tree in the back next to the dumpsters. I recognize it now, Cole's car. That's who she was meeting.

"Do you believe him?"

She shrugs. "Why would he lie?"

I think about Lia and Cole, the word *revolutionaries*. What was Lia thinking? How did they plan on getting the answers for the test? And why? Lia was impulsive, but she wasn't the type to take huge risks.

Then again, she did hate school and everything it stood for. The tests, grades—"tools of oppression," she once called them.

Hunter and Lia have been together for only a few months. She doesn't know Lia like I do. She might not know Lia hated it all because she never, ever felt good enough.

9.

Spring break, junior year. Or maybe it was earlier, the moment Lia and I found out we'd be spending the summer apart, our first since the age of six. In the fall, we'd applied for Stanford's Frontier Scholars program together, eight weeks in Palo Alto taking classes and living in dorms.

Stanford was my dream, though, not Lia's. On the other side of the country, it might as well have been on the other side of the world from Meadowlark. I wanted it to be a taste of what was to come, of what our lives after graduation could look like: the two of us on our own, the two of us free from high school, from nagging parents, from people who thought they knew us.

But then Lia didn't get in.

"I won't go," I told her. "We'll spend the summer here, get tutoring jobs, spend August in Maine like always." Every year, her family took us to Kennebunkport for the last month before school.

"It's okay," she said, hands cupping mine. "It's only eight weeks."

I was relieved. "If you're sure."

"Go." She kissed me. "It'll be over before we know it."

We'd spend the summer apart, then I'd fly directly into Portland and the Vestianos would send a car to drive me to Kennebunkport for the last two weeks. I thought that was the end of it but Lia had second thoughts.

"What if I went with you?" she asked right before spring break. We were at her house, spread out on the floor of her bedroom, books scattered everywhere, studying for exams. "I'll find an internship in San Fran. My mom knows a ton of chefs in the area."

"I thought you hated that stuff." As kids, we liked going on set, getting our makeup done, and pretending to surprise her mom on the show. But the older we got, the more Lia resented it.

"I wouldn't *cook*," she said. "I'd intern with management. Maybe at a hotel even. Learn the business side, that kind of thing." Her mom was connected and I had no doubt she was right, that she could get whatever she wanted.

"I'll be in Palo Alto," I said.

"That's close. We can hang out on the weekends."

"I'll be busy."

"But never too busy for me," she said with a smile, leaning over to place a kiss on my cheek.

"No, but . . " It was hard to explain the dread I felt, even to myself. Lia may have resented her mom, may have called all the times Jo made her go on the show "exploitation" once or twice, but she wasn't afraid of using Jo's connections. As much as Lia claimed independence, she *always* fell back on her mom. Me, I worked for everything I got. Getting into Stanford's summer program was the result of dedication, not a call from my parents.

Lia could slack because she had her mom. She'd end up doing something amazing no matter what, Stanford or not, perhaps running her own food and travel empire someday, the one that was practically waiting for her.

But back then, it was hard for me to put into words how I felt, and even more impossible to tell Lia.

"What do you think?" she asked.

"No!" I said suddenly and without thinking, startling both of us.

"Why not?"

We both stared at each other for a while, eyes wide. Then I looked away. I could never hurt Lia. And she was right—it'd be nice to see her on weekends, a way to salvage our plans. Still us against the world. Still a glimpse of our future out of here, together.

"Never mind," I said softly. "You're right, it'd be fun."

Lia searched my eyes, her wariness eventually melting into warmth. "I knew you'd like it."

But my resentment still grew.

"What do you think of this apartment?" she's ask about an expensive studio in the Mission. "Or how about this loft? Ooh, should we buy a car? We could go on road trips, drive along the coast."

"I'll be busy. And there'll be things on the weekends that I'll have to go to," I'd remind her. "I can't just leave whenever I want."

"Yeah, yeah," she'd say, and then continue on like I hadn't said anything at all, planning a road trip out to Tahoe or a long weekend in LA for July Fourth.

Then finally, she snapped at me one day when I reminded her for the millionth time that I couldn't blow off classes. "Chase. Come on." We were in Montauk, on her boat but still docked at the marina, the waves rocking gently against the side.

"What?" I got up to shut the doors, not wanting anyone else to overhear.

"It's just summer camp. Get over yourself." The memory still burns from the way she said it, *summer camp*, like it didn't mean anything.

"No. I'll be taking classes. With Stanford professors. I told you," I said, sick of the same argument.

"Whatever. Don't be so selfish."

"*I'm* being selfish?" I remained by the doors, back pressed against the glass. I can still feel one palm pressing into the steel frame, the other gripping the handle.

"Yeah."

I actually laughed at her, at the absurdity.

"Do you ever stop to think about anyone but yourself?" she asked, her voice rising. "I mean really, really think about anyone else."

"Do you?" I shot back. "It's always about which ridiculous apartment you're going to rent or what trips you want us to take."

Lia grew quiet for a moment. "How about when I found out I didn't get in?"

That stopped me cold.

She looked away, eyes on the floor. "When I found out they wanted you but not me." For a moment, it was just the sound of the water against the boat, and we were two girls filled with regret.

"Lia—"

"No, seriously. You'll be gone for eight weeks." We'd never been apart for longer than one week, let alone— "Eight whole weeks. What am I supposed to do without you?"

"Do you just want me to stay?" I asked, that same dread sitting in the pit of my stomach. *Please say no*, I thought.

"No, of course not," she said, but the relief was fleeting. "It's not like I really have a choice though, do I? It's fucking *Stanford*. Your big dream. Your destiny," she scoffed.

Dread grew into an anger that coiled tightly around my heart. I'd worked so hard to get in. I put in more hours, more blood, sweat, and tears than anyone into everything I did. I *deserved* it, and I won my spot fair and square. "Don't shit on something just because you couldn't cut it. You know I wanted you there. I helped you with your application and everything." That was the exact wrong thing to say. Seeing the hurt on Lia's face, I tried to backtrack. "I didn't mean that. I'm sorry."

"No," she said. "I think you meant exactly what you said. *Lia's not good enough. Lia always needs my help.* And, what, even with your help, I couldn't get in? You must think I'm pathetic." She looked on the verge of tears.

I didn't know how we'd ended up here. I walked over, sat by her side in contrition.

"Listen, I want you to go, okay?" she said. "I want you to go because I love you and I want you to have everything you've always wanted, but don't pretend you would've stayed if I'd asked. Don't pretend you were really asking my permission to go. You were going to go no matter what. You always do whatever you want, you always get whatever you want."

"*I* always get what I want?" I asked, shifting away from her. "I never get what I want *except* this. I can't just get an internship at some fancy restaurant. I can't just get whatever apartment I want or buy a car just because."

"So what?" Lia said, getting up to pace around the living space.

"*So what?*" I repeated. "If you haven't noticed, my family doesn't have a yacht, doesn't *summer in Maine*."

"Your dad's a big shot at McKinsey. You live in Meadowlark. It's not like your family's exactly struggling." Lia crossed her arms, leaned against a counter by the sink. "And besides, none of that stuff matters."

"How can you say that? That stuff is the only thing that matters. You can do anything, be anything. You don't even have to try!" I was shouting, and in some ways, the words that burst out of me were inevitable, an explosion of everything I'd felt in all the years we'd spent together, things I couldn't say. Things I couldn't feel because they were disloyal. Things I felt anyway and buried, a betrayal.

"What do you mean, I don't even have to try?" Lia asked, her eyes narrowing.

"Forget it." I looked away. No, I turned my whole body. I couldn't face her, or maybe what I couldn't face was how I felt.

"Say what you're thinking."

"I said forget it."

"Say it."

"No."

"Just say it!" she shouted. "Tell me what you think of me and my family, what you really think of us."

I remained quiet, stuck between what I wanted to say and what I wanted to have—Lia. Finally, I turned to her, stood up, and walked over to hold her in my arms. "I love you," I said. "I'm sorry."

Lia froze, stiffening at my touch, angry. Then she began to cry, shaking against me. "I love you too."

I kissed her, cupping her face, thumbs brushing away her tears.

"Come here," I whispered. "Let's not fight."

She nodded and closed the distance between us.

That was supposed to fix things, and it did, for a while.

10.

That night, I text Cole, tell him I need to re-up even though it's early. He texts me back right away.

Cole: So soon? :)

Me: Yeah sorry just stressed

Me: Can you come tonight?

Cole: Sure

He stops by around midnight, after Mom and Aidan have gone to bed. "Say no to drugs, kids," is the first thing he says to me after he pulls up, grinning at his own awkward joke.

I force a laugh and slip him cash for the fresh tin.

"Seriously though. Take it slow, Chase. Don't want an OD. Bad for business," he says, and I can't tell if he's still joking.

"Right," I say. "Can you even OD on Focentra?"

"No idea," he says. "But don't push it."

"Don't worry about me," I tell him, then lean into the passenger side to keep him from leaving. "Hey, wait."

"What's up?" he asks.

"Lia."

He sighs, looking away. "Like I said, I don't want to be in the middle of any of this."

Like I said? He must be talking about what he told Hunter earlier. Does he know that Hunter spoke to me? Did Hunter tell him after?

"I'm not asking you to get in the middle of anything. I'm just worried. Do you know where she is? Where she could be?"

He hesitates, almost like he wants to say something, but shakes his head. "I have no idea where Lia is." I don't know if I believe him, but with nothing else to say, I step back finally and let him leave.

Something doesn't make sense, that's all I know. Lia's disappearance, what Hunter's told me, and now Cole. Pieces that don't quite fit together.

Checking my phone again, I see nothing from Lia. It's been four days and she's still missing. The Physics test is on Wednesday, and I have a million things I have to do, but I climb out to the roof from my bedroom window and lie down on the cold shingles, stare up at the sky through the limbs and leaves of the big magnolia in our backyard.

We used to do this, Lia and I, grab a blanket to lie on and sip hot cocoa in the fall and spring, iced tea lemonade in the summer. I haven't been out here in almost nine months, since the last time we were here together. If I close my eyes, the November chill feels almost as cold as the February freeze.

"You're hogging the blanket," Lia said, but what she really wanted was for us to snuggle closer, so that's what I did, scooting over and wrapping it tighter around us.

"Better?" I asked, my breath visible in the wintry moonlight.

"Better," she said, drawing me in for a kiss.

"I love you," I whispered, wanting to keep the words only for us.

"I love you too," she whispered back.

"How long?" I wanted to know.

"You first," she said.

"Since May."

"After my breakup with Jana?"

I mock-gasped. "We do not speak of Jana."

Lia laughed. "Fine. After my breakup with she-who-shall-not-be-named?"

"More like she-who-doesn't-deserve-to-be-named," I said. "But yes. After that witch."

"Chase!" Lia laughed harder.

I bumped her shoulder in admonishment, but because we were tangled so tightly together, it caused us to almost roll. "Shit, sorry." I righted us with a free hand, knocking over my mug, then catching it before it fell off the roof. Luckily, it was empty.

Lia was still laughing.

"Stop it," I whined. "You almost caused us to die."

She only laughed harder. "*I* did no such thing."

I pouted and she kissed me, longer this time, lingering, and for a moment I forgot myself, forgot where I was, forgot who I was. For a moment, I was just a girl so deeply in love I could float up to the sky.

Later, I remembered my question. "When?" I asked.

"Hm?"

"When did you know?" We were back in my room, chased inside by the cold.

Lia turned to me and in the dark, the two of us barely separated by an inch, and said, "I've always known, Chase. I was just waiting for you to know." I melted against her, kissed her softly, then fiercely. She pulled back, our noses nuzzling, breaths mingling, to tell me, "I want you to know that I was prepared to wait my whole life." This she said solemnly, and I believed her with my entire being.

Did I know then, that this would be the last time? I want to reach into the past, grab my stupid self by the shoulders and shake her. Remember this, I want to yell. Remember this because it was the last time on the roof, just the two of us. Remember this because it didn't have to be the last time.

It didn't.

It doesn't.

11.

Sleep is impossible. So late Monday night—early Tuesday morning, almost 3 AM—I lace up again, run by Lia's house. The lights are on, and I think about where she is and who she's with and how we ended up here—her missing and me outside of her house, more alone than ever.

When I return, I find my mom waiting for me. "Sorry," I say. "Did I wake you?" I run the water in the kitchen, tilt my head to drink straight from the faucet.

"Chase," she begins, then stops.

"What?" I ask, toweling off and kicking my shoes to the side.

"We need to talk. You should sit down." She sounds so serious that I obey, but before she can continue, Aidan interrupts us.

"What's going on?" She comes down the stairs. "Why is everyone up?"

"Sorry, Dani," Mom says. "Go back to bed."

"Why?" she asks.

"It's okay," I say. "She can stay."

Mom hesitates as Aidan joins us, sitting next to me and leaning against my side. I wrap an arm around her. We're not as close as we used to be during the divorce three years ago, when it felt like just the two of us and I had to shield her from the fallout. But she's only eleven and some of that protectiveness still lingers.

"Okay," Mom starts again, and I'm beginning to worry because I can tell she's blinking back tears.

"Did something happen with Dad?" I ask, feeling a sudden coldness in the pit of my stomach. He had a mild heart attack the year before, though since then, he's largely followed doctors' orders and gotten back in shape.

"No," she says quickly. "It's not Dad. It's Lia."

"Did she come back?" My grip around Aidan tightens and all the air disappears from the room.

"No," Mom says slowly. "She's—she's gone, Chase." Her words float past me, leaving me confused, disoriented. *Gone.* "They found her body. Late last night. Montauk. Washed up on shore."

"What?" It's Aidan who asks, not me. My mom's words echo and bounce off the walls, their reverberations growing in volume.

"They don't know how it happened yet."

Late last night.

Montauk.

Washed up.

She's gone.

Found her body.

Nothing makes sense and the world is spinning out of control. I stand up and nausea overtakes me. I fall to my knees and bile comes up.

"Chase!" Mom jumps up, running over to catch me after my collapse.

"Sorry," I manage to say, though it's not enough. The sobs tear through me, crushing me like a rip tide until I'm drowning. "I'm so sorry."

Late last night.

Montauk.

Gone.

She's gone.

They found her body.

Washed up on shore.

Lia, my Lia.

Dead.

12.

Meet me in Montauk. That's what Lia said to me. Her last words. But I didn't go, not soon enough. She was found out there. What happened to her?

My alarm buzzes and I shut it off. It's six in the morning and Lia is dead. How long has it been? I don't know.

Mom held me and let me cry and rage and scream that I was sorry until she thought I ran out of tears and lost my voice. Then she sent Aidan to bed, led me back to my room, and curled up behind me in bed, smoothing my hair and rubbing my back until my ragged breath evened and she thought I fell asleep. She left a kiss on the side of my head before leaving, closing the door soundlessly behind her.

But I'm wide awake. And I haven't run out of tears or lost my voice, not even close. I stare at Lia's message from four days ago and the ones I sent in response yesterday. Lia wasn't ignoring me, I know that now.

Me: Listen, I'm sick of this bs

Me: Don't text me again

I read and reread the words and feel worse and worse until I want to die. Lia was in trouble. She needed me and I told her I was sick of her bullshit.

Meet me in Montauk.

I was just there but I need to see it again. What I really need is to see Lia again, but she's gone. I wipe away my tears but it's futile.

By the time I make it to the LIRR, it's almost seven and the station is filled with commuters. For a moment, I think I see my father, but then I remember that he's moved back to the city, that he may help Mom with the house payments but he doesn't live here anymore. Besides, it's a Tuesday and he's probably in LA or Chicago for the week. I look straight ahead at the platform and try to ignore the headache building behind my eyes. I'm not supposed to be here. It's true that I'm not skipping a test or presentation, but it's fall semester senior year and I don't have any margin for fuckups. It's too much, and I feel like I'm about to crack under the pressure of the last few days, the pressure that's been building my whole life. I slip another pink pill and feel only a fraction better.

On the train, I try to study for the SATs but my eyes glaze over. All I can do is think of Lia, each memory a new stab in the heart. None of it matters, not school, not grades, not extracurriculars and my *high school career*. Not when Lia's gone.

Once there, I walk to the marina even though it takes almost an hour. I don't want to order a car, make small talk with the driver. I don't want to see anyone except the one person I can never see again.

That's why I'm infuriated when I reach Lia's boat: Hunter's already there.

"Hey," she says, standing up, and I can't explain the level of overwhelming rage building within me.

It takes me a long time to respond, the silence stretching taut between us. She has a right to be here, I have to tell myself over and over, but I just can't stomach the sight of her here, where Lia and I spent so much of our time together. Where we were in love. I feel possessive of this stupid boat with its stupid name, this stupid marina, all of Montauk, the whole of Long Island. No, the entire world, because it felt like it all belonged to us, Lia and I, and only to us. Because the world made sense when we were together and now it doesn't.

"What are you doing here?" I manage to say.

"Where else would I be?" she answers simply. It's then that I can see how wrecked she is, the swollen eyes, stringy hair, the pallor, and it punches a hole in the pressure building inside of me. Hunter is just as devastated as I am.

"When did you find out?"

"Middle of the night," she says, and even though I can't help wondering if Jo called her before she called my mom, for once it doesn't bother me like it did before. Because for once, we're not locked in some kind of competition. Because there's nothing left to fight for.

Lia, the person we loved, is gone.

I walk onto the boat and we both begin to cry. She pulls me in and I don't have the energy to resist, so I let her hold me. We sob and sob and sob until there's nothing left.

"Come on," she says finally, breaking away. "Let's go inside."

"You have the key?" I ask, but of course she does. It's Lia's spare, probably the one that used to be mine, the exact one I flung at her back in May.

She nods and unlocks the slider. It's just as cold inside, the heat off. I walk the small living space, dragging a hand along the kitchenette counter, glancing at my reflection in the tiny bathroom, looking inside the bare bedrooms, and finally sitting down on the couch. Memories of us haunt every corner. There we are, snacking on cheese and crackers and watching *Eternal Sunshine* for the millionth time. In the kitchenette, we're burning eggs and toast because of the shitty stove. In the second bedroom, we're curled up, a tangle of limbs and laughter, soft touches and tender moments. It's all I can do to not cry again.

Hunter doesn't bother following me, remains standing by the door to survey the space, and I'm grateful for the time alone.

"When was the last time you were here?" I ask.

"Two weeks ago," she says, eyes still sweeping the area.

"What are you looking for?"

"I don't know," she says. "It looks different somehow." I follow her gaze, try to see what she sees, but it's been months since I was last inside of the boat. The only thing I notice is Lia's favorite hoodie on the floor. I pick it up, dust it off, and place it next to me, folded. The cord that lines the hood is missing and I can't find it anywhere. Even though I know she's gone, I can't suppress the urge to fix it for her and my heart breaks a little more.

Finally, Hunter sits opposite me, and the two of us are quiet. It's a strange, almost eerie kind of quiet. Not uncomfortable but still unsettling. Our grief is overwhelming, Lia's presence palpable.

"It just doesn't make sense," I say, breaking the silence.

Hunter swallows painfully, like she's holding back tears too. "No," she agrees.

"What was she doing out here by herself?" I ask.

"It's too cold to swim," she adds.

"Was it some kind of accident?" I say.

"It makes no sense," Hunter repeats. "She obviously didn't take the boat out."

"What happened?"

13.

Mom's waiting for me at home. She must've taken the day off. I glance at the clock—it's too early for me to be home from school so she must know I skipped, but there are no angry words, only concern.

"Come here." She holds me and I lean against her, let the tears fall yet again. None of it makes sense and all I want is to press rewind to a time when Lia was alive, to a better time. A headache snakes up my neck and snatches my skull in a death grip until I can barely breathe. The ground is shaky and I lean into her embrace, let her hold me up.

"Do they know what happened?" I ask, my voice so, so small.

"Jo hasn't called again," she says. "But she texted and let us know we can come over anytime." Then she pulls back, hands firm on my shoulders keeping me steady, thumbs rubbing in comfort. "We'll go when you're ready."

The pain in my head sends shots of lightning through me. "Let's go," I manage.

"Right now?" she asks.

I nod stiffly, limiting movement in the hopes of quelling the shockwaves in my brain.

"Maybe you should get some rest first."

"Please," I beg. Jo will know more and I need to know how Lia—How Lia died.

My vision swims with tears.

"Okay," Mom says. "Okay, okay. Just let me see if Aidan can stay at the Campbell's for dinner."

It takes us almost an hour to leave. Mom pushes me into the bathroom for a shower and she quickly throws together a casserole.

"It's Jo," I remind her as she wraps it in foil. Jo Vestiano, celebrity chef extraordinaire, doesn't need our baked leftovers.

"I know, I know, but it feels wrong to show up empty-handed."

It's a short drive, only a dozen streets over. My parents would never admit it, or Dad won't at least, but the reason we no longer live across from the Vestianos is because of the divorce. Even with Dad making partner at McKinsey and Mom's promotion at the ad agency to senior copywriter, we couldn't afford to stay on the best block in Meadowlark. Divorce meant two households.

I used to think about that period all the time, only two years ago, when Lia and I were best friends but not yet together, and how I probably could've moved in with the Vestianos. How I would've, if not for Aidan, who was just starting fourth grade. Someone had to stick around for her, not that I've been the best older sister lately.

Rob, Lia's father, answers the door. "Come in, come in," he says, taking the casserole from Mom.

"I'm so sorry, Rob," Mom says, and they hug.

"Chase," he says in acknowledgment, resting a hand on my shoulder, and I can't hold it in any longer, tears slipping down my face. It's too much and Rob begins to cry too, swiping at his tears with his thumbs. Then he looks away, blinking furiously. "They're in here."

In the formal dining room, Jo sits at the head of the table, eyes bloodshot, face stripped of her usual makeup and professional smile. She's flanked by two others, a man and woman, one in uniform, one in plainclothes.

"Chase," she says when she sees me, jumping up to embrace me. In her arms, I only cry harder. When we break away, she turns to the police to introduce me: "This is Chase, Lia's . . " she trails off, unsure of what to call me.

"Best friend," Rob says from behind us.

"Best friend," Jo says in agreement.

I dry my eyes, will the tears away by focusing on the pain in my head, that ever-present companion. I trace a bolt of it from one ear to the other, and it feels like my skull is cracking itself in half.

One of the officers gestures for me to sit and I do, pressing a palm against the table to keep from stumbling.

"I'm Detective Ryder," the woman in plainclothes says. "This is Officer Alvarez. We had a few questions for Mr. and Mrs. Vestiano, but maybe you can help too."

I nod. Do they know what happened yet? My mom's words echo through the remnants of my mind: *Montauk. Found her body. Washed up.*

They both turn back to Jo and to Rob, who is now standing behind her, hands on her shoulders. They look a million years older. Lia was their only child and no matter what Lia thought, I know they loved her.

"What can you tell us about Lia's state of mind in the last few days?" Detective Ryder asks.

"She seemed fine," Jo says haltingly.

The question only confuses me. What do they mean, *state of mind*?

"Like her usual self?" Officer Alvarez says.

Rob nods. He's trying to put on a brave face but I can tell he's on the verge of tears again. "She didn't say anything, or, or—or do anything out of the ordinary."

"Sometimes these things happen without warning," Detective Ryder says. "Sometimes there are no signs."

I'm so lost. What does she mean by *these things*? Lia's disappearance? Or something else?

"What about you, Chase?" Detective Ryder turns to me. "Did you notice anything?"

Suddenly everyone is looking at me. But the truth is that I don't know Lia's *state of mind* from the last week. From the last few months, really.

Jo saves me. "Chase and Lia weren't in touch the week before Lia disappeared." More like several months, and in that moment, I can't help but think of what Lia called her—fake. But it's unfair, because Jo is just being kind, letting me be known as Lia's best friend, letting me have that in this unbearable time.

Ryder and Alvarez ask more questions about Lia, where she was, when did they realize she was missing, and it's clear they don't have any new information. But they keep returning to that first question—Lia's state of mind—until it finally cuts through even the worst of the pain in my head.

They think the person responsible for Lia's death is Lia herself.

I'm reeling, my hands gripping the seat of my chair, knuckles white, vision swimming in tears. They continue to talk, their voices muted in the background as I silently drown in this realization. *No*, I want to say. *You're wrong*. But I stay quiet, too shocked to say the words.

I knew Lia. We didn't talk in the last few months, but I *knew* her. Knew her in a way no one else did, not her parents, not her teachers or other friends, not Hunter. Especially not Hunter.

Lia was a fighter. She didn't give up like that, she *wouldn't*.

Would she?

It's not until my mom sits beside me and places a hand on my arm that I snap out of it.

"Chase?" she asks.

"What?"

"Do you know Lia's password?"

I turn to see Lia's laptop on the table, opened to the login screen.

"We haven't been able to locate her phone, but this will help," Ryder says. "If we can get access."

I reach for it but hesitate. Maybe she's changed it. Maybe Hunter would know, not me.

"Try 'nomnomnom,' no spaces," I say. Alvarez types it in and it works, it still works.

Jo laughs in a mix of surprise and relief and sadness. "Of course," she says, tears in her eyes, and I can't help but laugh a little too. "That's *so* Lia."

"She still used that?" Rob asks, shaking his head but laughing with us, and this moment feels so impossible, so brutal.

The police offer us kind smiles, shutting the laptop and sliding it off the table.

"What about her phone?" Ryder asks. "The passcode, in case we find it." They're getting up, everyone joining them, making our way to the front door.

Everyone turns to me. I used to know it, but I'm certain she's changed it.

"Even a guess," Alvarez says.

"She's definitely changed it," I say.

"Well, tell us what it was before," Ryder says.

"Try '0714,'" I tell them. My birthday.

Once they're gone, Jo and Rob show my mom and me to the family room, where we sit among a sea of flower arrangements large and small.

"They've been coming in almost nonstop," Jo says.

"Network people," Rob explains with a shake of his head. "Local news stations, even."

We sit and we talk, but I'm not really there. Mom covers for me when I lose the thread of the conversation. We're talking about Lia, but I can't stand it, can't stand that we're talking *about* her instead of *to* her.

That she's really gone.

14.

Later that night, I lie awake haunted by the questions the police asked. How they focused on Lia's mood, on whether she was acting out of the ordinary in the days before she disappeared. Or maybe what really bothers me is the questions that weren't asked. The Vestianos didn't ask about suspects, didn't ask if the police had any working theories or any new information. Everyone acted like they all knew what'd happened.

Like Lia *chose* this.

It doesn't make sense.

But nothing else does.

And then it's all I can think about, all I can picture—Lia out there alone, stepping into the cold October water, swimming out into a dark, midnight sea. Is that what happened? But how could she? Detective Ryder's voice drifts in like a faint echo: *Sometimes these things happen without warning. Sometimes there are no signs.*

I curl up on my side as the image of Lia walking into the water plays on loop and fresh tears erupt. Was that true, that there were no signs? I think of Lia, of the sadness she held, one I thought we both shared sometimes, one that came and went—the pain that was just part of being alive.

One night an eternity ago, Lia and I were at the beachside cottage the Vestianos rented in Maine, just the two of us on the sand, eyes up at the clear sky, a galaxy of stars glittering above, a very different midnight sea before us, warm and peaceful. It was the summer before junior year, when weeks and weeks of longing bloomed into love. We were together by then, but it was new and we hadn't told anyone, sneaking glances and holding hands under blankets, our little secret. We wanted to hold onto the freedom we had as best friends, not knowing if things would change, if there'd be new rules from our parents to contend with.

"What do you think happens after we die?" Lia asked in her characteristic, unexpected way. I loved that about her, the way her mind worked, always surprising me.

I turned to glance back at the cottage. Her parents' bedroom was dark, and I shifted closer, kissed her slowly. "I don't know."

"If you had to guess," she said, kissing me back but then pulling away like she really wanted to know.

"Nothing," I answered truthfully. "Nothing at all."

She looked disappointed.

"Why? What do you think happens?"

"I don't know," she said, "but not *nothing*."

"Come on," I laughed. "You don't really believe in heaven and hell, that kind of thing."

"No," she admitted. "But not nothing."

"Then what? If you had to guess," I said, voice teasing.

"Isn't it fun to think we could come back as someone else? Wouldn't it be amazing, finding each other again in another life? A different one?"

I laughed softly, thinking she wasn't serious. "Sure."

She nudged me with her shoulder. "I mean it. What if you and I have met before, if you and I have been here before. What if we're connected?" Then she looked over, expression worried, like she didn't want to scare me away with her intensity. It'd only been a month since the first time we kissed, but I was already so in love with her. Maybe I'd always been so in love with her. "I just mean—" she said defensively.

"It's okay." I kissed her again to reassure her. I liked what she was saying, the idea that we were somehow meant to be, that we belonged together and always would.

Later, when we were inside, snuggled under the same quilt, she said my name to pull me back from the clutch of sleep. "Do you really think nothing happens?" she asked.

"Maybe," I said, not wanting to disappoint her. "Maybe not."

The truth was, I did believe that, and maybe that was why I was the way I was. The way I still am. Because in my bones, I believed this was it, our one wild and precious life. Our one chance to make a mark on the world. To leave it having lived a life that mattered. Maybe that was the true difference between us, Lia and I. She never felt that rush of blood, that persistent whisper in her ear: *more, more, more*. Never safe, never stop running.

I think about that memory now, hold it softly in my hands as if it might crumble under the slightest pressure. I think about that moment now that Lia is gone. *What happens after?* I want to ask her, my heart broken.

I want to believe what she believed, that this isn't the end. That I would see her again, that the connection we shared could endure time and space. That she was somehow waiting for me on the other side, hand outstretched, soft smile on her face, and she'd tell me she was prepared to wait forever.

But then I think of something else she said, about coming back as someone else. Someone different, another life. Why?

Why did she want to leave this life behind, escape being Lia? What was so awful she felt she had no other choice but the most terrible of choices?

15.

"You don't have to go, you know," Mom tells me Wednesday morning. I'm already dressed, backpack over a shoulder, car keys in hand.

"Physics test today," I say, but it's not the only reason I'm going to class. I can't stand to be here alone without Lia. There are no answers in Meadowlark, no answers in Montauk, no answers anywhere. I can't take it anymore, wondering what happened to her, not knowing. She's supposed to be here with me, not gone. Forever.

"You work too hard," Mom says, then hands me a sheet of paper folded in half. "Here, for yesterday."

I take it and skim the signed letter excusing my absence Tuesday for being sick. "Oh." A rush of gratitude at her simple kindness almost causes to me to cry. I feel so fragile, so brittle, like the lightest breath could cause me to shatter. "Thanks," I say and turn so she won't see what a mess I am. Alone in the car, I take a deep breath and half a Focentra just to survive.

At school, Hunter and I share an accidental glance and immediately look away as if repelled by the strength of our shared grief.

We're in our usual seats, Hunter three spots ahead to the right, Lia's empty desk beside hers, and I watch her keep her eyes pointedly forward as Mr. Richter counts out and sets stacks of tests upside down on the desks in the front row. I grab a copy as the stack makes its way to me, leaving it upside down until everyone gets theirs and it's time to start. The flutter of packets wakes me from my trance and I focus on the test. AP Physics is my hardest class, but I manage to finish with time to spare. It's not until after I double-check my answers that I glance up and notice it—Hunter slowly slipping her phone from a pocket and resting it on her lap.

Mr. Richter is making his way up and down the desks but he's on the other side of the room, pausing to answer a question. That's when Hunter pulls it out, taking a shot of the first page, then the second. She quickly slips her phone back down and takes a peek in Mr. Richter's direction. He's back to pacing up and down the room, and she impatiently taps her pencil against her wrist, biding time.

I can't believe what I'm seeing. Hunter is cheating, taking snapshots of the test to share later. Doing exactly what she claimed Lia was planning. I'm so shocked, it takes me a second to look away as Richter makes his way toward us.

My hands are gripping the desk so hard, the edge is cutting into my skin. It's not just difficult to believe, it's impossible: Lia is gone and here is Hunter, busy cheating on the Physics test. Anger pulses in building waves that crash through me. I'm furious at Hunter, who's clearly not in mourning, but strangely, I'm even angrier at Lia. All I can think is, This *is the person you chose?* This *is the person you loved?*

The person you chose in place of me. The person you loved instead of me.

I check the clock and then Hunter, who seems acutely aware she has less than one minute to get the rest of the test. *Good,* I think. *Because fuck you.*

Then someone else raises a hand, and as Richter goes to answer, Hunter pulls out her phone again and snaps pictures of the last three pages.

This is bullshit, and I refuse to let her get away with it. My hand shoots up just as the bell rings. Richter moves quickly to me. "Yes, Chase?" he asks as others begin to get up, trickling to the front to drop off exams on his desk. Hunter turns around, our eyes locking, and in that second, I swear she knows everything I'm thinking. She looks frantic, eyes wide, and shakes her head ever so slightly—half-warning, half-pleading—and I falter, suddenly unsure. Her desperation feels strangely familiar, and I don't understand what it means.

"Chase?" Mr. Richter asks again.

"Sorry," I say. Hunter has turned away, bag over a shoulder, heading up to turn in her test. She glances back one last time, a sad smile on her face, like she's resigned to her fate, to me telling Richter what she just did. "I was just wondering," I hear myself saying instead, "is there going to be extra credit like last time?"

As Mr. Richter gently chides me for asking for extra credit before I know how I'll score, Hunter stares at me, looking just as stunned as I feel.

We both know I just saved her and neither of us knows why.

16.

The blood is pounding so hard in my ears that I can barely hear. The rest of the morning flies by in a blur. Stupid, so stupid. I can't believe what I just did. All I had to do was tell Mr. Richter what I saw. He would've taken Hunter's phone and she would've been finished. But instead, I hesitated and let her get away with it.

For a second, I let myself make excuses. Maybe I wasn't sure of what I saw. Maybe I imagined it. Or maybe it would've been futile—Hunter's phone was almost certainly locked, and if they weren't able to get in, I'd have no proof. But I know they're just excuses, because I *didn't* just imagine it and I know they'd believed me over her. Me, Chase Ohara, student council president, captain of the cross-country team, likely valedictorian, and favorite of her teachers, against her, Hunter van Leeuwen, a senior new kid who got kicked out of Phillips Exeter.

Then I think back to what Hunter told me at the beginning of the week, when neither of us knew what'd happened to Lia yet, about this very Physics test and what Lia and Cole were planning. Had she been lying then? Had *she* been the one who made those plans with Cole?

By the time lunch arrives, I'm ready to kill Hunter, rushing out of class to find her in the cafeteria. But I've been distracted, first by the test and then by what Hunter did during it, because I don't get very far before running into Logan Williams, the vice president of student council, who stops me in the hall: "Chase!"

I want to walk past her, but she holds on to my arm. "I'm so sorry," she says, and I realize everyone's looking at me. Or trying to pretend they're not looking at me.

"What?" I ask, still intent on finding Hunter.

"Lia," she says. "They made an announcement yesterday when you were out."

My eyes immediately find the floor, my vision soon obscured by tears I don't want to shed in front of the growing crowd. Suddenly, my mind cuts through the fog of the last few hours obsessing over Hunter's actions and I belatedly recognize the looks of pity and curiosity on everyone's faces. The teachers, the classmates, the strangers in the halls between classes. All of them, all morning. Somehow, I'd managed to escape a direct confrontation until now.

"I'm sorry," she repeats. "I know you were close." Logan is one of those genuinely nice people who isn't always thinking of how a decision will pay off three steps down the line, unlike me. She means well and she's a reliable ally on council, but I can't stand to be near her and her kindness right now.

"Thanks," I manage, shouldering past her.

"I'm here if . . " she trails off.

"Okay," I say, not turning back.

I run into a few more people on the way to the cafeteria, all members of student council or cross-country, and I have to suppress the urge to escape to my car and hide.

Then I see her.

Actually, it's Hunter who finds me before I find her, leaning against the wall near the entrance to the caf, eyes scanning the crowd.

"Hey," she says, coming toward me.

"I can't believe you—"

"I can explain." She sounds so confident it throws me off.

I take a deep breath, try not to lose it. "Then explain."

"Not now," she says, eyes not on me but still searching for someone in the hall. "I have to be somewhere. But after school."

"This is such crap," I say.

Then she surprises me: "I know we don't really know each other, but I need you to trust me." Now she's gripping me by the shoulders, really looming over me.

"But that's just it," I tell her. "I don't trust you." That's not completely true. I did, or I was starting to, before this morning. It felt like maybe we were going through something together. It felt like she understood, even if she was part of the problem, because she loved Lia like I did and I wasn't completely alone.

Hunter seems to spot someone in the crowd streaming into the caf. I turn in the same direction and see Cole. "You're a fucking liar," I tell her. "You said Lia and Cole were—"

She claps a hand over my mouth. "Shut up."

The sharpness in her voice stops me. I rip her hand off me. "What the fuck?" I whisper-yell.

"Sorry," she says, surprising me with the apology but still sounding agitated. "Look, I have to go. We can talk after school. Meet you at the bus bay. Or you can just do whatever you're going to do."

Lia's voice suddenly echoes in my mind: "You always do whatever you want, you always get whatever you want." Something she said to me in a fight, and it cuts in a new way.

I watch Hunter make her way to Cole and pull out her phone. Then they both slip away, and it feels like everyone's eyes are on me again. I run to my car, think about skipping but decide against it. Briefly, I consider going to Mr. Richter and telling him what I saw, but it's probably too late now. Hunter's smart. She wouldn't just leave photos of the test on her phone.

When the five-minute bell rings, I'm still fighting the urge to just *go* when I get a message from an unfamiliar number.

Unknown: Hey it's Hunter. Sorry about earlier.

I stare at it as I walk toward my next class. How did she get my number? In the short time she's been at Meadowlark, we've never had a shared project, a reason to exchange info. For a moment, I think she must've gotten it from Lia, but then I remember her walking away with Cole, who's the more likely source.

Hunter: I do want to talk.

Hunter: Meet me after school, bus bay like last time?

I stare at the texts for a long time before answering. I don't owe her anything, but I still want to know.

Me: I have xc

Hunter: I'll wait.

Me: Fine

When I show up to practice though, the conversation stops and everyone looks at me like I'm a ghost. "Ohara," Coach Gimmly says with a frown. "I didn't really expect you today."

"Why not?" I try to say casually, bending to retie my laces so I don't have to receive everyone's stares.

"Um." He scratches the back of his neck. "You were out sick yesterday. Why don't you take it easy. Tad can take over for a few days."

"I can do it," I say, standing straight, adjusting my ponytail.

"Go home," Gimmly says. "You don't look so good." It's true, I probably look awful, because I've never felt worse in my life.

"No," I say, this time with force. "I can't."

I've thrown him off. "What do you mean, you can't?"

Then I play the only card I know he'll accept: "My best friend just died. I need this." We were more than best friends, everyone knew that. But now it's what Lia's parents call me and it's what gives me a small measure of comfort now. And before the year we were together, we'd been best friends for over ten years. Maybe that matters more. Maybe that's always mattered more and why our breakup was so devastating. I didn't just lose my girlfriend, I lost my best friend. And now I've lost both.

There's nothing he can really say, and as predicted, he acquiesces. We take a familiar route, one I must've completed over a hundred times, and I try to lean in to that familiarity, lose myself in it, but I still struggle. My legs burn and my head's spinning. It feels like the world is closing in on me and I'm crumbling under the weight of it all. But I have to keep pushing. It's who I am. Chase Ohara, future Stanford grad, future power broker.

I think of my dad, how he got into Stanford but couldn't afford to go, how he grew up poor in Cali within a prosperous Asian American community. How he always reminds me and Aidan to "stay hungry, take nothing for granted." Except now I'm not just hungry, I'm *starving*, and the thing I want most in the world isn't a thing at all. Isn't Stanford, or grades, or the perfect SAT score.

It's Lia, and I'll never have her.

Maybe I never did.

As we run against traffic like we always do, a scary, familiar image bursts into my mind: the oncoming bus heading toward us, a single misstep at just the wrong moment.

I can see it. I can almost *feel* it, my feet suddenly unsteady, off rhythm, and my body tilting as if pulled by the street.

And in one second, it'd all be over. No more struggling to breathe through this impossible pain in my chest. No more struggling, period.

"Hey," Tad jogs up to me. "You okay?"

I shake all of it from my mind, put a smile on. "I'm fine," I lie.

We finish and I quickly pack my things to avoid conversation. The image is gone but this time, the idea lingers. Somehow, I imagine it'd be painless. Somehow, it'd be over in an instant.

Somehow, I'd be free.

17.

I find Hunter on the same green bench at the edge of the bus bay, headphones on, feet hanging off the side, laces of her boots untied. Eyes closed, she looks almost peaceful, and it only infuriates me more. The same wave of anger burns through me as before, an anger almost directed more at Lia than her: how could she have ever loved someone like Hunter? But Lia is gone and all my questions will forever remain unanswered.

Hunter seems to sense me approaching, sits up and slips her headphones off, leaving them around her neck. "Hey," she says, like nothing is wrong.

My hands curl into fists at my side but I know all my rage won't get me anywhere, so I force them open.

"Let's go for a walk," she says. "Come on."

I follow behind as we head south on the sidewalk along Rockaway toward Merillon in a loop around campus. I was just here running with Tad and the rest of the team, and as I watch a bus pass us, my chest tightens in dread, the image from earlier flashing into my mind. But this time, I don't feel the pull of the road, my feet steady, the temptation abated. This time, I'm in control, so I let out a breath.

"Hold on," I say, and put a hand on Hunter's shoulder. "I don't have time for this. Just tell me what you were doing."

She doesn't slow, just shrugs my hand off. "I don't know if I can trust you yet."

I almost laugh at the absurdity. "Is that supposed to be a joke? I'm the one who can't trust *you*."

She turns around, but she doesn't meet my eyes.

"You're the one who acted like you actually cared about Lia. And then today in Physics—how could you? You said Lia wanted to cheat on the next test but it was a lie, wasn't it? *You're* the one who wanted to get copies of the test. Why?" I have to hold back from screaming, from grabbing her by the shoulders and giving her a hard shake.

"Do you want to know the truth or do you just want to yell at me?" she asks, and it throws me off, the calm in her voice.

I do want to just yell, but I want the truth more so I hold back, shove the rage down.

Hunter notices her laces and drops to one knee to tie them. The seconds crawl forward and I can't help but feel like she's trolling me. "Come on," she says, and we resume walking. "I'll tell you everything, but you have to promise it stays between us."

I nod, exasperated.

"I might have left out that I was part of it, Cole's enterprise," she says as she sneaks a glance at me.

It doesn't surprise me so I just say, "Go on."

"But I was pretty new so I didn't know much about it," she continues. "I needed help in a couple classes and Lia brought me in. I only found out they were getting access to tests last week." I can't figure out if she's telling the truth, but I also can't see why she'd lie.

"What does this have to do with this morning?" I ask as we turn off Merillon back into Meadowlark's parking lot.

"I didn't know what happened between Cole and Lia, just that she said he'd convinced her they'd be some kind of revolutionaries." Then she takes a deep breath. "But now I think she was just trying to make it seem like it was her idea. Or that she was on board at least."

"What do you mean?" We've stopped moving, both of us staring out at the nearly empty parking lot, the redbrick building beyond, the glimpse of tennis courts behind it. The entire place hums with anticipation, and I'm almost scared of what Hunter will say next.

"I think she was pressured into it," Hunter says, turning toward me. The wind picks up, sending her hair dancing lightly across her face. "Cole called me last night out of the blue. Insisted on meeting up. Said he was sorry about Lia, that he couldn't believe it." Her eyes are pinning me in place, and I can't look away. "Said he was even more sorry to do this but the group had talked and come to a decision. I had to get them the Physics test or I was out."

"You're joking," I say in shock. Cole and I aren't exactly friends, but I've known him since second grade. I can't imagine anyone being this cold, not days after Lia's death.

"No." Hunter looks grim. "At first I was like, I'm fucking out, whatever. But I couldn't stop thinking about it all night. What if that's what Cole told Lia?"

I feel sick again, and as everything Hunter tells me falls into place, blood pulses in growing pressure behind my right eye socket, a thousand needles stabbing in unison as pain explodes through the rest of my skull like fireworks. My eyelids flutter desperately in an attempt to shut it all out, but I can't.

I knew Lia was struggling. I knew she'd struggle without me, and now I know what she did to survive after we broke up.

All I can think about now is something I said to her back in May, at the end, when we were breaking each other's hearts: "Maybe that's the real reason you're mad, that you'll never be like me or your mom. That maybe you'll never be good enough. That you'll always have to rely on one of us. That you need us because you'll never make it on your own." The words had burst out of me like gunfire, fast and dangerous, designed to inflict maximum damage. They were impossible to take back once spoken—though I later tried, apologizing and begging—because I was really issuing a dare, taunting Lia to prove me wrong.

Is that what led her to seek out Cole? I can't imagine he approached her the way he approached me—Lia didn't exactly have the same reputation, wasn't at the top of the class. We never talked about it explicitly, but I know it bothered her, the comparisons: two Asians in an overwhelmingly White school, one at the top and one middling. There were things teachers might let slip, like curiosity over a difference in our performance as if I matched their expectations but Lia fell short, seemingly innocent questions from classmates about her adoption like Lia had the genetic goods but was missing some key cultural element. Even little comments from Jo gently admonishing Lia to be more like me, which came off as awkward compliments but probably stung. They were all just small moments of friction that had to grate and grate on her. And then I said what I'd said, out of weakness, lashing out in a desperately painful moment, but also because I knew it would cut deep.

So I dared her to prove me wrong, and alone, she must've turned to Cole. But I know it couldn't have been easy, being part of his little gang. That to receive help meant you had to contribute too. And with us, I always let her take whatever she needed, never asking for anything in return. I can picture her struggling still, maybe even imagine Cole's frustration with her. And then finally, a breaking point, and he asks her to get them the Physics test or she's out. Is that what happened?

"Do you have any proof?" I finally ask Hunter, but I'm not sure what it would even mean now that she's gone.

"No," she says quietly. "But that's why I changed my mind, told him I'd do it."

I'd almost forgotten that this is the reason I'm even here in the first place. The Physics test from this morning suddenly feels like a lifetime ago.

"It's actually why I wanted to talk to you. Even if you hadn't caught me," Hunter continues. "I could use your help."

"With what?"

"Getting proof," she says, like it's obvious. "Look, I know I'm not as smart as you." This admission seems to pain her, but she pushes on. "I'm not as smart as Cole or his friends. Getting the test just means they're not cutting me loose—yet. I'm hanging on by a thread. They'll never let me in, not really. I'll never be one of them, but you could."

"You're joking." I let out a short, stunned laugh. "You want me to *infiltrate* Cole's crew of cheaters and then what, get some kind of proof of them pressuring Lia to cheat? Don't be ridiculous."

"What's ridiculous about it?" she asks, staring me down.

"Everything." I shake my head and begin to head to my car, Hunter trailing after me. "What kind of proof are you even looking for? And what would you do with it, turn him in? For what, exactly—asking a member of his cheating ring to cheat?" After we arrive at my car, I lean a shoulder against the door and level a look at her. "Have you even thought about what this would do to Lia? To her reputation?"

"Who cares about any of that?" she asks, exasperated. "She's *gone*."

I flinch at the raw anger in her voice. "It's *someone's* fault." A tear spills over followed by more as she quickly swipes them away. "And maybe that someone is Cole."

It feels like a desperate theory. I don't think she's intentionally lying—everything she's saying, she believes. But each link feels weaker than the one before it. According to her, Lia had agreed to steal the test, maybe even wanted to. And then Lia disappeared Thursday night, almost a full week before the test. Could it really be the reason she left?

I think of the police, sitting in the Vestianos' dining room: "Sometimes these things happen without warning. Sometimes there are no signs."

But Hunter's words cut through: "It's *someone's* fault. And maybe that someone is Cole." Maybe this is what she needs to believe because nothing else makes sense. Because the person we love is gone and we need it to make sense. Because if we can trace a line between Cole's actions and Lia's death, then it will mean something, even if we can't bring Lia back. I look at Hunter's face. Her heartbreak, so raw and aching, sparks a recognition in me and the anger I felt earlier begins to soften.

I almost tell her yes, if only so she'll feel less alone. But the truth is that people like Hunter van Leeuwen don't have to weigh risks the same way the rest of us do. She got lucky the first time, but we have a quiz or test almost every week, and that luck will run out eventually. If she gets caught and kicked out, there are any number of fancy schools that would take her, along with a very generous donation. Or perhaps her father would simply call the right school board member, write a check for the football team or a new media lab and smooth a hiccup in Hunter's high school career. The kind of hiccup that would derail my entire life.

I'm about to tell her no again, gently this time, but she speaks first: "I know we were together for only a few months. And I know you and Lia have this huge history, but you weren't with her near the end. I'm telling you, something wasn't right."

The last five months of being on the outside looking in, of missing Lia and what we had, of longing and desperation and mystery. The last five months of not knowing Lia, what happened to her, a black hole I can't see into. Our breakup changed me, made me brittle and lost. A different person.

I think of the moments I saw her in the hall, how much of a stranger she'd become. The moments our eyes met and how it hurt so much we had to look away.

Maybe Hunter is wrong about Cole and Lia, but maybe she's not wrong about Lia near the end. What made her do it, wade out into the midnight sea, disappear under the water? I have to hold on to my car to stay upright as the wave of grief slams into me, threatening to pull me under.

What was Lia going through? What was she doing? With Hunter, with Cole. And here it was, the perfect opportunity to find out.

I'll never have Lia back, never have these last five months back, but maybe I can find out what happened. "I don't know," I tell Hunter, but I can feel myself caving.

Anything for Lia, always.

"Please, Chase," Hunter says simply.

Meet me in Montauk, Lia had texted me and I didn't show up in time.

I take a deep breath, then say yes. I owe it to her to show up now.

Some risks are worth taking.

18.

Cole Landau and I go all the way back to middle school track. But it wasn't until second semester freshmen year that he moved up from an acquaintance to dealer. I showed up to tryouts after an all-nighter looking like shit and feeling worse.

"Hey, Ohara," he said, eyes cutting up and down. "Wow, you okay?"

"I'm fine." I just wanted to be left alone.

"You look like you're about to collapse," he said, taking a few steps my way and dropping his voice. "Here." He slipped an Altoids tin out of his track shorts, knocked out a small white pill onto his palm, an offer. "It's not a big deal, just Adderall. Half the team's on it."

"No, thanks," I said, but I hesitated.

"Seriously, not a big deal," he said. "And you don't want to fuck up tryouts your first year, do you?"

I looked out at everyone else warming up. Was he exaggerating that half the team was on it? I felt awful, light-headed and dizzy with the beginnings of a migraine. And worse, he was right—these were new coaches who'd never seen me run before, and I was the only Asian kid there. Maybe it wouldn't have mattered, but I felt this pressure, like I had to be the fastest to prove I belonged on the team.

"Okay," I told him. "Thanks." It went down easy with a sip of water, and by the time we crouched at the starting line, the pressure and exhaustion seemed to lift, a rush of freedom in their place. Everything seemed to sharpen—my eyesight, my mind. It was easier to *breathe*.

I felt invincible.

Near the end of sophomore year, he introduced me to Focentra when I complained that Adderall didn't pack the same punch anymore.

Beginning of junior year, he told me about a new "initiative" he was starting, how he'd gotten some of the top kids in our class behind it.

"Who?" I'd asked.

He gave three names: Lena Harrison, Josh Hendon, and Rebecca Degray. Josh was the president of debate, and both Lena and Rebecca were direct threats to my future as valedictorian. He had to know that.

"I don't believe you."

"Ask them yourself," he said with a shrug, and I knew he wouldn't bluff about something I could so easily verify. "Anyway, you should join us."

"What are you planning to do?" I asked.

"Nothing big," he said, remaining cryptic. When he saw my skepticism, he relented a little, adding, "Just the usual. Share notes. Homework. That kind of thing."

"No, thanks," I said.

"Aren't you sick of all the shit we have to do? School, classes. Homework and tests. All the crap we have to do *for college* like we're circus animals made to do tricks. It's bullshit and you know it." It surprised me, the sudden passion in his voice. Cole never struck me as anyone who cared that much about school. He was one of the smarter kids, often in the same honors and AP classes with me, but lacking the work ethic to be real competition. "It doesn't have to be like that, not if we all work together."

Maybe it was *because* he'd never been seen as real competition that he wanted to do this.

"Look, it's not that different from what you're doing now," he said, and it took me a moment to understand what he meant.

The Focentra.

"Don't be ridiculous," I said. "It's not even close."

"Isn't it?" he challenged.

"It's totally different."

Wasn't it?

It was.

Cole had been right back when we were freshmen: half the team was on Adderall. Only now, it was more like most of the team. Everyone was on *something*, and it was just part of the game.

Maybe he had a point, that all the crap we had to do *for college* sucked. The sleepless nights, the endless cramming, the mountain of extracurriculars, the impossible standard of coming off as a relatable, regular teen while also trying to prove you had the potential to lead the nation, or invent the next life-changing app, or become the voice of your generation. You were supposed to be passionate and extraordinary at something specific but still well-rounded. Perfect but also humble. Driven but not ruthless. Work hard but make it look easy.

"No," I said for the final time. It was tempting, more than tempting. Cole was promising a world where we might actually achieve something like balance, where we might sleep more than four hours a night and still ace our tests. I also understood why he told me who he'd already recruited. The threat was implicit: if I didn't join, they might overtake me, leave me in the dust. But what I feared was the opposite—that we'd all get complacent, our performance converging. Or worse, our complacency would lead us to slip and get caught.

High school wasn't a team sport. There was only one valedictorian.

"All right," Cole said. I was surprised he didn't push harder. "But the door's always open."

19.

Hunter texts me the next night to tell me Cole's interested in meeting the following day. After school, she takes me through the busy halls to where Cole is leading Speech and Debate practice in one of the English classrooms.

"I've already talked to him," she reminds me out in the hall after she's waved at him inside. "He's agreed to give you a trial run."

"What exactly does that mean?"

"He'll give you an assignment. You'll do it. Turn it in."

"That's it?"

Hunter nods. "That's it."

"Look who's back," Cole says, joining us outside, broad smile directed at me. It's a strange thing to say, as if he knew I couldn't stay away forever, but his expression isn't gloating. It's welcoming. Kind, even.

"Hey," I say, awkward.

He leans against the door frame, arms crossed but demeanor friendly.

"You sure?" he asks, producing a small packet, folded in half. The assignment Hunter told me about. He holds it out, but only halfway between us, forcing me to reach for it.

The truth is I'm not sure at all. There's still time to back out, though Hunter will be pissed. But I'm not doing this for her. I'm doing it for Lia. I search Cole's face, really look, but he's unreadable. If he's nervous, he's not showing it. No sign of guilt or shame. Nothing to hide.

I take it from him and stick it in my backpack quickly, afraid of being caught, and he raises an eyebrow in amusement.

"When do you need it by?"

"Sunday," he says. "That doable?"

Lia's funeral is on Saturday. I have no idea what it is or how long it'll take me, but I nod.

"Good." Then he drops his voice: "And you know the drill"—I glance over at Hunter, who just shrugs—"no texts, no e-mails, call if you absolutely have to. But otherwise, just meet me back here if it's a weekday, and my house on the weekend."

"Yeah," I say, even though I hadn't known any of that. These rules are slightly different from the way we've always done things. Whenever I needed to re-up on Focentra, all I had to do was text asking if he wanted to hang out. This feels even more secretive, but maybe it's riskier too, or just more complicated.

"And one more thing," Cole adds, this time sounding a little hesitant. "I'm sorry. About Lia." He looks over at Hunter too, but only briefly. "It sucks."

She tenses visibly but says nothing. I don't know what to say so I remain quiet too. My mind lingers on his words, trying to decipher if there was an apology under his condolences, if "I'm sorry" could hold hidden meaning, a sense of responsibility.

Cole uncrosses his arms, hand hovering near my shoulder for a second before he retracts, and I'm grateful. "All right," he says instead and heads back inside, leaving me and Hunter in the hall.

Leaning over, I pull out the packet he gave me just enough to unfold it inside my backpack.

"Oh," I say.

"What?" Hunter asks. "Is there a problem?"

It's just a lab from AP Bio, which I took junior year and still have all my notes and homework. But even without all that, it'd be easy to look up most of this online. He gave me something easy on purpose. Maybe that's what the trial run is. Or maybe he feels sorry for me, because of Lia.

"No," I say. "No problem."

"Okay," she says. "Thanks."

"What for?" I zip up my backpack, sling it over my shoulder as I head toward the gym for cross-country practice.

"For doing this. For believing me."

Our eyes meet and it unsettles me a little to see her gratitude because I don't know what to believe at this point.

All I know is that Lia is gone, and I want to know why.

When I'm finally home later that night, I head down to the basement, where I keep old notes and homework. I lift the lids of a couple plastic tubs before I find my AP Bio binders, neatly stacked and organized from last May.

Lia and I took AP Bio together last year, one of the two classes we managed to share during the same periods, sitting next to each other and partnering for all the labs.

It takes me a few minutes to find the right lab on cell respiration. I take it upstairs and begin to copy my notes over, careful to change the wording a little here and there.

And then I turn to the last page and my heart stops. On the top right corner is Lia's handwriting: "Love you," the two words encased in a loosely drawn heart.

I remember feeling annoyed when she did it. "You know I hate it when you do that," I told her.

"You love it," she said, nudging me with her shoulder. We were at her house, lying on the floor working on the lab write-up together, which of course meant I was doing most of it and she was distracting me. "Besides, what's more important, perfect notes or your girlfriend telling you she loves you?" She leaned over, kissing me.

"Ugh, you're impossible," I said, and she laughed.

The memory leaves me in pieces and I have to push away from my desk to avoid crying all over the packet Cole gave me. I unclip my notes from last year and curl up in bed, holding the pages to my chest, pressing Lia's words to my heart. I miss her so much I can't breathe.

It's been three days since I heard the news and it still feels like it just happened, like it's happening right now.

I wish I could go back in time, to a year ago when we were at her house. I wish I could tell her that she was right, that I love this little reminder of her love.

I wish I could tell her that I loved her too.

When I finally manage to come up for air, I sit in a slightly stunned daze, just staring at her words, that loose heart. Then I run downstairs to the basement and begin to tear through each tub until I collect everything from AP Bio and AP US History.

I spend hours transfixed, flipping through each page, my heart stopping every time I stumble upon Lia's handwriting. I can't believe I ever found her scribbles intrusive, annoying.

"You're cute," she wrote on one page.

"This is so boring!" she wrote on my notes on mitosis vs. meiosis.

"Montauk tomorrow?" she asked. I check the date, try to remember when this was. Last December. Bitter cold. We went straight to the boat and shivered the whole time because it wouldn't heat up enough. We couldn't stay overnight, driving back in my car late Saturday night and sleeping over at Lia's.

I think about the last five months and what I've missed, everything I've lost. I want it back, more than anything, but it's gone. This is all I have left now, just little fragments of her words and a heartbreak that will never, ever heal right.

20.

It's a short, quiet drive to the church Saturday morning. We arrive too early but still struggle to find parking. I already know the attendance will be huge because of Jo. There might even be press. Lia would've hated it, all these strangers who never even knew her.

"Is Dad coming?" Aidan asks.

"No," I say.

"Oh." I can't tell if she's disappointed or unsurprised.

"He called this morning," I tell her.

Mom looks over at me in slight surprise. "He did? I've been trying to get ahold of him all week."

I can still hear his gravelly voice: "Sorry I can't be there, Chase." He made the usual excuses—a big deal in San Francisco and McKinsey couldn't spare him. Even though he'd watched me and Lia grow up together, even though we used to vacation as families, even though we *were* all family, once upon a time. "You've got to keep your head up," he said at the end of the short call, and I understood the subtext. Don't lose sight of the goal, no matter what. Can't forget the bigger picture, not even if you're dying inside, maybe especially if you're dying inside.

I wanted to throw my phone across the room. But I just ended the call without a goodbye, let my silence speak for me.

"Does he know?" Aidan asks. "About Lia?"

"He knows," I say, and try to bury the anger.

As we circle the area, I distract myself by scanning the sidewalks for Hunter. I think of the things she's told me about Lia, about these last five months. How the Lia I knew and loved became the Lia who swam out to sea by herself. I can't shake the feeling that Hunter's not telling me everything she knows. Maybe she's not hiding something on purpose, but she's holding something back. Or she's so wrapped up in her pursuit of Cole—of finding someone to blame—that she's blinded herself. I don't know what to think, what to believe, but all I know is that the only person I've ever loved is gone and I want to know why.

When we finally find a parking spot a few streets away, we join the stream of black coats and scarves. Aidan takes my hand and tugs.

"I miss her too," she says quietly.

"I know," I whisper back, already blinking back tears.

She gives me a small squeeze. "Look," she says, showing me the necklace she's wearing. At my confused expression, she adds, "Lia gave it to me, remember?"

"When?" I ask distractedly. We're getting close, the crowd thickening.

"September. For my birthday," she says.

"What are you talking about?" I ask, giving the necklace a closer look. It's a teardrop in sapphire, Aidan's birthstone.

"You were there," she says, but I definitely don't remember. Maybe she's talking about last year, when she turned ten. After her birthday party, Lia and I had taken her out for late-night pizza, just the three of us. Had Lia given it to her then?

Before I have a chance to ask, I see the Vestianos near the entrance, greeting everyone as they come up. Jo spots us at the bottom of the steps. "Chase!" she calls out, waving us up. She hugs all of us in turn, me the tightest and longest. When we break, there are tears shining in her eyes but I can see something else too, a glassy blankness behind them. Lia once told me she found a bottle of Valium in Jo's beside table, and I wouldn't blame her for taking something today. I wrap my arms around her again and hug her tight.

Inside, ushers escort us to our seats, handing us program cards printed on thick, creamy paper. I look all around us, at the mountains of white lilies and baby's breath, the celebrity chefs and executives from the network. This was the exact life Lia wanted to avoid and now it's how she'll be remembered. I scan the space, steal glances at the door searching for Hunter, but she's still not here.

"Is it closed casket?" one of the people beside us asks her companion, and I can feel my whole body tensing. I don't recognize either of them.

"Yes. They didn't want to do a viewing. All that time in the water," the other says, and I immediately turn toward the casket at the front of the chapel. It didn't occur to me to think about whether it'd be open or closed. I've only been to one funeral before, for my grandfather, but it was years ago and I can't remember the details, just the oppressive air of grief, the shock of having to say goodbye. And now I have to do it again, this time to the person who matters most to me in the world.

"So sad," the first one says. "Only seventeen."

"Yes," the other agrees.

All that time in the water. It's all I can think about now. Lia floating, adrift in the sea. For how long? Hours or days? It must be days, but how many? I can't bear the thought of her out there alone and lost.

Lia, my Lia.

I let the tears fall, hear them splatter against the program card. The strangers beside me notice and seem to freeze in discomfort. After a brief and awkward silence, they get up and I never see them return. *Good,* I think. *Go gossip somewhere else.*

Breathe, I tell myself. I have to get it together. Wiping away my tears, I stare at the program, try to focus on that. A hymn, a psalm, a couple readings by her parents. A homily, prayer, and a closing hymn. No eulogies, no mention of heaven or hell—it's a Catholic funeral mass.

Lia was baptized and confirmed but never religious. The Vestianos go to church only twice a year, for Easter and for midnight mass at Christmas, but God is suddenly everywhere today. God is watching over her, the priest says. God is watching over all of us in our time of grief. She's with God now.

God, God, God.

Even though my parents were atheists, I was never as sure as them. Now I'm less certain than ever, torn between what I want and what I know: part of me longs for there to be an *after*, but part of me knows my time with Lia is over.

The man who delivers the homily clearly never met Lia. He talks about how she was adopted from Korea, about how close she was with her mother, about how much she loved the family trips to her birthplace. He's sticking to the facts but getting the details wrong.

I'm completely numb, just going through the motions. I stand when everyone else stands. I mumble when we're supposed to sing. But mostly I stare at the casket and the world fades away. This moment feels almost sacred, the last time I'll get to be near her. It's my chance to say goodbye and I'm not ready. Maybe I'll never be ready. This is the last time I'll ever be in the same room as her, and I have so many mistakes and fuckups to atone for.

There are so many things I wish I could say to her, memories I wish I could relive, so many moments I wish I could redo.

In this horrible, unending moment, I can't comprehend why I'd resented her for wanting to come out to California with me. Can't believe I'd pushed her away when we could've flown out together, still us against the world. I'd give anything to go back, give her the summer she wanted. Maybe she'd still be here.

When we stand to leave, I watch as Lia is carried out, and I still don't have the words to say goodbye. I'm frozen, and it takes Aidan tugging hard on my cardigan for me to move.

When we're outside, I think I catch a glimpse of Hunter by a distant tree as we stand in a circle around the casket and the priest commits Lia to the ground, but when I look again, no one's there.

21.

After the service, I drop Mom and Aidan off before heading to the Vestianos' house. Aidan has soccer in the afternoon, and I tell Mom it's fine, that I'll call her when it's over, that I'll only stay for an hour at most. She's reluctant to leave me by myself, but I don't want to be any more of a burden than I've already been, so I repeat my promise to call her after.

At the Vestianos', I'm surrounded by a sea of mostly unfamiliar faces. Lia and her parents weren't close to their extended families, something about their jealousy over Jo's success and their initial disapproval of Lia's adoption that left lingering bad blood, but I was never really sure since Lia rarely saw them and didn't like to talk about it. "Mom always says family is who you choose," Lia used to tell me, and it was understood Lia meant me too.

I scan the room, unsure of who I'm hoping to find. No Hunter. No one else from school, actually. I saw some of them at the funeral, a few from the volleyball team, one or two from Science Olympiad, but I avoided everyone, too overwhelmed with grief. Feeling lost, I'm hit with the urge to run away when Jo catches me. She's sitting on the floor in the living room, part of a larger circle, and she waves me over, patting the place beside her.

"This is Chase, Lia's best friend," she tells everyone, and I say a quiet hello. They're sharing stories about Lia. Her first time seeing a lobster, her first time at the beach. Her first time back in Korea, her first time making and cutting fresh pasta in Italy. Jo and Rob seem to only talk about firsts because thinking about lasts is too hard. The last time I saw her, the last things we said to each other, the last few months of being shut out. But these memories, these stories they're telling don't quite feel real. It's true that they went to a kimchi museum and made a jar of it when she was ten—I've seen the episode—but none of it feels like *her*. Who she really was.

"Chase?" Rob asks. "Do you have a favorite story?" I look over at them, tears clinging to cheeks, exhaustion in their bones, grief etched in the lines of their bodies. He's asking for a reprieve—from talking, from remembering. I think of all the stories I could tell but come up empty. They're all too personal, or too insignificant in the way that life is made up of tiny, forgotten moments strung together one after the other. A past that becomes the present that disappears into the future, time pushing forward relentlessly, leaving scattered memories and fragments of dreams in its wake.

I can't think of the future right now. And everyone is looking at me. Suddenly, I notice that the circle around us has grown larger.

I could beg off with a quick apology. The Vestianos would forgive me, I know they would. My eyes find them again, hands and arms wrapped around each other, clutching, clinging.

It hits me then that this day, the day of Lia's funeral, isn't for Lia. It's for the people who love her and miss her. For her parents, for her friends, for me. It's for us to remember and celebrate her. I hear Jo's voice saying "That's *so* Lia" on Tuesday when I told them her password. These little details that make her feel a little more present, that lessen the loss of her.

Taking a deep breath, I begin. "Two years ago, right after the last hurricane, we discovered two baby squirrels near Lia's house. Their eyes were still closed and they were completely helpless. We kept checking on them from Lia's room but their mom never came back. We thought she was probably injured during the storm. So of course Lia adopted them."

A few chuckles and small, watery smiles from Jo and Rob.

"When she called rescue groups, many of them didn't take squirrels and were already overwhelmed with calls about injured or sick animals from the hurricane. Animal control said they'd have to euthanize them, and Lia yelled at them. They reminded her squirrels were considered pests, and she called them the pests."

The chuckles grow into scattered laughter.

"To be fair, squirrels *are* kind of pests. But Lia looked at these helpless babies and didn't see the future dumpster-diving monsters they'd become. She saw two critters who needed her. She fed them puppy formula out of a dropper. She checked on them round the clock, changing their bedding and keeping them clean, just like a mom would. She was the first thing they saw when they opened their eyes."

A hushed "aww" spreads throughout the room.

"And she named them Jo and Rob, after her parents." The Vestianos and I lock eyes, all three of us with tears streaming down our faces. When I finally break contact, I look up and see that we're not the only ones crying.

Only, the last part isn't true.

Jo didn't want pet squirrels and tasked her assistant with finding a shelter that would take them. Within a week, they'd found a sanctuary upstate that said they'd rehabilitate them and release them into the wild.

Lia told me she wanted to wait until she got to know them better before deciding on names, but then all of a sudden, it was too late and Lia never got the chance.

22.

People keep coming up to tell me what a touching tribute I gave and how Lia is smiling down at us from above. It makes my skin crawl and slowly, I shrink away from them, even though I know they're just trying to help.

When I finally catch a moment alone, I manage to slip away upstairs to Lia's bedroom where I can hide out for a few minutes. I lie on her bed, pull the back of her comforter over me without getting under it, and I cry. I know I shouldn't be here, but I can't help it.

I miss her so much and I just want to be with her. Squeezing my eyes closed, I try to shut out the world. Lia and I used to lie on this bed together all the time when we were little, doing homework, watching movies, daydreaming and telling each other all the things we'd do once we were grown up.

Once we were free.

"Let's travel the world," she'd say.

"Let's *conquer* the world," I'd say, and she laughed.

"That's so boring," she said, rolling onto her side to face me. Lia never had to carve out a place for herself in this world. She was already on top, safe with nothing to prove. In my eyes, she always had power.

"Fine, then *I'll* conquer it and *you* travel it."

"Okay, deal," she said. "But you better be a good little tyrant."

"Of course." I think even back then, what I really wanted was to *give* Lia the world.

A gasp startles me from my memories. Or dreams of lost memories. But I keep my eyes closed. I'm in that halfway state between here and gone. "It's okay, hon, you just sleep." Jo's voice is so soothing and Lia's bed so warm that I let go.

It's dark when I wake, and I can't remember the last time I managed to sleep longer than an hour or two. I don't belong here, but I can't help but linger in Lia's room, a place that once felt like home. At her desk, I pull open a drawer, fiddle with her pencils, and find her Tombow eraser, the one she brought home from Japan on a summer trip two years ago and adored. A second drawer reveals a clutter of pens and clippies, but also something else underneath.

My breath catches at the sight of the white card now pale yellow with age, the chalky watercolor heart I painted in second grade, little faded stars around it. I can't believe she's kept this, a valentine I'd made for her in the early days of our friendship. I pick it up, flip it over, see the words "I love you" in my shaky, eight-year-old handwriting. I'm frozen in shock, a million sharp pinpricks of emotion cutting me all at once.

I press it to my chest, my free hand clapped over my mouth to stop from crying out. It had to mean something that she never threw it away. It had to mean something that she kept it all these years, that she kept it even after we broke up. Even after she was with Hunter. It had to, it had to.

When I've recovered and wiped away my tears, I slip the card into my bag and notice another scrap of paper. It's floating among the pens and clippies. When I pull it out, it's a business card: Dr. Stephanie Quinn, PhD, LSW, in dark blue ink, followed by a phone number. A quick search on my phone pulls up her website, a simple landing page for a therapist.

Lia's therapist?

Lia's therapist.

She must've started seeing her over the summer. It's a shock but not a surprise. Of course Jo would've sent her to someone. Not anyone, but the best. But what's shocking is that Lia would be willing to accept help in the first place.

I put the business card back, then take the Valentine out and put it on top the way it was when I first opened the drawer. Lia would have had to take the card I made her out and place it over her therapist's card. Could it be a message somehow, for me? I blink and stare, then feel ridiculous. Maybe I need to believe Lia left it for me to find.

Still. It feels deliberate.

I take them both out again, stare at the business card as if it might hold clues to the mystery of Lia's last months. Maybe it does, or at least the person on it does. Maybe Dr. Stephanie Quinn has the answers I'm looking for.

I don't know how long I've been standing there when I hear a voice behind me: "Thought I'd find you here." Hunter. I slip both cards into my bag quickly.

Spinning to face her, I close the drawer behind me as quietly as possible. She's in the doorway, casually leaning against the frame like she hasn't just caught me looking through Lia's things.

"What time is it?" I ask, my heart beating so hard I can barely breathe. Maybe she really didn't see me.

"Almost midnight."

It's much later than I thought. I think of the Vestianos, and it's then that I remember Jo's voice from earlier that afternoon. It must've startled her, seeing me in Lia's bed. We don't look alike, but we have the same hair, the same build, and in the low light, if you wanted to see Lia, it wouldn't have been hard. But she let me sleep, and now I feel awful, the words of apology already forming in my mind.

"Come on," she says. "Let's get out of here."

"Okay," I say, following her.

The house is quiet, too quiet. We don't run into anyone until we're outside and see someone in a catering uniform packing up a crate of dirty dishes. He barely seems to notice us. I know I should find the Vestianos, say goodbye at least, but when I look back at the house, all I feel is a stab of anguish and I have to turn away.

"You hungry?" Hunter asks.

"Sure," is all I can manage.

We take my car, drive aimlessly at first. "Where are we going?"

It takes a beat before she answers. "Colony?"

The Colony Diner is the only place open at this hour. It's almost completely empty, and we sit in a corner. I order a coffee and Hunter orders nothing, just a water she doesn't touch. In the florescent glare, she looks like shit. We both do. I can feel a headache coming, the dull pressure at the base of my neck building. I instinctively reach for the Altoids tin in my bag but catch myself. I think about making an excuse, going to the bathroom, but press my hand flat against my thigh to try waiting it out.

"Why'd you lie?" Hunter asks, shaking me from my thoughts.

"What?" I say, surprised.

"Earlier, that story you told."

"You were there?" I ask. "I didn't see you. Didn't see you at the service either."

"I was all the way in the back, didn't really want to be seen. Lia told me about those squirrels, by the way. She told me all about how she had to give them up."

"I know," I say quietly, desperate to keep the dull ache in my head from exploding.

"Then why'd you lie?" Hunter's eyes cut right through me and I flinch.

"I didn't lie exactly," I say, looking away. "Okay, fine, maybe I stretched the truth, but you know what? Everything today—the funeral, this thing at the house—it was like that." The priest who didn't really know Lia, the estranged relatives crying at the house. "But Jo and Rob, they're hurting. Me, you, we're—"

"I know we're all hurting," she says. "But maybe we should be. Maybe this is exactly what we're supposed to be feeling when someone we love dies. Maybe we shouldn't tell ourselves comforting lies to feel a little better." Hunter looks more crushed than angry, eyes bloodshot, tears on the verge of falling.

The sharpness of her pain slices through the numb and grief, the sadness on my shoulders heavy almost like armor. Maybe the funeral, this day, was to comfort those who loved Lia, but Hunter didn't want to be comforted, didn't want to forget Lia, who she really was. "I miss her too," I say after a long silence. "The real her." Our eyes connect, and it's like looking into a mirror.

"I know," she says, blinking away her tears.

Strangely, the pressure building in my head begins to subside, the waves of nausea and splitting pain pulling away.

I think about the real Lia and what I found in her drawer. The valentine from second grade and the business card. I feel bad, like I'm withholding a piece of the puzzle, so I take out the latter and show Hunter. "Do you know who this is?" I ask even though I already know.

Hunter picks it up and glances at the thick cardstock embossed with Stephanie Quinn's name and number in deep blue ink. She flips it over to check the back before flicking it lightly to the side, where it lands next to the saltshaker.

"I think she was Lia's therapist," I add when she doesn't answer. "Did you know she was seeing one?"

"Yeah," she says, but she seems cagey, like she doesn't want to talk about it.

"Did Lia ever say anything about it?" I ask.

"Not really," she says, still hesitant. "You know Lia." At my confusion, Hunter adds, "She never wanted anyone to think she was weak."

It'd been different once upon a time. With each other, we were safe and things were easy, unguarded. But then I'd said what I'd said, all but calling her weak, telling her she'd always need me, that she'd never make it on her own.

"I don't fucking need anyone, and I certainly don't need you," she'd flung back, tears in her eyes.

I think about the Lia that Hunter inherited, and how our breakup changed her, how it changed me. The scars we gave each other, the love and sense of safety we destroyed. I'd give anything to take it all back.

"When did Lia start seeing her?" I ask, even though I think I know the answer. Even though I'm afraid of the answer. "Back in May?" I hate how I sound.

"I don't know," Hunter says, pretending not to hear my desperation. "Listen, it doesn't matter."

I look at her in surprise. How could it not?

"It's not like we can talk to her therapist. It's not like she can tell us anything," she says.

"That's not what I meant. I know she won't be able to tell us anything."

"Then what?"

"I don't know," I say, frustrated. "I just thought, if we knew *why* Lia was seeing her—"

"There's no point in speculating," Hunter says, cutting me off with surprising harshness. "We just have to focus on what's in front of us. What we can do now." On Cole, she means. On this theory she has. On finding out the truth. "Forget about this," she tells me, softer this time.

Still, when we get up to go, I linger for half a second, swipe the card from the table. I can't get over the way I'd found it in her desk right under my valentine. There weren't any other scraps of paper, just these two.

Maybe I'm reading too much into it. But then, maybe I'm not.

23.

On Sunday, I drive over to Cole's, assignment in hand. It takes a while for him to answer the door after I ring the bell. He lives a few streets over from the Vestianos, within the unofficial cluster of mansions in Meadowlark.

"Come on in," he says with a quick pivot and loose swing of an arm overhead. His parents are entertainment lawyers and the walls are covered with photos of them with movie stars. I follow him down to the basement where Lena and Rebecca are sprawled out on the carpet, papers spread around them. Cheat sheets, I realize. They both look up when we come down.

"Hey, Chase," Rebecca says.

"Hey," I say. They share a look, but I don't know what it means. Had Cole or Hunter told them I was joining? The three of us—Lena, Rebecca, and me—have all taken turns at the top. Meadowlark stopped releasing rankings years ago, but when you're at the top, you have a sense of who the competition is. Do they feel threatened, or is it something else?

"Here." I hand the AP Bio lab back to Cole.

"Cool," he says, taking it and placing it in one of the piles. It looks like madness, but it must make sense to them.

"You're not going to check it?" I ask, a little surprised.

"Why, should I?" He laughs like he finds the idea I'd somehow mess up completely preposterous.

I shrug. "What's next?"

"Right," he says, and begins rifling through one of the piles. "Here you go." He takes the pages and folds them in half again. "Wednesday, if you can."

"Sure," I say, sticking it in my backpack again.

"See ya," he says, picking up his phone and tapping out a text. "Don't worry about the door, just close it behind you."

"Actually, could you walk me out?" I ask, surprising both of us. Lena and Rebecca share another look, but I ignore them.

"Okay," he says easily, setting his phone facedown.

Upstairs, we stop at the door, me standing on the outside, him leaning against the frame.

"What's up?" he asks, and maybe for the first time in my life, I don't have a plan. Lia was the impulsive one, always ruining my plans in the best of ways.

But then, when Cole didn't bother checking my work, it felt like some kind of opening, like he could trust me.

And now he's standing here, just the two of us. No Hunter, no one to overhear us. I opt for honesty.

"When I was at the Vestianos', the police were asking about Lia and the week before she disappeared, about how she was feeling, how she was acting. If there was anything unusual," I tell Cole.

His eyes widen and he looks instantly uncomfortable, staring at his feet.

"I couldn't—I wasn't there for her then, but maybe you—" I don't finish, let the question hang in the air.

"She seemed sad," Cole says. "And distracted."

"Distracted?" I ask.

"Preoccupied, like she had a lot on her mind, which, I guess she did," he says, eyes still on the ground. "But we weren't that close, so I don't know. I'm sorry, Chase."

I can feel the pressure building behind my skull, the tears threatening to burst, the tightness in my throat. I have to look away, try to breathe.

"I should've talked to her," he says. "I didn't think she'd—I really didn't think"—he seems to struggle to find the words—"I had no idea she felt that way."

"I'm not sure if anyone knew," I say.

"Yeah." He takes a half step back, withdrawing back into his house. "Look, maybe it was too soon. Maybe this is all too much." He gestures helplessly at the whole situation. "If you need more time—" It takes me a moment to realize that he's asking me if I want to quit.

"No, it's good to keep busy," I say reflexively. But long after we've said our goodbyes and I'm driving aimlessly through Meadowlark, I'm not sure what I'm doing anymore. I think of Hunter and the way she's gunning for Cole. The things she's told me and the things he's said.

Hunter first said Cole and Lia seemed close, that they were both into the idea of Lia getting copies of the AP Physics test, but then she came to suspect that Lia was lying, that she was being pressured by Cole to get the test. Talking to Cole, he just seemed sad about the whole thing. And more important, he gave me an out, even though Hunter says he needs us to get the same Physics tests.

Something isn't adding up and someone is lying.

• • •

At home, I pull out the next assignment from Cole and it's not another AP Bio lab. It's not homework at all.

It's a test.

One I recognize from AP Calc junior year, on inverse functions. For a second, I think he must've gotten it from someone who took it last year, but it's completely blank.

When Hunter told me he'd started getting tests, I thought she meant past tests or people giving hints or copying answers day-of like she'd done with the Physics test. Because this—a test that hasn't happened yet—shouldn't be possible. I search my memory, looking for her exact words: "I only found out they were getting access to tests last week."

But how? And more important, did it have anything to do with Lia?

I get to school early Monday, head for the band room and wait for Rebecca Degray to emerge from morning practice. "Hey," I say, startling her.

"Oh, Chase. Hey," she says.

"Can we talk?"

The truth is that we don't know each other very well, despite being in a lot of the same classes and working on the same projects throughout the years. But she was friendly yesterday. Friendlier than Lena at least.

"Sure," she says, a frown of concern forming. I lead her away from the stream of band kids and we head outside where the sun is just waking up, the first streaks of light tinting the sky pink.

"Can this stay between us?" I don't know if I can trust her. I don't know if I can trust anyone. But I can't just sit around waiting for answers to fall from the sky. For Hunter or Cole to control the narrative.

"Okay," she says hesitantly. "What is it?"

I take a deep breath. "Where does Cole get the tests?"

Her eyes widen in surprise but there's something else in her expression I can't decipher. Like she can't believe I'm even asking. Like she's almost exasperated. "Wait, are you serious?" she asks.

I nod.

"I really don't know," she finally says. Hunter had said no one knew so it's not a total surprise, but I'd been hopeful.

"What about Cole and Lia?" I ask. "Were they close?"

Rebecca seems even more confused by this question. "I don't think there was anything going on between them."

"That's not what I meant." I feel heat creeping up my face, embarrassed that she'd think I was asking out of jealousy.

"I mean, I don't think Lia even wanted to be there, especially after—"

Suddenly, I catch Hunter approaching seemingly out of nowhere. I'd been so caught up that I wasn't paying attention.

"Thanks," I say to Rebecca and turn to go.

I'm hoping to dodge Hunter, but she catches up with me re-entering the building as the ten-minute bell for first period rings.

"Chase!" she calls after me.

"Hey," I say, not slowing down as I head for Physics.

"Wait up." She places a hand on my shoulder, forcing me to face her. "We're going to the same place." When she sees my expression, she pauses. "What's wrong? I saw you with Rebecca—did she say something to you?"

"No."

Hunter looks like she doesn't believe me. We arrive at our classroom but linger in the hall by the door.

"There's something you're not telling me," she says.

"Why does it have to be Cole?" I finally ask.

"What do you mean?"

"Have you always had a problem with him?"

For a moment, she's too surprised to speak. Then she clears her throat. "I never had a problem with him before Lia disappeared, before he asked Lia to steal the Physics test." She's trying not to sound defensive but it seeps through anyway. "Whatever Rebecca told you, she's obviously just covering for Cole. Seriously, you can't trust them."

The message: *I'm* the only one you can trust.

I'm not sure if I've ever completely trusted her. It doesn't seem like she's lying, but I can't shake the feeling she's not telling me everything. I run through everything she's told me, back to the very first time we talked. When she told me they'd had a fight. I think about the fight Lia and I had at the end, how brutal it was. What if it was a fight like that? All those months of Lia ignoring me until that Thursday night asking to meet in Montauk, our SOS.

What if they broke up?

"What was your fight about?" I ask. "The one with Lia, right before she disappeared."

Her expression shifts from surprise to anger almost instantly. "I already told you. Cole. The Physics test. Their plan to steal it."

"And that's it?" I push.

"That's *it*," she insists. For a moment, we just stare at each other, an impasse. Then the minute bell rings and she's the first to break eye contact, heading to class.

The way Hunter's zeroed in on this specific version of what happened to Lia, her certainty and defensiveness—it all but confirms she's hiding something. I can't help but think she might be blinded by guilt, a sense of responsibility for not being there for Lia when she needed her.

She isn't the only one who's failed Lia, the only one who wants to understand what happened. But I'm not interested in finding a scapegoat. I only want to know the truth. Later, when I'm home, I take out the two cards I found in Lia's drawer, my valentine and her therapist's card. I think about the way Hunter dismissed the idea of contacting Dr. Quinn, of trying to find out why Lia was seeing her in the first place.

On impulse, I take out my phone and tap out the numbers on the card. After a few rings, it goes to voice mail. "Hi, I'm Chase Ohara, Lia Vestiano's"—I hesitate, wonder if Lia ever told her about me—"friend," I finish. "I was wondering if we could talk."

24.

Dr. Quinn's office is across the street from a large strip mall not far from school. Inside, the walls are sparsely decorated with abstract art in neutral tones—muted pinks, beiges, grays.

She called me back within an hour of me leaving a voice mail and said she had a cancellation the next day, so I skip practice to meet her. I think about Tad and the team, my lackluster performance of late, and part of me knows I should care more but all of that feels farther and farther away each day.

I can sense another headache building and quickly slip a Focentra, swallowing it dry. As I sit down on the couch in the waiting area, the office door clicks open softly and a girl not much older than me walks out and makes a line for the exit without looking up. Soon, an older Black woman emerges. "Chase?" she says softly. "Come on in."

Inside the office, we sit at opposite couches. The walls are lined with bookshelves and a glass desk sits by the windows, a lone laptop on it, screen down. I set my bag on the floor beside me.

"I was very saddened to hear about Lia," Dr. Quinn begins, setting down her reading glasses. "As you know, it's been a while since I last saw her, but it's still a big shock." Why does she think I'd know? Then

I remember I'd introduced myself as Lia's friend, given the impression we remained close even after the breakup by coming here. "I wish I could have done more to help her." She takes a deep breath. "Tell me how you've been doing."

I start to speak but nothing comes out. The minutes stretch out before us, endless. I want to talk about Lia, ask about her, but I don't know how.

"It can be hard to talk about losing a loved one," she says. "I know you and Lia were inseparable."

I wonder what Lia's told her, what she already knows about me. Everything, nothing, somewhere in between. Me at my worst, me at my best. What I did, what I said. How I hurt her, how we hurt each other.

"Have you had any thoughts of harming yourself?" she asks, surprising me. The question seems to hang in the air. It sucks me back in time and I can almost feel the pavement hard under my feet, the rush of oncoming traffic, the pull of the street. One misstep and it'd all be over.

An accident.

A relief.

"No," I say, a little too forcefully.

I'm not sure she believes me but she doesn't push it.

"Survivors of suicide can often experience overwhelming guilt," she continues, and it's a shock to hear those words, to hear myself described as some kind of survivor. What's more, I'm beginning to realize that there's been a misunderstanding. That she thinks I'm here for help when I'm here for Lia. "It can feel like it's our fault, like we should have known or done something. That weight can be crushing."

I think about the text Lia sent. The call for help I'd ignored. *Meet me in Montauk*, she begged. And it feels like all the oxygen's gone. Tears are slipping down my face, but I can't lift my hands to wipe them away, can't reach for the tissues on the coffee table. It doesn't feel like I deserve them.

"It's not your fault," Dr. Quinn says softly.

"But it's *someone's* fault." The words fly out of me, but they're not mine. They're *Hunter's*, and now I'm parroting her. Is that what I believe? Is that why I'm here? Why I joined Cole's crew, why I'm searching for answers, trying to understand what happened to Lia?

Lia, my Lia, gone.

"Whose fault do you think it is?" Dr. Quinn asks, her voice even. "Mine?"

"No," I say.

"Her parents'?"

"No, no." I squeeze my eyes shut, try to disappear from the world.

"Yours?"

I don't answer.

"Lia's?"

My eyes fly open in shock and anger.

"Who do you blame, Chase?" she asks calmly.

"Are you saying it was just inevitable?" I say. "That no one could have helped her? That she was—it was somehow unpreventable?" The headache I'd pushed off earlier comes knocking at the base of my skull. I can't remember the last time I got a full night's sleep, and even with the Focentra, I'm not sure I can stave off the pain this time.

"No, that's not what I'm saying," she says. "But let's look at the facts. Lia had been suffering from severe depression. I began working with her after her hospitalization but only saw her a few times, you know that. Was what happened inevitable? No. But was it all one person's fault—was it all *your* fault? Also no."

My head is spinning. The pain has sliced through the barricades and is spreading like an angry wildfire determined to burn this body down. But it's her words that have completely unmoored me.

Her hospitalization, Dr. Quinn said. I had no idea Lia had been hospitalized. Had she been in an accident? I search my messed-up mind, try to remember the times I saw her at school, if she had a scar, if she looked hurt.

Only saw her a few times, you know that. Has Dr. Quinn confused me with Hunter? I can't think of any other explanation. If she only saw Lia a few times months ago, it wouldn't be that hard to mix up a girlfriend with an ex-girlfriend. If that's true, then this is the thing Hunter's been holding back. Is that how they met? A boating accident? A car crash in Kennebunkport?

But soon, the pain consumes any ability I have to concentrate. I touch a hand to the back of my neck, press a useless finger against the cradle of pain at the edge of my skull and feel it pulse out like a shock, spread like tendrils of lightning.

"Chase?" Dr. Quinn says, but her voice sounds tinny, far away. "You okay?"

"I'm sorry," I manage, grabbing my backpack to go.

I don't remember how I get to my car, the drive back home. The streets and taillights seem to blur, the ground unstable, my hands shaking. I don't remember how I make my way up the stairs, collapse onto my bed. I shiver as I press another pink pill onto my tongue, and after what feels like eternity, the pain subsides enough for me to get up. These days, the Focentra seems to provide only temporary relief, a way to keep going.

It's dark out. The clock says 9:32 and I haven't touched my homework, haven't solved the Calc test for Cole. By the time I'm done, it's almost 1 AM.

I lace up, tell myself it's to make up for missing practice, and hit the street. It's drizzling, a light mist dancing in the streetlights, the dark roads glistening. I try to focus on each step, the occasional squeak of my sneakers. No music, just me and the night.

Then, out of nowhere, a car swerves in front of me as I'm crossing an intersection and screeches to a halt. For a moment, time seems to freeze, the car's headlights illuminating every droplet of water hanging in the air as my body nearly collides with speeding metal.

The shriek of a car horn shakes me awake and the driver gets out, shouts, "Get out of the street! Kill yourself on your own time! Christ."

I stand limply in the crosswalk, stare after him as he gets back in and peels off. I look up at the pedestrian signal, the hand drawn in red lights. I could have sworn it was green. I could have sworn the street was empty.

The stranger's words echo in my mind as the drizzle turns into heavy rain. I make my way across the street and wonder if that's what I really want—to kill myself. It's what Dr. Quinn wanted to know earlier too.

Finally, I sit on the curb, let the rain soak deep into my bones as the tears run hot down my cheeks and my body shakes with sobs.

Nothing makes sense anymore. Nothing will ever make sense again, not with Lia gone. I don't know what I'm doing, I don't know *why* I'm doing any of it. What does it all matter anyway, with Lia dead? Understanding what happened won't bring her back.

I've never been so devoid of hope. Never felt so alone.

Then my phone buzzes, Hunter's name flashing on the screen. It's almost two in the morning, but she's awake and calling.

"What's up?" I try to straighten my voice, hide the crying.

"Want to go for a drive?"

It's late and I should go home, try to get some sleep. I say yes.

"Can't sleep these days," she says when I pick her up. "Thought maybe I wasn't the only one."

"Oh."

For a while, we just drive around town, but soon I take us north until we hit the water. I pull into a parking lot and stare out as the rain pours over the windshield in heavy sheets. I know the ocean is out there, but I can't see it. Lia and I used to do this when we couldn't make it out to Montauk or escape into the city. It always felt good just to inhale the salt air. I thought I might feel closer to her here by the water, but I don't feel anything at all.

"Did you know about Lia's hospitalization?" I ask, still staring straight ahead. I'm so exhausted, so drained, I can't think of a better way to ask.

"Yeah," Hunter says. "How'd you find out?" She sounds curious, not angry or defensive like I would've imagined.

"Went to see her therapist," I say. "Why didn't you tell me? What happened? Was she in an accident?"

"Something like that," Hunter says. "It wasn't relevant."

"How can you say that? Was she hurt badly?" This time, I turn to face her.

"It wasn't the thing that killed her," she answers.

"Her therapist seemed to think it was important," I say, confused by Hunter's evasiveness.

She shakes her head. "All you need to know is that she recovered."

"I want to know everything that happened," I say. "Tell me everything, don't leave anything out."

Hunter seems to study me. "I've already told you everything you need to know."

"Why don't you tell me everything and I'll tell you which parts I need to know."

"You first," she says, eyes challenging me. "Tell me everything that ever happened between you two."

That stops me.

"I get to keep some things between us," she says, but this time the defensiveness doesn't seem out of place. "I get to hold on to our past. It's the only thing I have left."

"Fine," I say finally. I still have a million questions, but I know I won't be getting any answers from Hunter.

25.

On Friday after school, I drive over to the elementary school and pick up Aidan. It's Dad's weekend with us. In the settlement, he didn't even bother fighting for custody because being a management consultant means he's gone most of the week, so he asked for standard visitation, two weekends per month, but we barely manage one these days.

It was a major point of contention between Mom and Dad because he moved out and immediately signed a lease in Tribeca. I still remember Mom screaming at him on the phone.

"It just doesn't make sense for me to stay in Long Island," he told me and Aidan later. "Not for two weekends a month. And you know I'd love to see you girls more but I'm gone most of the week."

Neither of us protested because there was nothing to say. We barely saw him even before the divorce. He flew out before we woke up Monday morning and flew in late Thursday night, leaving for the Manhattan office early Friday, back late, often working through the weekend.

Nothing really changed after. Some of our weekends with him were spent largely by ourselves at his loft, ordering takeout for every meal, Aidan watching movies and me studying. Lia would sometimes join, I think out of pity, and she'd make it fun, take us out for fancy dinners or start an impromptu dance party just the three of us.

But sometimes we didn't go to Dad's for two-month stretches because of scheduling. His work, our everyday things—a birthday party Aidan didn't want to miss, a student council meeting or track booster club breakfast for me. Saturday-morning meets during cross-country and track seasons.

When I pull up to the front of Aidan's school and wave at her, she comes over to me, surprised.

"It's Dad's weekend, remember?" I say.

"I totally forgot."

I sigh. "Mom didn't pack a bag for you?"

"She did," Aidan says, getting in. "But it's at home."

"It's fine, we'll swing by the house."

"Do we have to go?" she whines.

"It's been, like, two months," I say, but I'm wondering the same thing. I know it'd be easy, a quick text to him with some made-up reason. Even the thinnest excuse won't be questioned. Maybe he'll be relieved too.

But there's a part of me that wants to go, if only to get away. There's something soothing about the city, the feeling of invisibility. I can run a million blocks and not see a single person I know. I can breathe, in a way.

Then, as soon as we pull into the parking deck beside Dad's building, I get a text from Jo.

Jo: I know it's a little last minute, but Rob and I would love to have you over for dinner Sunday.

I turn off the car but don't move, trying to figure out what to say. Then I remember the way I'd left without saying goodbye, slipping away from the house in the middle of the night.

"What is it?" Aidan asks, seat belt off and ready to go.

"One sec."

Me: Sure. What time?

Jo: Six okay?

I feel like I can't say no. Once upon a time, Sunday dinners at the Vestianos' were religiously attended by my family. After Dad left, Mom came a couple times alone but soon it was just me and Aidan, and then just me. But it's been over six months since I've been there, and it's strange, the sudden invitation.

I wonder if I'm the only one. If Hunter will be there too, if Hunter had completely replaced me in my absence.

"Chase, I'm cold," Aidan says, waking me up.

"Sorry. Let's go."

We're a little late, but it's not a surprise to find Dad's loft empty. Aidan heads straight for the couch and plops down. "What do you wanna watch?" she asks.

"Whatever you want," I say. "What about dinner?"

"I don't know," she says, already searching for something to play. "Noodles, maybe?"

I smile. Aidan always wants noodles. "Okay," I say, and order ramen.

By the time Dad gets home, Aidan's asleep upstairs and it's just me and him in the living room, dark except for the muted TV on in the background.

"Sorry I'm late," he says, starting the usual dance of apologies.

"It's fine." I don't even bother telling him to text next time because he'll forget. Or tell one of his assistants to call me like he did once and I had to listen to him apologize on Dad's behalf for five minutes.

"Aidan?" he asks me in a whisper.

"Upstairs." We have to talk quietly because it's a loft, and while the second floor's spacious, everything's open.

After he's done taking off his shoes and hanging up his bag and coat, he comes over and sits next to me. "Sorry I couldn't be there last week."

"It's fine," I say, because there's no point.

He almost missed his own father's funeral. Grandpa Ichi, who always carried peppermints in his pockets, tucking them carefully into our hands when we were younger. Grandpa Ichi, who came to live with us after Grandma Lily died of cancer when I was six and before Aidan was born. Grandpa Ichi, who tried to teach us violin until Dad forbade it, as if it were a disease we'd catch. Who defiantly filled the house with music at night during the years Dad was hustling to make partner and rarely home. Who helped Mom with baths and bedtime, regaling us with wild stories he made up starring imaginary forest animals, a bear who was mayor of Beartown, a goose detective solving funny mysteries.

Who, in the two years before he passed away, had to move into an assisted living home where Mom took us on the weekends for short visits. Where the air never smelled right and he was too dispirited to tell any more stories. Where the violin sat in the closet gathering dust.

Where he'd ask why Dad never came and Mom would make some excuse. An important deal in LA, a crucial project in Atlanta. Next time, she'd say, and we all knew it was a lie.

And then our last Christmas together. They'd kept the peace tenuously, Dad and Grandpa Ichi. The only real fight we'd witnessed was over the violin. But there was always this tension underneath that we were too little to understand.

"You work too hard," Grandpa Ichi told Dad when he came home late Christmas Eve, his dinner set aside and long cold.

Dad's eyes flashed with anger but he kept his voice in control. "I'll be partner next year. It'll be different." It'll be worth it, he was saying. All the late nights, the absences, the broken promises.

"We both know it won't be different," Grandpa said.

"Oh, so you know all about how management consulting works?"

"No, but I know how you work," he said simply.

Dad slowly put the fork down, every muscle in his hand and arm tight, and for a second, I feared he'd hit Grandpa.

"It'll never be enough for you, whatever it is," Grandpa continued, not even looking at any of us, staring off like he was already far away. "I wish I could've shown you a better path. It's my fault."

Dad started laughing, and it scared us.

"Come on, girls," Mom said. "Let's go upstairs, get ready for bed."

"No, let them stay," Dad said. "They're old enough to know." Our eyes grew big at the anger coiled tight within his voice, ready to strike.

"You're right," Grandpa said. "They're old enough to know you're never home, to know you always choose work above all else."

"*How dare you?*" Both of us jumped from the sharpness in his voice. "You could never understand the sacrifices I've made. You've never sacrificed a day in your life! It was always Ma who took care of everything, who worked herself to the bone."

Grandpa grimaced, remaining silent.

"Everything I do, I do for the girls. Maybe they can't understand that now, but they will one day. Everything I do is for this family. *Everything*. Who pays six thousand a month so you can get the best care?"

"I never asked for it," Grandpa said. "I never asked for anything!"

"You never had to."

"I'll move out tomorrow."

"And where will you go?" Dad asked. "Don't be ridiculous."

"I'll find my own way. I always have," Grandpa said.

"You're eighty-five years old," Dad said. "You can't remember how to tie your shoes half the time. You can't drive anymore. You get lost walking in the neighborhood."

I'll never forget the tears that ran down Grandpa's face. The anger and helplessness in his eyes.

"Enough," Mom cut in. "Girls, let's go." Aidan and I remained glued to our seats at the table.

Dad ignored her. "You don't understand why I work so hard because you've never worked hard a day in your life. You couldn't possibly begin to understand."

"There are more important things in life than work, than money," Grandpa said quietly.

Dad shook his head. "Don't you get it, old man? You can sit there and pretend you're above it all, but the truth is that you were nothing without Ma, and now you're nothing without me."

"Joseph!" Mom stood, picking up Aidan and yanking me by the hand. "You're just being cruel."

And at the age of eleven, I was old enough to know that's exactly what it was—cruelty. That our father's words were designed to cut, that our grandfather was hurting on what would be his last Christmas with us.

But still, the words hung in the air as I tried to sleep that night. *Who pays six thousand a month so you can get the best care?* The helplessness in Grandpa Ichi's eyes. *You were nothing without Ma, and now you're nothing without me*. The tears running down Grandpa's face.

It was all so cruel, but what was worse was that it was maybe also true. For the first time ever, Dad made it crystal clear just how much we needed him. How much power he held over all of us. How much control.

In this family at least, he made all the rules, but it was impossible not to see the source of that power. The long nights, the hustle for one promotion after another, the money and prestige. He could make all the rules because he was our source of security, the one who paid for the house, the cars, the clothes, and meals out with friends—all essential to living in a place like Meadowlark. There were only two kinds of people: those with power and those without, and I couldn't stomach the thought of being under another person's thumb my whole life. Of being completely at the mercy of anyone, least of all someone like my dad. Maybe what I wanted most wasn't simply to escape him but surpass him. Beat him at his own game.

That following February, Grandpa Ichi passed away and Dad barely made it home in time for the funeral because of some project in London, because he didn't want to tell his boss that his father had died. It didn't matter that he was family, didn't matter that Aidan and I were inconsolable, that we needed our dad. Why should I've been surprised that he didn't come to Lia's funeral?

I used to think the price he paid was high but ultimately worth it—that this was what you had to do if you wanted a life of consequence, of security. If you wanted to control your own destiny. But now with Lia gone and this black hole in my heart, it feels like my center of gravity is shifting, like what used to be my center can no longer hold.

"How're you doing?" he asks now, as if he really cares.

I shift away, look at my feet. I think about everything he's missed, everything that's happened since the funeral. The work I've done for Cole, the meeting with Lia's therapist, the near collision a few nights ago. I haven't run in the dark since. "Shitty," I tell him.

He sighs. "I know this is a hard time for you right now, but you can't lose sight of your goals. First semester senior year is arguably the most important, and when are you retaking the SATs, early December?" he asks even though he already knows. It's probably on his work calendar. "That's less than a month away."

"Don't worry about it," I tell him, getting up and reaching for my bag. It's almost midnight and I feel exhausted.

"It's my job to worry," he says, turning off the TV and letting the dark envelop us. "You're so close. So, so close, Chase. I'd hate for you to lose everything after how hard you've worked. I'd hate for you to get distracted—"

"I'm not distracted!" Lia's death isn't simply a distraction. It's my entire universe caving in. The sun and stars and galaxies collapsing into darkness. Her death is the end of time and space, and he can go fuck himself.

"I'm just saying that if you can stay focused for a few more months, you can deal with everything else after you've turned in all your applications and you're done with the SATs."

Everything else. Lia is not *everything else*, I want to shout, but before I do, I remember where I am and look up to where Aidan's sleeping.

"Look, just let me worry about my own crap, okay?" I say. "When have I ever, *ever* failed you? Since I was little, I've gotten perfect grades, did everything you ever asked of me. My applications are all done, essays written before school started, recommendations already lined up. Just tell me, when have I ever let you down?"

He opens his mouth, and suddenly I realize what he's going to say. The first time I took the SATs and fucked up, my scores far from terrible but not high enough for Stanford.

"The SATs," I say for him, because I can't bear to hear him say it.

"Actually, no, that's not what I was going to say," he says, like he's about to list some other thing I messed up. "Never mind. Forget it."

"What?" I ask.

"No, no, forget it. Let's just go to bed."

Upstairs, we quietly take turns washing up. Then I climb into the lower bunk under a sleeping Aidan.

Only, she's not asleep after all. As soon as Dad turns off the bathroom light, she climbs down soundlessly and gets in bed with me, curling up next to me, and I have to blink away the tears.

As I lie awake, Aidan beside me, I think about Dad, sleeping on the other side of the room, and the things he said. The worst thing that's ever happened to him was not being able to go to Stanford. That's it for him, his most significant trauma. Not losing his parents. Not losing Mom, and not losing us. That's the moment he's chosen to define his entire life, and the reason he wants so badly for me to go. But even then, even if I get in and go, I'm not sure it'll be enough for him. I'm not sure anything will ever be enough for him.

I wrap an arm around Aidan, give her a small squeeze and she holds my hand. I think about Lia's death and how it's now my most central trauma, the black hole I'll be circling my whole life, and I feel sorry for him. That he'll never love anyone more than he loves himself.

Maybe that's not quite right.

Maybe it's that he'll never love anyone more than he's terrified of not having enough—enough money, enough power, enough status.

I close my eyes, try to remember the good times Lia and I had, the years of friendship, the final year when we fell in love. I'm so grateful for everything she's given me, everything she's taught me about life and about myself.

As I silently cry myself to sleep, I try to hold on to Lia's love, even though she's gone and even though she probably didn't love me anymore when she died.

Someone like Lia Vestiano loved me once and maybe that's enough to know.

Maybe I can finally be worthy of that love.

26.

To the surprise of no one, Dad has to work on Saturday and Aidan seems relieved when I tell her we have to leave earlier than usual on Sunday. I have dinner at the Vestianos', and before that, I have to go to Cole's house and drop off the next assignment, an AP Bio test.

"I miss her too," Aidan says when we get in the car to go home, when we know we're alone. "Lia was like a bonus big sister."

"I know." I take her hand and wonder just how much she overheard the night before, the tense whispers between me and Dad.

"Last summer, I went to her house," she says, and I almost drop her hand in surprise.

"What?"

She's looking out of the window now, staring at the too-bright parking garage.

"When? Why?" Had she seen Lia? Had she spoken to her?

"It was the week after you left for Stanford and I guess I was just lonely. I got up to their front door and stood there for a while feeling kind of stupid."

"You never told me," I say, and it comes out more accusing than I intend.

"Because nothing happened. I didn't knock, just walked back home."

"Why'd you go?" I ask, softer this time. "What'd you want to say to Lia?"

"I don't know," Aidan says, turning back to look at me. "I guess it just felt like the divorce all over again, but maybe worse."

Shocked, I don't know what to say. Back in May, when Lia ended things, it'd felt so final, so devastating, but all this time, I'd been thinking only of me, of us.

"When Dad moved out, and Mom was crying all the time, I still had you guys. I know you weren't together back then, but it still felt like—"

"Like family," I finish for her, as fresh tears run down my face. She was only eight when they decided to split, and where I turned inward, closing myself off to everyone except Lia, Aidan had turned outward, her friends multiplying until she was almost never home, always busy with this friend or that. I thought maybe it meant she was okay, or more okay than me. I thought it meant that outside of the big, tense moments—the screaming fights, the crying parents—she didn't need me as much. But maybe Lia saw through her, through both of us, and knew we needed the silly dance parties, the trips out for ice cream, the long walks just the three of us. Lia, she was there. And she made it better.

When I lost Lia, our whole family lost her too. And now we've lost her forever.

Aidan starts to cry with me. "Sometimes it just hurts, growing up, losing people," she says. "Most of the time, I don't even remember what Grandpa looks like anymore. I have to look at a picture of him, and then when I can remember, it's just the picture I remember. Is that what'll happen to Lia? I don't want that to happen to Lia." She cries harder.

I pull her toward me, hold her tight. There's nothing I can say that'll make her feel better, that'll make either of us feel better. There are no words for the pain we're in, no words that can bring Lia back to us.

"Hey," I say after Aidan's cried out. "I love you, you know that, right?"

"Love you too."

"I'm here. I'll always be here," I tell her.

Aidan pulls away, rubs at her eyes. "How do I know I won't lose you too?"

"You won't," I promise fiercely, and she finally nods, but I can tell she doesn't believe me. Because there are no guarantees in this life, no promises that can't be broken.

We spend the rest of the ride mostly in a pensive silence and at home, Aidan runs right in, giving Mom a quick hug before darting up to her room.

"Why are you back so early?" Mom asks. She's in the living room, wrapped up in a blanket, a book in her lap.

"Oh, I need to meet up with a friend. Then I'm going to the Vestianos' for dinner. Is that okay?" I ask, not really expecting any pushback, but the hesitation on her face surprises me. "What?"

"Nothing. It's fine," she says.

I drop my bag, sit down across from her. "*What?*"

"It's just—why are they having you over for dinner alone?"

"I don't know," I say. "Do you want to come? I can ask."

"It's not that," she says. "Never mind. I'm being silly. You go, have a good time, tell them I send my love."

"Now I really want to know," I say.

She sets her book down on the coffee table. "This is going to sound so stupid, but during the divorce, they"—she blows a puff of air at her bangs in irritation—"they kept offering to take you guys to help us out. At first it was kind of embarrassing, but then even after I told Jo no a million times, she kept pushing. It started to feel like she was, I don't know, trying to take you from us. Or at least imply she and Rob would be better parents. It sounds stupid. Never mind."

I laugh a little out of surprise. "What?"

"See, it's ridiculous. Sorry I said anything." Mom laughs too. "Hey, how was Dad's? You okay?" Then she sees my expression. "Uh-oh. What happened?"

"Nothing," I tell her. "It's fine. Everything's fine. I don't want to talk about it."

"Okay," she says, softening. "I'm here if you ever do want to talk."

"Thanks."

The thing about our mom is that she means well and loves us, but growing up, she wasn't always there for us like she's trying to be now. I couldn't see it then, but she was too wrapped up in Dad, making sure he was happy, making sure he was taken care of, making sure she was doing her part to fulfill his vision for life.

During the divorce, Mom came home after a rough meeting with Dad and the lawyers and in an angry rush told me how she'd been a playwright before she met him, even had a few shows at festivals that ran sold out for weeks. But after they got married, Dad kept pushing and pushing her to make a switch, which is how she ended up becoming a senior copywriter at an ad agency specializing in pharmaceutical marketing. "Dick pills," she told me in between sobs. "I sell dick pills."

Now, she reads books on empowerment and will occasionally ask me and Aidan if Dad is brainwashing us, to which we never have an answer.

She's always been a little fragile, and it was sometimes easier to deal with shit myself instead of telling her only to end up having to comfort her.

But maybe that's not fair to her anymore, because since the news of Lia's death, she's been nothing but reliable, there for me, writing that sick note when I skipped school, holding me until I stopped crying. Maybe she's not the same mom I thought she was. It's been two years since the divorce—at least twenty self-empowerment books ago.

So I take a chance and ask something I've wanted to know forever: "Why did Dad hate Grandpa so much?"

Her eyes widen in surprise. "Did something happen? Did Dad say something?" I can tell she's instantly on edge.

"No," I tell her. "I just want to know."

For a moment, she looks like she wants to deny it, but then she just sighs. She doesn't owe Dad anything anymore. "It's complicated," she begins. "Your dad didn't have much growing up, but more than that, I think he's always wished Grandpa Ichi were a different kind of father." She doesn't have to protect him, doesn't have to make him look good, but it's still her first instinct after all these years.

"You don't have to defend him anymore," I say.

"I'm not finished," she says. "I told you it's complicated. Grandpa Ichi didn't want you to know, but I think you're old enough now."

"Know what?"

"Well, he was born in San Francisco in 1931," she says, peering up at me like I'm supposed to understand something. "He was eleven when Japan attacked Pearl Harbor."

I gasp with realization. "I never thought about it. I can't believe I never thought about it."

"It wasn't just the internment itself, being imprisoned four years for a crime they didn't commit, not knowing when the war would end, if its end even meant release—his family lost everything. They had a store and a house. When they returned, another family was running the store, someone else lived in their house. Grandpa Ichi never talked about it with me, but I can't imagine what that did to him, to his whole family."

"I had no idea," I whisper.

"Me neither, for a long time. Until one day I realized just how old Grandpa Ichi was. Then I asked your dad and he told me the whole story eventually."

I sit down on the armchair next to the couch, a new, overwhelming sadness washing over me. "I can't believe I never pieced it together." It feels like I've failed Grandpa, like I've lost him all over again. He passed away when I was only eleven, and there are just so many things I'll never know about him.

"Grandpa didn't want you two to know. He never talked about it, never wanted to talk about it. I tried to ask him one time but he shut down and left the room."

"Why?"

"I'm not sure. I got the sense he didn't want anyone to feel sorry for him. But I don't know."

"But what about Dad? Did he just not care?" He was the one who told Mom, so he knew the whole story. All I can think of is his disdain and coldness toward Grandpa.

Mom looks thoughtful for a moment. "I used to think your father was just completely unreasonable. How could he not see the pain Grandpa Ichi was in? How could he not muster any compassion for him? But I don't know, after the divorce, the distance helped me see him a little differently. That yes, maybe he should have tried to have some empathy for his dad, but also, maybe it wasn't possible for him because of the way he grew up."

"What do you mean?"

"He used to tell me about seeing other Japanese families with parents who went through the same thing put it all behind them and work hard to provide for their kids, heads down, nose to the grindstone kind of thing. Totally stoic. But then there was Grandpa Ichiro, schlepping his violin downtown every day and begging hotels and restaurants to let him play. Or sometimes he'd set up on busy street corners, all with very little to show for it, according to your dad.

"If you grow up hungry, maybe your father's struggles don't matter to you. If every day feels bleak, maybe it's impossible to feel compassion for someone else's decades-old trauma."

I think about something he said all the time when Aidan and I were younger—"always stay hungry, take nothing for granted"—and connect it to what Mom's saying now. It sounded so trite, just well-worn words that didn't mean anything, but maybe he meant it literally.

But then there was the way he treated Grandpa Ichi long after he'd left home. Long after losing Stanford. Long after he was no longer hungry. Long after their roles reversed and Grandpa was under his care. He couldn't change, couldn't forgive. Couldn't move past the trauma and unfairness of his youth. Dad was just stuck.

Maybe that's what everyone in this family was—stuck. Grandpa Ichi, who always lived in the moment because he watched the world snatch away everything his family had built. Dad, who was still hungry, still desperate to prove himself. Mom, still fighting the ghost of Dad.

I don't want to be stuck, don't want to be defined by the things that happened to me, don't want to spend the rest of my life forever circling them. But then I think about Lia, about losing her, and an unbearable chasm opens up inside me. I have no idea how or even if I'll ever bridge that rift within me, but in this moment, I feel differently about my dad, and about Grandpa Ichi.

I see their pain. Like I see my own pain.

And then I think about Lia, but not just about how lost I feel without her. I think about *her* pain. About how she kept it from everyone the way Grandpa Ichi kept his carefully hidden behind peppermints and silly stories. A facade built with little lies of omission. Because he wanted us to be happy, because he never wanted to be a burden to anyone.

Was that how Lia felt? What pain had she hidden away?

27.

At Cole's house, it's Lena who answers the door. "Hey," I say, surprised.

"Hey." She passes me a folded packet, and it takes me a second to figure out that it's the next assignment. "Cole said you had an AP Bio test?" she asks.

"Oh." I hand it over.

Cole's been avoiding me. Rebecca too. When I turned in the Calc test Wednesday, he gave me the AP Bio test and practically ran.

"You all right?" Lena asks. I didn't think she cared, but she doesn't seem insincere.

I shrug, because I don't know how to answer.

"I'm sorry," she says. "Dumb question."

"No, it's okay."

She offers me an apologetic smile as we say our goodbyes.

As I drive to the Vestianos', I think about everything that Hunter's told me and whether it would've been better to stay quiet like she wanted me to, build up more trust with Cole by getting more Physics tests. Lia used to tell me I was the most impatient person she'd ever met but it never annoyed me because it was just who I was—who I am. That rush of *more, more, more* in my blood, that whisper of *never enough* in my ear. All the things I've learned in the past week were hard won, even if the more I discover, the more questions I have. Maybe tonight, I'll be able to get some answers.

I slow down in the Vestianos' neighborhood, drive past our old house, the home I spent most of my childhood in. It used to pain me to see it after the divorce, but once I fell in love with Lia, it felt like home was a person, not a house.

In the driveway, I take a deep breath, try to clear my head. But I don't get much of a chance because Jo soon steps out, waving at me. She must've heard me pull in.

Inside, she and Rob take turns giving me big hugs, and I feel knocked off-center, looking past them as if Lia would appear like she used to. Jo sees my glance and smiles sadly. "Just us, I'm afraid."

"Sorry."

"Don't be," Rob says. "Come on in, come on in."

I take off my coat, hang it on the owl stand by the door, and follow them to the kitchen. On the way, I spot a box sitting in the corner of the formal dining room. Strange.

Once in a while, a camera crew would show up and film an episode at the house, but the Vestianos always kept their house photo-ready even with the cameras off. The cardboard box sticks out against the long farmhouse table and tasteful decor.

Rob catches me staring. "Oh, that's some of Lia's things that the police returned. We haven't gotten around to . . " he trails off awkwardly.

"Did they ever find her phone?" I ask, eyes still on that box. I can see the silver of her laptop sticking up at a slight angle.

"No," he says. "Unfortunately. We haven't canceled her line

though, just in case." In case of what, he doesn't say. Her case's been closed as far as I know. No one is out looking for it.

But part of me is grateful because I don't want to let her go either. I like knowing that I can still call her number, listen to her voice, even if it's just telling me to leave a message.

In the kitchen, Jo has made enough food for an army.

"I hope you're hungry!" She manages to inject each word with forceful cheer, as if we weren't just talking about Lia's things.

Jo's made all of Lia's favorites: lasagna, pork chops, fettuccine carbonara, cast-iron deep dish pizza, and cheese cake. It's overwhelming, and I don't even know where to begin.

She notices my expression and deflates. "I made way too much."

"I tried to tell you, hon," Rob says gently.

"No, no," I clear my throat. "It's nice. It's like she's here." I fill my plate up with a little of everything and make a show of eating it all even though I'm not hungry.

It's been months since I've been here for one of these dinners and it feels so strange to be back now, without Lia. Jo and Rob don't exactly avoid talking about her, but it's clear they don't want us to spend the entire night sobbing.

"Beautiful memory, thank you, Chase," Jo tells me at one point, referring to the story about Lia I told on the day of her funeral.

"Yes, beautiful," Rob agrees. We don't talk about the squirrels. We don't talk about the truth.

They ask about school, about my plans for the future.

"I don't know," I say. "Same plans, I guess. Stanford, hopefully."

"If anyone can do it, it's you," Jo says. "Haven't I always said that, Rob, about Chase? Such a smart girl."

"Yes," he says.

"Do you think you'll come back?" she asks, and they share a quick glance that I don't understand. "After graduation?"

I answer honestly: "I don't know. I don't even know if I'll get in. Maybe I'll end up somewhere else." And then I really think about it. Would it be so bad, if I didn't go? I wasn't happy last summer. This dream, I always knew it was what Dad wanted, but I thought I wanted it for myself too. That urgent press of *gotta keep running*, of *never enough* used to mean gunning for a perfect life that was always somewhere in the future. But with Lia gone, I can't even imagine a future anymore. "Maybe it wouldn't be so awful, if I didn't get in," I say, almost testing the idea out loud.

"Don't say that. You worked so hard. If anyone deserves it, it's you," Jo says with confidence I wish I had.

"I don't know. Maybe it's not a good fit. Last summer—"

"Don't think about last summer. It was rough for everyone," she says, and I almost bump into my pasta leaning forward to listen. I stay quiet, hoping she'll reveal more. I want to know everything that happened that summer. Lia's accident, her hospital stay, and maybe most of all, the piece of the puzzle no one else has: the direct aftermath of our breakup in May.

"It was awful," Rob says. "Lia, she—"

"I don't want to go there again!" Jo says sharply, cutting him off. Her tone surprises all of us and she slumps back in her chair, defeated. "I don't want to think about it, not ever again."

This is somehow more devastating to hear than anything they could've told me about Lia that summer. Jo sounds traumatized, like Lia herself was traumatized.

By *me*.

Suddenly, the room feels too small even though we're in the biggest kitchen I've ever seen, in the one of the biggest mansions of Meadowlark. The air feels thin, my throat tight.

"Excuse me," I say quickly, and force myself to walk, not run, to the bathroom. Inside, I close the toilet lid and sit, just trying to breathe. My heart's pounding, and I can feel the pressure building in my head. It explodes and I see stars.

"Hon, it's been a bit, you okay in there?" Jo's voice comes in through the door. *Been a bit*—how long have I been here?

"Fine," I manage, and stumble to the sink to turn on the water. "Be right out, sorry."

I splash my face, take a sip from the tap, and spit it out. My reflection looks terrible, and I'm shaking in the mirror.

Just. Breathe.

I start to count then. One. Two. Three. Dry my face, try smiling, and fail. Finally, I stop shaking. And more important, my throat seems to loosen and I can breathe again, just barely.

Outside, I focus on surviving the night. We make small talk, but I think we all know the evening's finished.

Jo walks me out, following me to my car. "Thanks for coming," she says. "It means a lot to us. And we've missed you."

"I missed you guys too," I say, and it's the truth.

She smiles, and it's the first time I believe it. "Do you think—" She sounds hesitant. "Do you think we could make it a regular thing? Sunday dinner?" She wraps her arms around her, shivering in the cold without a coat.

I hesitate, thinking back to us at the table trying to recreate memories that once made us happy but failing because that past was gone. I don't think I understood, back when we were all happy, how much Lia meant to me. Even in all my lonely desperation after we broke up, it was the hope of being with her that carried me from one day to the next, one breath to the next, and now all of that hope is just gone.

I've taken too long to answer and Jo tries to hide her disappointment. "We'd understand if you were busy. I know you must be busy," she says, giving me an out.

"No, that sounds nice," I say quickly. It's the least I can do, and her whole face seems to light up. Maybe we're both realizing the same thing: how impossible it was to know how much we needed Lia, how impossibly we'd miss her.

"Okay, okay," she says. "I promise I won't make so much food next time. It'll be different, you'll see."

"Okay," I say, and attempt a smile.

Jo's right. I'm busier than ever with the SATs in less than a month, Hunter and Cole, the cheating ring assignments, not to mention extracurriculars, but I can't bring myself to say no, not after everything.

At home I take a cold shower and two Focentra before starting on Cole's next assignment, an upcoming AP Stat test.

28.

On Monday in Physics, Mr. Richter hands back the tests and announces a quiz for the end of the week. At lunch, Hunter pulls me aside on my way to my car, where I've been spending lunch most days.

"We have to get answers for Cole," she says as I keep walking toward the parking lot. "It's our opportunity."

"It's too risky," I tell her. I'm not sure if I could ever do what Hunter did, take pictures of the test.

"It's important."

"Cole's never even mentioned it to me, how can it possibly be important?" I ask.

"Trust me. AP Physics is the only class he can't get tests for. He has it fifth period. And he's failing." At my expression of surprise, she adds, "Okay, not *failing*. But in B-minus territory." Which might as well be failing if you're trying to get into a top school. "It's the key to getting him to trust us."

"I talked to Cole," I say. "He was sad about Lia. Sad he didn't talk to her. Honestly, he just seemed sad about the whole thing." I don't know why I'm defending him. If I'm even trying to defend him or if I just no longer trust Hunter at all.

"When did you talk to him?" she asks, eyes narrowing.

"Last week."

"Have you ever thought about the possibility that he's *sad about the whole thing* because he had something to do with it? Maybe he feels guilty for pressuring her to get him the Physics tests, have you ever thought about that?"

"I'm not doing it," I tell her again after she's finished, firmly this time.

"Fine," she says, getting out. "I'll do it myself." She slams the door and is gone.

Later that night, I text Cole.

Me: Wanna hang out?

It takes him almost an hour to respond.

Cole: Sure, tomorrow?

Me: You free tonight? I can drive over.

Cole: It's fine, I'll swing by.

I know he's not happy. He knows this isn't a reorder. It's been only two weeks and I usually last the month. But I have to see him, and I have to do it when Hunter's not around.

It's almost 1 AM when he pulls up. I get into the passenger side. "Thanks for coming," I begin.

"What is it?" He sounds impatient.

"Here," I hand him the AP Stat test.

"Always the overachiever," he says, sticking it into his bag and pulling two more packets out. "Somehow I knew you'd finish it in one day. Here's the next one. And here's a copy of the AP Econ test with solutions for next week. Lena finished early too. I swear to God, you guys are gonna run the world one day."

"What?" I take the next assignment—a Calc II test, and glancing at a few of the problems, I can tell it's likely the next one I'll face in class—and try to give the Econ test back.

"Don't tell me you're gonna actually study for it," he says with a laugh. "Just take it. In case."

"I don't know," I start to protest.

"Just keep it. If you don't use it, then whatever."

"Fine," I say to avoid arguing, and fold them up.

"You know all this could've waited until tomorrow," he says.

"I know, but I needed to talk to you. Alone." I feel nervous all of the sudden, like Hunter knows I'm here, talking to him somehow. Or worse, that Hunter's right and Cole isn't to be trusted.

"Okay, so talk," he says. "Sorry if I sounded mad earlier. I'm just tired." He tilts his head back, eyes closing. "Sometimes I'm not sure if this thing's worth it."

"What do you mean?"

"Just, you know, all the work," he says, but I don't know. "You think it'll save you a ton of time, but then you end up spending all your time doing this shit. Copying out cheat sheets, delivering them, whatever."

"Oh," I say, a little surprised at this admission. "Why don't you just quit?" He can't need the money—his family lives in Meadowlark, his brother goes to Columbia, and besides, he's got the Adderall and Focentra side business.

"You know how sometimes you start something and it just kind of gets away from you? You forget why you did it in the first place but now you can't stop." He's talking to me like we're friends, not acquaintances. Maybe he's just exhausted, but there's this vulnerability I've never seen before and it makes me want to trust him, even though I'm not sure if I do yet.

"Why not?" I ask, genuinely confused.

"All these people are counting on me now," he says. "I can't just stop." It's hard to see the guy Hunter sees, someone cold and calculating. Someone who knew Lia needed help and pushed her over the edge. "Anyway, what did you want to talk about?" he asks. "If you want to renegotiate your cut, it's not going to happen." Renegotiate? I've never negotiated my cut in the first place. But then I think of Hunter. Maybe she did it for me already.

"It's not about the money," I tell him, because I don't really care about that. "It's about Lia."

That gets his attention and he turns to look away.

Hunter's voice echoes in my mind: *Maybe he feels guilty for pressuring her to get him the Physics tests, have you ever thought about that?*

"The test," I say. "Was that your idea, or hers?"

He takes a deep breath. "What did she tell you?"

"Nothing. She never told me," I say and instantly regret it. Now Cole can say whatever he wants.

"It was my idea, not hers," he says, surprising me. He could've said the exact opposite, but he didn't, and now I know he's telling the truth.

"All right."

"She didn't want to do it, and I didn't push it. That's *it*," he says. "I promise."

"Okay," I tell him.

"I need you to believe me," he says, sounding more sincere than I thought he was capable.

"I believe you."

He sighs in relief and it's one more thing that makes it hard to imagine he had anything to do with Lia's death. I want to ask him about Hunter, but I'm not sure what's really going on. How close they are, what Hunter's trying to do. All I know is that I don't understand any of it. And that I don't want to play anymore.

"You okay?" he asks softly.

"Yeah," I say, and stare out the window. It's quiet, and in moments like now, it's hard to imagine we're only miles away from New York City.

"Have you been sleeping?" he asks, and I release a little empty laugh. "Seriously, you should cut back if you're not sleeping."

"Now that's ironic, my drug dealer telling me to cut back," I say. It was meant as a joke, but he looks unexpectedly wounded.

"I'm not a drug dealer," he says, and when I shoot him a flat look, he adds, "I don't give people hard shit. No painkillers, no cocaine, nothing you can OD on. Just a little Adderall." And Vyvanse, Ritalin, Focentra, maybe more. But I get his point. "And I don't give it to just anyone. I never sold to Lia, even though she asked." He sees the shock on my face. "You didn't know?" he says in disbelief.

"I had no idea," I say. "When was this?"

"A few months ago. But when she told me she was also on antidepressants, I wouldn't give it to her. You really didn't know?" he asks again, and I shake my head.

"She was on antidepressants?" I repeat.

"Wellbutrin and something else," he says. "I don't remember. But I didn't know how Adderall would play with them, so I said no. I really thought you knew. I thought—never mind."

"What?" I ask.

"Nothing, just surprised, I guess. You guys seemed so close," he says. "But maybe she—" He doesn't have to finish. Maybe she started the antidepressants after the breakup. "I'm sorry."

"Me too." I keep my eyes focused on a streetlamp, just trying not to cry. How much of Lia's life did I miss, and more important, how much of it did I fuck up? I remember what Jo said about that summer, how awful it'd been for her after the breakup. Is that when they put her on antidepressants?

Then it hits me: Lia's accident and hospital stay over the summer. I'd been picturing a car crash, a boating mishap, but what if it wasn't that kind of accident? I think about the times I felt the tantalizing pull of the street into oncoming traffic. One misstep and it'd be over. An accident, a relief.

Is that how Lia felt?

She was sad sometimes, but I thought it was the same sadness I felt sometimes, more of an exhaustion with life, really. This feeling of being stuck on a track, running to nowhere, but I'd always been able to shake it off, refocus on what I wanted. I thought Lia's sadness was the same, easily banished with a day of sun in Montauk.

But what if it wasn't?

Or worse, what if it was, only the breakup threw everything off balance? I know it turned my entire world upside down. I can't help but feel responsible for all of it.

Then, suddenly, I wonder if Hunter blames me too. *It's* someone's *fault*, she'd told me. My mind spins as I try to run through everything she's ever said to me. She'd made it all about Cole, but what if it had nothing to do with Cole?

29.

Hunter's not in class the next day, but I know she'll find me, and she does. The day's over when I see her after practice, the sky long dark. She's sitting on the hood of my car, cross-legged, hunched over her phone.

"Hey," I say, throwing my things in the back seat.

"Hey." She hops off, gets in the passenger side without an invitation.

"Where were you today?" I ask.

She shrugs. "Didn't feel like coming."

"But you're here now."

"Cole said you wanted to talk to me?" she says.

"Cut the bullshit. Look, I talked to Cole, okay? He doesn't care about the Physics tests or quizzes. Says it was his idea, but Lia didn't want to do it so he dropped it. What kind of game are you trying to play?" I twist to get a better look at her, pushing an elbow against my seat. "Is this some kind of trap, some kind of fucked-up revenge fantasy?"

She laughs. "Of course you think it's all about you. Of fucking course."

"This whole thing with Cole's been a lie from the beginning. It's me you want, and it's been about me the whole time."

"Unbelievable." Hunter shakes her head.

"I figured it out," I tell her. "I figured you out. You blame me for Lia's death, don't you? You decided it's all my fault, so now you want to destroy my life, is that it? Convince me to help you cheat on the next Physics test—"

"Quiz, actually," she says, ever so casually, mocking me.

"Quiz, whatever! Convince me to cheat and make sure I get caught. That's it, isn't it?" It's the only thing that makes sense. I spent the whole night tossing and turning, trying to come up with something, anything, that made sense. The Physics tests, that was the answer. It was always about them—she's been trying to get me to help her get them from the beginning. But it couldn't be for Cole, who doesn't seem to care that much. And it obviously wasn't for her. So it had to be some kind of trap.

Then suddenly, I remember that Lia's phone is still missing. Maybe she left it on the boat. Maybe Hunter found it, saw the text she'd sent me. The call for help I misunderstood and ignored. Maybe that's what this has been all about.

Maybe she's been after me this whole time.

"Yep, you got it all figured out," Hunter says with a hollow laugh. "Chase fucking Ohara, smartest cookie around."

"Fuck you." Angry tears fall down my face and I wipe them away quickly.

"Yeah, fuck me, right, for caring. Because while you're busy befriending Cole and having dinner at the Vestianos', I'm running around trying to figure out what really happened to Lia." And then she pops the door open and slams it shut on her way out, leaving me stunned and more confused than ever.

It's only long after she's gone that something jumps out in my mind. I'd never told her that I'd seen the Vestianos that Sunday. No one outside of Mom and Aidan knew.

So how did she find out?

For the rest of the week, Hunter doesn't show but I can't shake the feeling that I'm being watched. Is she following me? I begin looking over my shoulder all the time but I never see her tall frame, the electric blue streaks in her hair. I'm being paranoid, I tell myself. I just need to get more sleep.

On Friday, the day of the quiz, she's still absent, her seat empty. On Saturday, I finally cave and text her.

Me: You okay?

Me: Let's talk

She doesn't respond until Sunday, after I've already pulled into the Vestianos' driveway.

Hunter: Meet me tomorrow, 11AM. The boat.

Me: No. I'm not skipping class.

Me: Meet me at school. Or the diner after. I'm not going all the way out there.

Then I have to put away my phone because Jo and Rob have descended upon me, ushering me in from the car. I think of Hunter then. How they didn't invite her last week and probably aren't planning to invite her to one of these, ever. How they won't even utter her name. I wonder if she ever came over for dinner when she and Lia were together, if they did the formal meet and greet. Or maybe it's her personality, the abrasiveness.

Inside, we make small talk about the weather, school, and I notice the box is still sitting in the corner of the formal dining room.

"We missed you," Jo says, her smile a little brighter than last week.

"Missed you guys too," I tell them, sitting down at the kitchen table.

She's made chicken marsala. The first bite reminds me of home, and I tell them that.

"You used to make this all the time," I say. "When we were little."

Jo and Rob share a look, like they're about to cry.

"Oh God, I'm sorry."

"No, no, it's fine. It's good," Rob says, and Jo nods.

"Listen, Chase," Jo says when we're done. "I've been thinking. How would you like to join me for the Christmas special?"

"We talked about this, Jo," Rob says, a gentle warning in his voice.

"I know, I know, but I was planning this tribute to Lia, and it wouldn't feel right without Chase." Now they're both staring at me, waiting for my verdict.

"I don't know. When is it?" I ask, but I can already feel myself caving in. How can I say no?

"First week of December."

"I'm retaking the SATs then," I say.

"Oh," Jo says, visibly deflating.

"Maybe next year?" I suggest, feeling awful.

"What if we moved the shoot to the second week of December?" she asks—no, begs. "Please?"

"Okay," I say because I don't have an excuse ready, and her whole face lights up.

"Really? Okay, it'll be great, Chase. You'll see. I'll send a car to pick you up from school, or maybe I can talk your mom into letting me borrow you for the day." She keeps talking, excitedly planning it out, and I feel myself shrinking.

Instead of focusing on her words, I glance past her at the dining room, the box inside. When she's finally done, I excuse myself and head for the bathroom, but loop around the other side of the house instead and make my way to the dining room. Lia's laptop rests on the top, and I grab it. Below it is a notebook, a journal maybe, and I take it too. Under that is a bag of clothes and shoes, stained and covered in sand—what she must've been wearing when they found her—and I have to stifle a sob.

Staying out of their sight, I quietly make it to the front door and fold my coat over them. Later, when I leave, I gather everything up quickly and dash out to the car before they notice.

30.

At home, I run upstairs, toss my keys and coat on the floor, but before I can open Lia's laptop, my mom knocks on the door and I have to shove everything under the bed.

"How was it?" she asks.

"Fine," I say.

"Why are you so out of breath?" she says.

"What? I'm fine," I answer. "Just ran up here, I guess. Still have a few things to do for school."

She sighs. "I can't believe they're asking you to come over *every* Sunday." I haven't even told her about the Christmas special.

"It's okay," I tell her, because I'm desperate to be alone. "Sorry, I gotta, you know."

"Oh. Okay," she says, a little hurt. "Love you."

"Love you too."

Finally, she leaves and I close the door firmly behind her. I slide out Lia's laptop, type her password in, and poke around.

The first thing I pull up is her e-mail, but after a couple hours, I don't see anything odd. Then I go through her documents. Still nothing. When I look at the time, it's almost two in the morning. I get up, stretch, then remember the notebook and pull it out from under my bed.

Inside, there are no dates, just a short paragraph on each page, a few lines really. When we were kids, Lia used to spend hours practicing her penmanship and it kills me now, seeing the familiar curve and slant of her words, every stroke perfectly tucked in.

> *Wish you were here. No. Wish I were where you are. Or anywhere but here.*

That's it for the first page and it jolts me. Who was she addressing? Me? Hunter, her mom, someone else?

> *Remember when we were always busy busy busy? Now all I have is time and nothing to do. They took my phone. No win devices, they said. We can't be trusted. No contact with the outside world. Mom brought me books but I can't seem to make it past the nrst pages. She won't bring me the things I want. Too sad, she said. You won't get better that way.*

I have to put the notebook down. Where was she? Where did they put her? It has to be during the summer when I was in California and she was here. I don't remember her missing any school this fall. Oh, *Lia*, I think. What happened to you? I wipe a tear away and keep reading.

> *Can't sleep. The pipes clang all night long. They do checks every hour and even the night tech heard it. She grabbed the nurse on the moor and*

> *of course the moment she got here, the clanging stopped. Of course. She just stood there staring at me like I was fucking crazy. And I guess I am, but not like that. Wait, I told her. That other lady heard it. After a million years, the pipes nnally fucking clanged. Sorry, she said, we're all booked up, like we're at the Waldorf or something. You can sleep in the time-out room, but it's just a mattress on the moor. She's not kidding. It's a padded room with a bare, plastic-sealed mattress on the moor, a drain in the corner. The straitjacket room, the others call it. A girl hit one of the nurses on my nrst day and spent a day there. Solitary connnement, with only a small porthole window for us all to gawk. No, I told her, because all I could think was that they were going to nnd me there in the morning and think I belonged there. A prison within a prison. Hope it's better where you are.*

I read and reread her words, my chest tightening with a sob tearing its way up my throat and soon I'm a mess of tears just clutching Lia's journal, pressing it to my heart. *This* is the hospital stay Dr. Quinn mentioned, and I can't wrap my head around it. Something must've happened. They wouldn't have hospitalized her unless something happened.

The room feels like it's closing in on me again. The thought that she hurt herself over the summer is incomprehensible. The thought that she took her own life is just as unbearable. It's the truth that we've all been stepping around, unable to say out loud, acknowledge.

But I don't have the whole truth yet, so I force myself to push on.

I don't want to miss you, but I do. I don't want to be here, but I'm here. I don't want to be Lia Sophia Vestiano anymore, but I am.

I wipe and wipe at my tears, then flip the page.

Mom and Dad came to visit again. I asked her when I could leave and she said when the doctors say I can. We argued. I told her being here makes me want to kill myself more and she minched. Dad cried the whole time, but Mom didn't shed a single tear. She kept glancing around the room like she was worried someone would recognize her. You're pathetic, I told her. Pathetic. Maybe you should cry, in case someone notices. Because that would be normal. Because then you could look like the caring mother. Shut up, she whisper-yelled. Shut-up-shut-up-shut-up, she said. Your daughter tried to kill herself! I yelled back. That's not fucking normal, stop trying to act normal! Then a nurse came over and asked if everything was all right and we all knew what she meant so we just shut up.

It's a shock reading Lia's words, but maybe not a surprise. I close my eyes and I can picture the three of them. Rob, silently weeping. Lia, angry. And Jo, a steely calm. I remember Hunter's voice: "She loved her, yes, but in this very specific, limited way." Was that what Lia had meant every time she called Jo "fake"? That Jo didn't just pretend on TV but in real life?

All I could see growing up was this happy family helmed by Joanna Adriana Vestiano. All I could see growing up was my parents fighting, my father domineering, my mother giving in. But across the street was this other family that I sometimes felt part of. They were always laughing and feeding me pasta, and I thought it was perfection.

But maybe it wasn't.

Maybe Lia was trying to tell me all this time and I didn't want to see it.

When I nrst arrived, everything was so rushed and they wouldn't even let me go home to grab my things, like I might somehow pull it off sitting in trafnc. Mom packed a duffel with underwear, socks, and what she called comfy clothes. Just leggings, baggy T-shirts, sneakers, and my favorite hoodie—you know, the gray one? But they said no strings, so we had to pull out the laces and the cord threaded through the hood. Now my shoes kind of mop around when I walk and I can't tighten the hood around my face. It's not like I ever used it before, but now when I look in the mirror it looks wrong without it. Incomplete.

Even this journal. First, Mom brought a normal spiral-bound one, but they said I could take the metal out, fashion it into a weapon, so now I'm stuck using this composition notebook like I'm in elementary school.

It just drives me crazy. I look around and all I can see are the ways I could hurt myself if I wanted to. The mantel over the plastered-up fireplace has corners sharp enough to take out an eye. This pen, which they allowed, could end everything with a quick stab to just the right spot in my neck. I could do it at night and no one would know, not even the checkers.

They pretend all the rules are to make us safe, but we're not safe here. We're locked behind barred windows. We're not allowed to go outside. We're trapped here. How anyone's supposed to get better is beyond me.

I call Mom and tell her all these things. Well, not the part about the pen—I'm not stupid. She listens and just sounds sad. They don't have yoga? she asks. No swimming or hydrotherapy? No aromatherapy or massage? She asks these things like she's surprised and I want to smack her. No, Mom, it's not a fucking spa. It's not summer camp. It's hell and I want to go home.

But I can't, and we both know it. Even if she wanted me home, the doctor won't allow it. I'm not better, they say, even though they spend less than twenty minutes with me each day. It doesn't matter what I tell them because they just don't believe me.

I think of her hoodie, sitting on the couch in the Vestianos' yacht, the missing cord. How Lia went into the hospital and was forced to take it out. How we could re-thread a new cord into the hood but we'd never be able to replace *her*.

> *Maybe what I want more than anything else is not to die but simply not exist anymore. If I could just blink and just disappear, that would be enough. That would be everything.*

Each word feels like another knife to my heart. She never, ever told me these things. Yes, sometimes she was sad, but I thought it was the same sadness we shared, a kind of heaviness that was just the price of being alive. I thought it was that feeling of drowning under the weight of always having a million things to do. I thought it was just feeling overwhelmed and stressed, nothing a day in Montauk couldn't fix. Nothing a day spent with each other couldn't heal.

But Lia's sadness wasn't just stress. She didn't just feel overwhelmed. She wanted not to exist.

I want so badly for her to be here right now, for her to be in my arms so I can hold her and tell her that I love her. I want that love to be enough to save her. I want it so much it hurts, the tears a never-ending stream that I can barely see.

I want to go back and not fight about stupid things. I want to give her everything, the summer in California she wanted, the road trips and weekends in San Francisco. I would give her anything to have her back, *anything*.

The sobs are crashing through me too quickly and I'm gasping for air that isn't there. It takes forever to finally calm down enough to flip the page, but when I do, I see that the next page is written in Lia's handwriting but the ink is blue, not black, and I can't explain it but it looks almost recent even though there's no date.

> *Meeting you was the best thing that ever happened to me.*

It sends a jolt down my spine. Her words here remind me of something she once said to me, about how I was the best thing that ever happened to her. There are a few more paragraphs like that, and then:

> *You are the only person keeping me sane. I don't know what I'd do without you. I still can't believe you spent every single day at the hospital with me.*

Her words stop me cold and I feel my heart shatter into a million pieces. She's not talking about me at all, but Hunter. For a moment, I let myself cry harder, but when I come up for air, I press one hand hard against my heart, try to stanch the pain.

I press my free hand against these pages, try to feel how happy Lia was, and it's bittersweet.

At least she was happy, I try telling myself. I repeat it over and over again, hoping to feel anything other than excruciating devastation.

She was finally happy. *Finally.* But it wasn't with me.

I skim the next few pages, unable to read every glowing word about Hunter van Leeuwen. And then I flip the page to something different.

> *You . . . left. You just left. I tried to explain,*

but you wouldn't listen. It's over, you said. It's fucking over.

No, I said. Please don't leave. You don't understand. I need you. You can't go.

Watch me, you said. Fucking watch me.

I'll die, I said. I'll die without you.

I can't live like this anymore, you said. I'm terrined. I'm always terrined of you. You have to nnd a way to live without me.

And then you were gone.

But the truth is, I know I can't. I need you.

And that's it.

I flip and flip and flip but there's nothing else. "Oh my fucking *God*," I whisper. "Fuck, fuck, fuck."

I scramble for my phone, call Hunter. It rings and rings and rings but she doesn't pick up. I check the time—it's almost four in the morning.

It was *her*. It wasn't me. It was *Hunter*.

I punch the floor and slam the heel of my palm against it helplessly. She's the reason Lia's no longer here.

31.

It's 7 AM and I'm at the Meadowlark LIRR. The station is full of Monday-morning commuters but the platform I'm on is pretty empty. Everyone's heading into the city and I'm going out to Montauk.

I'd drive, but I haven't gotten any sleep. Even with two Focentra, my vision blurs a little every so often and I'm barely hanging on. I can't remember the last time I slept. I can't remember the last time I felt anything other than helpless and scared.

And so completely without hope.

I watch other trains come and go, everyday commuters filing in without a problem, but I'm afraid of standing too close to the edge.

I can't trust my legs, wobbly and weak. I've been barely surviving the cross-country practices and still skipping my night runs.

Each time a train pulls near, the air hums with tense anticipation followed by a sense of potential release. Then I panic and step farther away from the edge.

No, I tell myself. *Don't you fucking dare*. I blink, trying to clear my vision, but it's useless.

Finally, the right train arrives, and I get on.

I call Hunter again, but she doesn't pick up. I send her another text.

Me: I'm coming. You better fucking be there.

It doesn't make me feel any better, and she doesn't respond because of course she doesn't. Alone on an empty car, I try to get some sleep in the almost three hours I have on the train. The pain in my head, an almost permanent companion these days, only settles in deeper.

When we pull into the Montauk station, it's just as empty as the train, and I'm the only one who gets off. It's freezing, the sharp wind coming off the water snatching my breath away. I tighten my coat around me, rewrap my scarf, and order a car. Soon, I'm at the marina, standing in front of Lia's boat alone. Hunter's late. Of course she's late.

I kick the glass door in anger and the pain that shoots up my toes to my shin shocks me into tears. I lean against the door, sobbing. I've been crying so much it's almost a surprise that I have anything left. I'm crying for Lia, for everything she went through, for what we had and what we might've had.

All this time, I've been focused on the past, but now I'm not just mourning all the moments of laughter and love—I'm grieving the loss of a future that could have been ours. Maybe we'd never be together again, maybe we'd never even be best friends, but I can't imagine a life without her in it, our fates strung together from the age of six. But that thread between us has been severed, permanently, and it feels like I'm the one lost at sea, unable to find a way back to shore.

Hunter emerges from the side, coming into view, the keys dangling from her fingers.

I dry my eyes, try to hide my tears. Square my shoulders, focus on my anger.

"You lied," I begin. "About everything."

"Come on," she says, and I follow her in.

Inside, the air is stale and everything is as we left it. I see Lia's favorite gray hoodie lying on the couch, still folded, still missing its cord.

"How could you tell me Lia's hospitalization was irrelevant? She was obviously struggling!"

"It wasn't the thing that killed her in the end," Hunter says simply. Then she sits on the floor, cross-legged, her back against the sectional, and pulls the hoodie toward her.

"Don't touch that!" I cry.

"Why not?" she asks, holding it up against her chest.

"You don't deserve it," I say, but she doesn't budge, only clutches it tighter. "How can you talk about the thing that killed her in the end when you're the real reason Lia's gone? You blamed me for everything, but it was you. She needed you and you just left her." I collapse from exhaustion onto the couch and my vision doubles for a second, everything zipping apart then back together. "I found her journal. I read it. I know what happened."

Hunter laughs and it cuts through me. "You don't know anything." Then she pushes herself up, taking Lia's hoodie with her. "You don't know *anything*." She heads toward the cabins, and I get up to see her disappear into Lia's room. *Our* room. The bed where we spent so many hours laughing and studying and watching movies. Kissing and sleeping, tangled up in each other. Some of my favorite memories, my most important memories.

I slam the door open so hard it almost knocks back into me. "Hey!" I'm about to scream at her but there's no one there.

The room is empty.

"What the fuck?" I shake my head hard, rub my eyes. I tear through the boat, barge into Jo and Rob's stateroom, check the bathroom, then come back out to the living area, scanning the kitchen and sectional.

Hunter is nowhere to be found.

32.

A spark of intense pain travels from the back of my neck up along the middle to the top of my head and it feels like I'm being split open like a melon, my skull cracking in half.

"Hunter?" I call out. "Hunter!"

But I'm all alone.

I search the boat once, twice, three times.

"This isn't funny!" I cry, and then I hear laughter. It sounds distant, distorted at first, but then it grows and grows and grows until it's all I hear.

"Boo." Hunter scares me from behind.

"What the *fuck*?" I yell, startled into falling down, my heart punching against my rib cage. "Where were you?"

"Where were *you*?" she asks, a deranged smile on her face.

I must be losing my mind. It's the sleepless nights. Or too much Focentra. Or the pressure, the unrelenting pressure. Seventeen years of perfection and I'm finally breaking.

"Have you figured it out yet?" she asks, back by the couch, Lia's hoodie still in her clutches.

"Give me that." I lunge for it, for her, and miss. "You don't deserve to have it. You don't deserve to fucking *touch* it. You killed Lia. You left her. She needed you, and you just left. Who *does* that?"

Hunter grows serious, leans in toward me but still out of reach. "*You.*"

"What?"

"*You,*" she repeats. "You, my darling, fucked-up Chase. You did that."

Then she disappears again, this time before my very eyes. And when I look down, I see Lia's sweatshirt limp in my hands like I've been holding it the entire time.

"You did all of it." Hunter's voice floats in and out of focus, but she's nowhere to be found. "You made it all up!" Hunter shouts. "You made *me* up. You made up this entire story so you could fucking forget. Isn't that fucked up?"

Then she answers for me: "It's *so* fucked up."

I stumble around, my head ablaze with pain, my vision blurry, my heart ready to break out of my chest. I am so broken, so confused. My world feels like it's shrinking in on me, and I fall back to the ground, curl up with Lia's hoodie pressed against me, just trying to breathe. Just trying to stay alive.

"It's not possible," I whisper. "It's not fucking possible."

"And yet," Hunter says, appearing before me, causing me to scramble away.

"You texted me," I say, trying to seize on something, anything.

"Check your phone," she says.

I pull it out, open my messages. "It was right here." I scroll through it again. "I texted you *this morning.*"

"No," she says calmly. "You *imagined* texting me this morning."

"You were at Lia's house. I saw you. We went to the diner."

Hunter just shakes her head.

"I've seen you close doors. My car. Cole's. At school. Here," I say. "Yeah, here! You opened the door. You have Lia's keys."

"Check your pockets."

I pull them out, stare at them in disbelief. "No," I whisper. "*No.*"

"Do you believe me now?"

Suddenly, everything makes sense and nothing makes sense at the same time. The Vestianos didn't avoid talking about Hunter because they resented her, they didn't talk about her because she didn't exist. Everything else about the last few weeks—no, the last few months—snaps into focus. Had Cole ever mentioned Hunter? Any of my teachers? Classmates? *Anyone*, ever?

"But you and Lia, together, holding hands," I protest.

"Never happened."

"I remember seeing you together." The memories of them laughing, Hunter's fingers brushing Lia's hair away, the way Lia's eyes hardened when she glanced my way. But these images in my mind, they feel wrong somehow but only now, when I examine them. They don't seem to belong anywhere. They feel like snapshots, not part of a real time line.

"You made it all up. You made *me* all up," Hunter says.

"I don't understand," I whisper, even though maybe I'm beginning to.

"I don't know how many different ways I can explain it to you," she says, every word laced with impatience. "You couldn't cope with what'd happened, so your brain created this alternate world where you could be innocent and free."

My brain. My fucked-up, drug-addicted, sleep-deprived brain.

"Innocent?" I ask, breathless.

"Yes, innocent. Here, in *this* story, you could be the good one. Here, in *this* version of events, you could be the one free from blame. Here, in this *fantasy*, you could hate the person who took Lia from you: me."

"You keep talking about innocence and blame, about how I couldn't cope with what'd happened," I say, squeezing Lia's sweatshirt even closer to my chest. I've spent all this time trying to keep everything under control, not realizing until now that I'd already lost it. "What the fuck happened?"

PART II

33.

Early May, Lia and I were weeks away from flying out to the West Coast together, weeks away from what was supposed to be an epic summer. Me at Stanford, her interning at a Michelin-starred restaurant in San Francisco. After our big fight on the boat, we were careful to keep the peace, tiptoeing around each other. Lia stopped pushing so hard for me to meet her in the city every weekend, stopped making new plans for big road trips, and I relented on the two trips she wanted, a long weekend in LA for July Fourth, and a drive up to Portland, Oregon, but only after my program ended.

Still, it wasn't enough. Those quiet weeks were only the calm before a storm. It was just a matter of time, even without the stress of final exams and papers.

The weekend before finals, Lia insisted on going out to Montauk again, and to avoid a fight, I caved like I always did.

We remained docked, staying in the smaller stateroom, sprawled out on the bed, books and papers surrounding us as the boat swayed gently in the water. I tried to focus on chem formulas and balancing redox equations, but Lia quickly gave up, flopping onto her back and occasionally looking over at me with a heavy sigh.

"Let's take a break," she said only an hour in.

"We just started," I complained, not taking my eyes off my notes.

"Come on," she said, snuggling up to me, tucking a wisp of hair behind my ears, placing a light brush of a kiss against my neck.

"Later," I said, stiffening.

"Fine." She rolled away and went back to her books. But soon, she collapsed on her side, curled up, and fell asleep. I knew she was behind in chem and needed to study, but I let her nap so I could focus without interruption.

She woke late, long after it'd grown dark. We ordered pizza but she barely touched it, staying unusually quiet as we ate in the kitchenette.

"Let's just stay here tonight," she said.

"Sure." I shrugged and texted my mom. We'd done it a million times, treated the boat like it was our own little getaway.

"Chase," she said later, when we were brushing our teeth. "Do you love me?"

It should've set off alarms, the tone in her voice—needy, yes, but also with the slightest edge underneath—but I was tired from studying all day, from the long morning on the train. From all the weeks of trying not to fight.

"Of course," I told her, spitting into the tiny sink.

She smiled, but it was tight.

With the lights off, a single shot of weak moonlight illuminated the bedroom through the porthole. She reached for me under the covers in the dark. "Come here," she said, and I slid over, my eyes already closing, ready to fall asleep with my face tucked under her chin, our limbs tangled, her breath on my hair, her heartbeat against my skin.

"Chase?" she whispered.

"Hm," I mumbled, barely conscious.

"Never mind." She squeezed me tight, and I let go.

But I woke in the middle of the night, cold and alone. Shivering, I wrapped the comforter around me and went out in search of Lia.

She was outside in her pajamas with her coat loose over her shoulders, looking out at the water, the dark horizon ahead.

I joined her. "Hey."

"Can't sleep," she said, eyes remaining fixed on the waves dancing under moonlight, the vast emptiness beyond the boats nestled in the marina.

"Come back to bed. It's cold." I tugged at her arm, but she was unmoving. "What's wrong?"

"Nothing." She folded her arms, not like she was angry but almost like she was hugging herself. Like she needed protection.

"What?" I nudged her gently with an elbow.

"Nothing," she said, annoyed.

"What?" I asked again.

"Nothing."

"Fine. Stay cold out here by yourself," I said, turning to go. But back in bed alone, I struggled to sleep. Soon I was stalking back outside, where Lia stood in the exact same place in the exact same position, a statue carved out of sadness. "What's wrong?"

"You don't want to know," she said, finally turning to face me. "Just forget it."

"No, I want to know." I stepped forward to hold her but she stepped back, away from my reach. "I do."

She shook her head slowly.

"Just tell me what I did this time and we can go back to bed. We have a chem final Monday, math Tuesday—"

"This is exactly it," she said, cutting me off. "This is the problem."

"That we have finals next week?" I asked, exhausted.

"No, it's you," she said. "You don't really want to know what's wrong, just for me to tell you what to say, what to apologize for so you can get enough sleep to study for finals. Look, I'm sorry I'm so inconvenient."

"That's not what I meant, I'm sorry," I said. "I was just—" I searched for the right word. "—frustrated. And stressed." But she was right. I thought her moody, needy. And yes, inconvenient. I let her nap so she'd leave me alone. I wanted her to tell me what to say so I wouldn't have to deal with her feelings. It felt like I was always the one caving, the one accommodating her, and for once, I wanted her to accommodate *me*.

"You're always stressed!" she said in a sudden explosion. "And you'll always be stressed."

"Okay, yes, I'm stressed," I said, still trying to placate her, always trying to placate her.

"But I think you secretly like it. I think it makes you feel important. I think it makes you think you're doing important things. Accomplishing something real when all you're doing is running in place." Then she turned ever so slightly toward me to catch my reaction out of the corner of her eye.

Her words sank in, leaving me stunned. All my hard work, everything I cared about, she was saying none of it mattered. That the things I wanted didn't matter. That, ultimately, my *life*, or at least the life I wanted, didn't matter.

It was cruel. Standing on that little deck, I felt very trapped all of a sudden. That even with the vast sky and ocean before me, I was locked on this boat, locked in this unhappy relationship with Lia.

Lia, the person I loved, and the same person who was, at that very moment, suffocating me. I wanted to lash out—I wanted to tear up the unspoken peace treaty and stop tiptoeing. Stop pretending everything was okay when nothing felt okay.

"How fucking dare you?" I exploded right back at her. "How dare you trash all the things I care about?"

She looked momentarily chastened, eyes cutting away from me.

"And I'm not just *running in place*. You know how hard I work. You *know*." That was what crushed me the most, the idea that I was a hamster on a wheel. That *Lia* thought I was only a hamster on a wheel. Lia, the one who had everything, who never had to fight for anything. Lia, the one who had this grand future sitting on a platter for her taking, fame and fortune, and who could dismiss all my hard work because she'd never really had to work for any of it.

"I know," she said finally. "I know how hard you work, and as someone who cares about you, I'm worried, okay?"

"You're not worried about me," I said. "You're just selfish. You just want me all to yourself. You don't care what I want, just that I come when you call."

"*I'm* selfish?" she asked. "You're unbelievable!"

"You wanted to come out here, even though it's finals week, and what did we do? We came out here. It's always whatever you want. I always give you whatever you want, don't I?"

"You're here, but you're not here," she said with a sad shake of her head.

"What's that supposed to mean?"

"You came, begrudgingly, like it was this huge ask, but all you've done is study on the train and study on the boat. I might as well be here alone."

"It *is* a huge ask! We have finals next week. It's junior year. Come on, Lia, don't be an asshole."

"Yes, it's finals week, and yes, maybe I shouldn't have asked you out here, but it's always something with you. There's always a reason to say no to me. There's always a reason you're stressed out of your mind. Before finals, it was student council elections, and before that, it was Science Olympiad. Before that, it was getting into Stanford's summer program, and before that it was first-semester finals."

"So?" I began to pace, tired of feeling like a trapped animal, but there was hardly any space to really move, which only fed into my claustrophobia. "So what if I'm always stressed? This is what I want. This is all I've ever wanted. It's the life I want, my fucking dream! You knew all this about me, and you've known forever. You knew who I was, you've known all along, and you still wanted to be with me. This is who I am, this is the whole thing." All of that was true—I had never, ever lied to her about who I was or what I wanted.

Lia watched me pace, a spark of defiance in her eyes. "It doesn't have to be this way." What she was really saying: *I* didn't have to be this way. "Maybe I don't want that kind of life. Maybe I don't want to spend our whole lives living like this. One finals week to the next. One emergency to another. Look at our parents. Look at their lives. At the people in Meadowlark, in New York City. All they do is work and it's never enough."

"What are you saying?" I stopped moving, turning to stare right at her as she prepared to break my heart.

"Maybe I want something else," she said after a breathless moment. The sea breeze picked up, pushing her coat against her body and she slipped her arms through its sleeves, wrapping it tight around her. "Maybe I want a different kind of life," she said. "Maybe I want the kind of life where we're happy. Where we can just be ourselves and it would be enough."

"But that's what I'm saying. This is who I am, this is what I want."

"No, Chase, it's not. It's what your dad wants. It's what my mom wants. It's always chasing after the next thing and never being satisfied because that's just complacency. It's never being happy, not even with making partner at McKinsey or having a hit cooking show. Because there's always something else better, but better never comes."

"That's not how I see it," I said. "Better will come." I wanted to believe that more than anything. I wanted to believe that if I did everything perfectly, then I'd be the master of my own destiny. Then I could do anything, be anyone.

Be in control.

Lia shook her head sadly. "Aren't you tired of winning at any cost?"

"What do you mean?"

"What about student council elections?" she asked. "When you promised everyone you'd give them prom at the Schwarzman Building? You lied just to win." The Schwarzman Building was New York Public Library's flagship branch, known in movies and TV shows for its grand steps and glamorous interior. I'd made it part of my campaign, knowing it'd win the election and knowing it was impossible.

"Look, everyone knew it'd be a stretch, okay? I didn't promise them. I just said I'd fight for it." That was true enough, but I hated the way she talked about it, the insinuation, the judgment.

"But you're not going to, are you?" she pointed out. "You said it just to win, and you have no intention of even trying."

"So what?" I said, face growing hot. "It's not like I'm the only one who did it. Jenna Smith ran on a bullshit platform of getting the school to pay for a ski trip to Aspen." I didn't understand why this was the thing she wanted to criticize me for, why she chose that moment to bring it up.

"But aren't you tired of playing the game? Aren't you tired of pretending to care? How many more times will you have to do it? You're just like Jo. Fake," she said, and it infuriated me. I could feel the pressure building inside of me with every word she spoke, the rage and rush of blood pounding in my head. All I could see, all I could think, was that she'd taken a knife and aimed straight for my heart. That she was attacking the very core of who I was, calling me fake, a term she'd previously reserved only for her mother. That she was measuring me against her standards and found me not just lacking but pathetic somehow.

All I could see was her contempt for me and the things I wanted. The things I'd worked so hard for my whole life. All I could see was someone who'd never had to work. Who'd never have to work for anything.

All I could feel was her complete betrayal. She was the one person I loved, the one person I trusted, and she was just standing there, breaking my heart like it meant nothing at all. Like it was easy.

And in that moment, all I wanted was for her to feel the same way. In my mind, she'd already destroyed everything between us, and so in my mind, I was free to burn it to the ground.

"It's funny," I began. "You act like your mom is the worst fucking thing that's ever happened to you, but you're so full of shit. You complain all the time but you don't have a problem using her money or her connections. You don't have a problem waving her credit card and spending weekends on the yacht she paid for. Getting an internship in San Francisco, renting a studio downtown for the summer, buying a car so you can go on road trips. You never say no to spending every August in Maine. You never say no to the trips to Italy and France, Korea and Japan. I've never been *anywhere.* God, Lia, is this what the rest of our lives is going to look like? I work my ass off and you just get whatever you want because your mom knows someone?" I knew I hit a nerve even before I finished, watching as Lia's expression turned from shock to hurt to anger. I knew I'd crossed a line I'd never be able to walk back. That even though everything I was saying was the truth, it was the kind of truth you weren't supposed to say out loud.

"You know what?" I couldn't help continuing. "Maybe that's the real reason you're mad, that you'll never be like me or your mom. That maybe you'll never be good enough. That you'll always have to rely on one of us. That you *need* us because you'll never make it on your own." Now I'd buried my own knife in her heart. Now I'd really killed whatever we had between us, our entire history. Our friendship and our love. The future we'd imagined. Us against the world.

Now it was me against her, and our world was collapsing in on us. For a moment, my words lay around us like the aftermath of an exploded bomb and we were in a daze, ears ringing, vision swimming, bleeding from the shrapnel.

"Fuck you," Lia said when she managed to speak. "You think I need you?" Tears streaked her face, her eyes ablaze.

I'll never forget the fury and raw hurt. The surge of power and satisfaction from dealing such a blow faltered and I was hit with uncertainty.

"I don't need my mom. I don't fucking need anyone, and I certainly don't need you." And in her rage, I could see the truth, the fire burning within her. "Everyone thinks I'm useless. That I'm not as smart as you or as hardworking or as strong. That I'll never amount to much or that I'll only follow my mom into the biz but fail. But you're wrong. You're all wrong. You'll see."

"Lia—" I didn't know what to say. I was suddenly struck with doubt. Had I misunderstood what she was saying? What was it that we were really fighting over?

But it was too late.

"Get the fuck off my boat," she said. "Get the fuck out of my life!"

"Fine," I said, but I couldn't just leave it at that. "You know what, I'm glad. I'm fucking *happy*, okay?" I shouted. "You're not my fucking problem anymore." Then I went inside and gathered my things before leaving what had been our sanctuary for the last time.

Every time I replay this night in my mind, I'm less sure of what exactly happened and how we got there.

But I'm more certain now than ever that she was right: Lia didn't need me, but I needed her.

34.

I stormed off, but I couldn't stay away. It ate and ate at me, the things I said to her. I called her but she sent me straight to voice mail. I texted to say I was sorry a million times, but it went unanswered. If she saw me approach at school, she turned and walked in the opposite direction.

I sent one final text, not expecting it to work.

Me: Meet me in Montauk.

She didn't respond for two days, but when she did, I fell to my knees as if grateful for an answered prayer.

Lia: Tomorrow, the 11:18 train.

Me: I'll be there.

But she didn't show the next day. Instead, I got another text when I arrived at the station.

Lia: Took the car, see you on the other side

Me: Okay

It felt like she'd planned it this way, intentionally avoiding me, but I didn't care. It didn't matter because she was waiting for me, because she was willing to see me at all.

"Hey," she said quietly when I found her outside Montauk station in her car.

"Hey," I said, getting into the passenger seat.

We drove in mostly silence to our favorite beach, her pensive and me anxious. I remember that it was a beautiful day, all sunlight and hope. The weather was just starting to warm up again, with a trickle of people from the city dotting the sand before the Memorial Day crush. For a while, we sat on our favorite bench, made entirely of one piece of driftwood nearly bleached white by the sun, and quietly ate sandwiches from the 7-Eleven nearby, the silence tense yet somehow protective, keeping us safe just a little longer. I touched the place where we'd carved our initials against the wood, faded but still there. "Remember this?" I asked, showing her.

"Forever ago," she said, but nothing more.

Then we walked along the water, the waves lapping at our ankles, the breeze soft against our skin.

"I'm sorry," I began. "The things I said—I'll never forgive myself." Every word was true, but they were laced with the heavy poison of fear that made it all sound forced, desperate. Almost like an act.

"I'm sorry too," she said quietly, and I could hear the breath of relief escape me. "You're not the only one who said awful things."

Everything would be okay. We were both sorry, we were going to be okay.

"Chase, I love you," she said, and stopped us, pulling me closer, her hand in my hair, steadying me. Our kiss was soft, her lips a little cold from the wind. Then she pulled away: "But I can't do this anymore."

"What?" I asked, breathless. She might as well have plunged another knife into my heart.

She couldn't look at me. Wouldn't.

"Lia, please." I was begging and I didn't care.

"I can't," she said, voice cracking. "I just can't do this anymore. We're just not"—she took a deep breath—"we're just not good for each other, you know?"

"You're not making any sense." Things were moving so fast and all I wanted was to stop the train.

"It's for the better. I don't want to be—" she broke off.

"Be what?" I could feel tears slipping down my face. I could feel my heart splintering in my chest.

"I don't want to be a problem for you anymore," she whispered. "I don't want to be a problem for *anyone*. A burden."

For a moment, I didn't understand. Then my words came back to me: *"You're not my fucking problem anymore."*

"It's better this way," she insisted, voice stronger this time. "I need to be on my own. I need to know I can be on my own."

"But I can't," I said. "I need you."

"No," she shook her head. "You're the strongest person I know."

"I'm not," I said. "I was wrong, okay? Is that what you want to hear? I'll say it a thousand times. I was wrong."

"No," she said. "I don't want to hear you say anything. I don't want anything from you. Chase, it's over."

All my hope and sunshine and desperation shattered into a thousand pieces. "It can't be." I didn't care that I was sobbing, that people were turning to stare.

"I'm sorry," she said, and I could hear the resolve in her voice.

"So you dragged me all the way out here, ditched me at the station and drove, just to fucking destroy me?" I pulled away from her, couldn't let her hold me anymore.

"I wanted to finish things here. Our place. It was important to me," she said, and I couldn't help but think that was just like Lia to pull something like this, think of only herself. It was always like that, I thought, and maybe it always would be. And like an idiot, I was still here. Like an idiot, I always came back.

"I love you, Chase, but—" She didn't finish, eyes cutting away.

"You love me, but not enough," I said, furiously wiping at my tears. "You love me, but you don't care enough to stick around, figure it out. You love me, but the last ten years meant nothing."

Lia remained quiet, let me yell.

I couldn't stand to see her like that, so stoic, no tears, no fear. Not even anger. I wanted her to feel something. I wanted to hurt her. But the only thing I could think of in that moment—the only thing I had—were the keys to the Vestiano yacht, so I tore the ring off my chain, threw it at her.

And ran.

"Wait, Chase!" she shouted after me, but I didn't want her pity and I couldn't stand the idea of sitting next to her in the car for even a second, let alone the ten minutes to the train station. So I ran and ran until the clouds above me began to spin and I collapsed to the sand, gasping for air.

When I looked behind me, there was no one there, just the awful memory of Lia breaking my heart.

35.

By July, I was at Stanford, miserable. Going to classes and trying to fit in but hating it. Everyone there was just like me. Too much like me. They didn't always look like me or sound like me but I knew that inside we were the same: all ambition and hunger. *Only* ambition and hunger. Winners, with chips on our shoulders. Everyone was the top of their class back home, the student council presidents, the captains of lacrosse or volleyball. The future leaders of our generation.

We were the best and used to it. But here, we couldn't all be the best. We couldn't all be winners.

Maybe I would've loved it if Lia had come. Or if Lia had been in San Francisco. She grounded me, kept me tethered. But there I was, standing in the place that I'd wanted for so long, completely miserable and alone.

All of that was true. I remember it.

But now another memory floats up too. A call, the fourth week of the program. I almost never picked up unknown numbers but it rang twice, so I answered: "This is Chase."

Silence, muffled voices.

"Hello?" I said.

"Hey."

"Lia?" I asked, shocked. She sounded so far away.

"I know you're probably busy," she began slowly, like she'd rehearsed the words before the call.

"I'm not," I said. "What's wrong?" I could hear people in the background, like she was somewhere crowded. "Where are you? Why aren't you calling from your phone?"

"Oh, that," she said, sounding slightly distracted. "It died. Listen, I just—" She took a deep breath. "I just wanted to hear your voice, okay? Please don't make a whole thing of it."

"I wouldn't do that," I said immediately. I knew the way we ended things left us shattered but I hoped not beyond repair.

"Okay," she said, relief in her voice.

"What's going on? Tell me what's wrong." *I love you*, I wanted to add, because it was true, because now that I had her on the line, all I wanted was to keep her there, to listen to her voice too.

"Nothing," she said. Then someone shouted behind her: "Get your hands off me!"

"Where are you?" I asked again, more alarmed. "On set?" I couldn't understand, then, where else she could've been.

"Something like that," she said without really answering. "I have to go."

"Wait!" I said.

"Bye, Chase," she said, and I heard a click, like she physically hung up on me.

I called her back on her cell, but it went to voice mail after several rings. Her phone wasn't dead. I called the number back and got an automated answer: "You have reached New York Presbyterian Westchester Behavioral Health Center. For our hours and location, press 1..."

I hung up, tried the number again. Same automated answer.

Nothing made sense. Was Lia visiting someone at the hospital? Had something happened to Jo, or her dad?

When I tried her cell again, it went through. This time, Jo picked up. "Hey, hon," she said, but without her usual cheer.

"Where is Lia?"

36.

Hunter paces before me now, walking the short length of the living space back and forth, back and forth.

"It's coming back to me now," I tell her, sitting up, Lia's hoodie resting on my lap.

She smiles tightly.

"You remember the call?" she asks, and I nod. "Then what happened?"

"Jo told me Lia had downed a bottle of painkillers a week before." My own voice sounds hollow and distant, the words foreign yet true. I remember now, the way Jo spoke, calmly at first, then crying as she told me how she found Lia, how Lia's stomach had been pumped, and how after she was out of the woods, they made the difficult decision to commit her. They picked New York Presbyterian Westchester because it was connected to Cornell and supposed to be one of the best, but it didn't take me long to figure out they'd also picked it for its distance from Long Island and Manhattan. Far enough away to safeguard a secret hospitalization, far enough away to keep Lia hidden.

I left Stanford early against the advice of the administrators and my professors. My dad called, yelling at me about how I was throwing away my future, but I didn't care. None of my classmates came by my dorm to say goodbye the night before I left, and I knew I wouldn't miss them.

I tell all of this to Hunter, but it occurs to me that she already knows. That she knows *everything*. More than me even. That somehow, she holds the key to a piece of my mind.

"What happened when you got home?" she asks.

Closing my eyes, I hunt through my memories. "I went to see her. Straight from the airport. Jo met me outside, walked me through. Lia looked awful. But she was happy to see me." I remember her appearance, pale and thin, hair messy and eyes tired, and I remember the moment we found each other: the light rushed back into her eyes and it was like pure oxygen and I could breathe again for the first time in a long time.

"Chase?" Her voice was barely above a whisper. "How are you here?"

I held her tight, squeezing her against my thumping heart, and all I could think was how I'd never let her go.

"I love you." I whispered the words into her ear and we began to cry. Everything awful between us melted away and it was just like it once was. Just like it was always supposed to be, just me and Lia. Us against the world. Us alone, together, and it was everything, everything. For a moment, nothing else mattered and the world seemed to disappear—the nurses, the other patients, the whole hospital. For a moment, it was just us and we were free.

Then Jo walked up to us, put a hand on Lia's shoulder and startled us out of our embrace. "Chase left Stanford early," she said. "Just to see you."

I stared at Jo in shock. Her words broke the spell.

"Oh," Lia said, already withdrawing into herself. "You didn't have to do that."

"No, it's—I wanted to," I told her, hands reaching for her, trying to hold on to her.

"It's not like we're together anymore," she said, her eyes shielded. "You should go back."

"Don't be so dramatic," Jo said with an exaggerated sigh. "I just meant—" I knew what she meant. Sometimes she'd say things like that to Lia once in a while. Things designed to elicit gratitude or guilt, a button to press. Lia used to complain all the time about it but it never seemed that bad to me. Until now. Seeing Lia like that, clearly sick and just hanging on, it was the last thing she needed.

"What she meant was that there's nowhere else I'd rather be," I told her. Lia hesitated, her hand still in mine. "You're the most important thing in my life."

I could see her soften.

"Please," I said, and I knew I hadn't lost her.

37.

It's so strange, this memory floating up from the dark and clicking into place. It's so strange, remembering something not forgotten but *new*. It feels like I'm there with Lia in the hospital, like I'm reliving these moments in the past somehow. That each step I remember, I walk at the exact same time.

"What do you see now?" Hunter asks, still pacing. She must know all of it, every second of every memory that's coming back, but she looks at me with distrust. Suspicion, even.

No, I have to remind myself. She's not pacing, she's not looking at me with distrust or suspicion. She's not *real*. She's not even here.

She's in my mind.

I squeeze my eyes shut and shake my head, hard, but she's still there when I open them.

"Trying to get rid of me?" she asks with a light laugh.

It's like I've been split in two and at war with myself.

"None of it makes sense," I tell her. "I *saw* you. You pulled your phone out. You took pictures of the test." There, I've said it. I exist in a space not of total disbelief but half belief. These new memories of Lia, they feel so real, not some misremembered dream, not an imagined past conjured up out of nothing.

Truth. They feel like the truth. So I believe some of the things she's told me, but not everything.

"No," she says. "*You* pulled your phone out and *you* took pictures of the test."

"*What?*" This is the last thing I expected her to say. "I raised my hand! I almost told Mr. Richter." I still remember that day, me sitting diagonally behind Hunter, her slipping out her phone, but when I close my eyes tight, try to bring it up, the image seems fuzzy around the edges, like something's not right.

"Glad you didn't," she says. "Would've looked pretty silly, telling on your imaginary friend."

"Is that what you are?" I ask, incredulous. "An imaginary friend?" I must be losing my mind.

"No," she says, not bothering to look at me. "Or maybe you're *my* imaginary friend." She laughs again and I shudder, shrink into myself.

"Shut up," I whisper, and close my eyes again, hold my hands over my ears to block her out. "You're not real. None of this is happening."

It's not, it's not, it's not.

But then I hear her sigh and walk over. I *feel* her sit next to me, the shift of weight on the couch. "How is this possible?" I ask, desperately confused, incredibly lonely.

"Let's start over again, okay?" she says, voice gentler this time. "I'm sorry. I know you're scared." She places a fucking *hand* on my shoulder and I flinch.

"I don't know what to believe anymore," I say. "I don't know what's real." I don't know what to trust. These memories—are they real, or have I made them up?

"Look in your e-mail," she says, because she can hear my thoughts. Because she's in my thoughts. Because maybe Hunter *controls* my thoughts. "You'll find the flight Jo booked you back in July."

Before she's finished saying the words, my phone is out and I'm already doing a quick search. It's there, on the screen. July 8, SFO to JFK, the red eye. I now remember holding out my phone, scanning the ticket at the airport. I remember not sleeping on the flight, being picked up by Jo and going straight to Westchester. None of these memories are fuzzy around the edges. These snapshots are new but bright and clear.

It really happened.

I really saw Lia there, pale and sick. Jo sat with us for the longest time and it was awkward in a way it'd never been before, maybe because Lia and I were still broken up, maybe because Lia and her mom had been fighting. But she left us be alone for a few minutes at the end when she spotted Lia's social worker and went to speak to her.

"Hey," I said, taking Lia's hands in mine.

"Hey," she said, and we were both on the verge of tears.

"I missed you," I said.

"Same." She sniffed, then looked away. "I'm sorry."

"Don't be. *I'm* the one who should be saying sorry." I wished I could go back in time, undo the fight, go out to San Francisco with Lia just like we'd planned. In that moment, I would've given anything just for it to be like it used to be.

This memory feels like déjà vu. I remember thinking all the same thoughts when I read Lia's journal. I remember how badly I wanted to take everything back, stick to our original summer plans, anything to make Lia happy. Anything to keep her from downing a bottle of painkillers.

Is what happened back in May the key to all of this? Was our breakup the last moment we could've prevented everything and we took a wrong turn?

It comes over me in heavy waves, the regret, my mistakes. If only I hadn't destroyed everything, if only I could've saved her. I cover my face as the sobs erupt, as a quick shot of nausea hits me at the same time.

"Let it out," Hunter says. "Don't hold back."

I keep my hands over my eyes and let the memory play out.

When Jo returned from speaking to Lia's case worker, we grew silent again, but I kept holding on to her until it was time for us to go. Visiting hours lasted until 8 PM, but Jo had an early morning on set the next day.

"I can stay," I told her.

"How will you get home?" Jo asked, picking up her big bag and hoisting it over a shoulder.

"I'll take the train, go to my dad's." I would've said anything to stay with Lia.

"It's Tuesday. Isn't your dad out of town?" she asked, distracted by something that popped up on her phone.

"I have a key—"

"It's okay," Lia told me. "Go. Come back when you can."

I remember how badly I wanted to stay, but I gave in, leaving with Jo. I remember how I held her hand until the last second. I remember not wanting to let her go.

"Go," Lia said to me, giving me a small push.

"I love you," I told her, and she looked a little surprised. Maybe not that I still loved her but that I said it.

"Me too."

And then the memory ends.

"No!" I shout now, on the boat with Hunter. I don't want it to end. When I open my eyes, I find my hands outstretched, like Lia is here in this room, like I was touching her only seconds ago.

"What happened?" I ask Hunter desperately.

"You went home with Jo," she says simply. I close my eyes and I grasp at the miserable fragments of being with Jo in the car, of going back to Long Island, tugging my luggage behind me.

"Then what happened?" I want to go back to the hospital, be with Lia again. I try to focus, force myself to remember. I search my mind, scanning for the next memory, but nothing comes up, and my tears turn angry. "Why can't I remember?"

Hunter has all the power, and I want to punch her even though I know it won't mean anything. But she doesn't seem interested in taunting me, at least not in this moment. She just looks sad, tired even.

"Maybe you're not ready," she says, not quite meeting my eyes.

"Tell me," I beg. "You know what happened. Just tell me." Put me out of my misery, I think. Please.

"I can't," she says with a sad shake of her head. "But they'll come back. Trust me."

I want to grab her by the shoulders and throttle her. I want to slam her against the wall hard enough to rock the boat. I want to force her to return these stolen moments to me, these memories of Lia that have been taken hostage by her. Trust me, she says, but all she's done is lie to me.

"You'll get them back," she tells me, hand heavy on my shoulder, "when you're ready."

Eventually, I nod, a capitulation because whether I trust her or not, I don't have a choice but to play along, to give in to whatever game she's playing.

I'd do anything to remember.

Anything for more time with Lia.

38.

On the train back to Meadowlark, it hits me and I can't breathe: if these new memories are true, then all my memories from earlier are lies. The memory of flying home in August and texting Lia to meet me in Montauk. The memories of Lia giving me the cold shoulder, of her and Hunter linking hands, all soft smiles and in love.

Every memory with Hunter.

It's all sinking in, the realization heavy and sharp, cutting me up inside.

What is real and what is a lie?

My vision blurs around the edges slightly and it feels like the train car is shaking violently.

Panic seizes me as I grip the seat in front of me to try and steady myself.

"Calm down." Hunter appears beside me. Or has she been next to me the entire ride?

When I let go, my hands tremble, so I press them against my legs, squeeze my knees until it bleaches my knuckles white and I can barely feel my fingers.

"Take a deep breath," Hunter continues. This time, she doesn't put a hand on my shoulder, doesn't touch me at all. She's barely even looking at me, eyes staring ahead. "Count to five, exhale. Do it again."

I hate her. I wish she would just disappear. I wish she would disappear forever.

No, that's not true, because she's the key to everything. And not just to my memories but maybe to what happened to Lia.

"I'll do it with you," she says, this time more insistent. I look over, watch as she takes a big inhale, holds, and releases. The world feels like it's spinning away from me again. The lights in the car flicker angrily. My wild eyes search the seats, but no one else seems to have noticed.

"What's happening to me?" I whisper, tears already running down my face. My heart's pounding so hard inside my chest that I hold a hand over it in an attempt to muffle the sound. Soon, it's so loud it seems to rattle the whole car with each beat. Again, no one else on the train seems to notice. "Am I doing this?" I ask.

Hunter claps both hands onto my shoulders, jerks until I'm facing her. "Yes, but you can stop it."

It feels like the way my chest seizes during a bad run, the way it rips me apart and snatches my breath. The way the bile rises up and threatens to erupt. But a million times worse. I shake free of her, reach for my box of Altoids, take two pills. My hands are unsteady as I wait for it to all melt away.

But it doesn't get better, only worse, until I'm shivering all over and my heart pounds so hard I swear my chest will crack open.

"You're having a panic attack." Even Hunter's voice sounds tinny, far away. "Try to breathe through it."

So that's what this is. A panic attack. It feels like I'm dying, like my world is collapsing in on me.

And worse of all, it feels like I've lost control of my body. Like nothing works, not my lungs, not my heart, not my hands, and definitely not my head. My fucking broken head.

"Count with me," Hunter says, hands still on my shoulders. I look up, finally meet her eyes. "One, two, three, four, five."

"One, two, three, four, five," I repeat, voice barely a whisper.

"Count to five as you inhale. Hold for a second, then count to five as you exhale."

I do as she says, even though the first breath is excruciating. I'm already choked for air, and now she wants me to breathe slower. The second is just as awful, but the third is a little better. By the tenth, my heart has begun to quiet and the lights have stopped flickering violently. The train seems to steady itself on its tracks, and I sit back against my seat.

I spend the rest of the ride counting my breaths, and by the time I get out of the Meadowlark station, I feel almost normal. At home, I think about the very first time it happened. The night I got that call from Jo, when I first heard Lia was missing. But it'd happened before I'd gotten the call. When I laced up and went for a run to blow off steam. When I saw the early-morning delivery truck round a corner and imagined falling in front of it.

Had that actually been the first time, or just the first time I can remember?

I take out Lia's journal and stare at it, uncertain. Finally, I put it aside and take out a fresh notebook and begin to write down everything I can remember, but only the things I'm sure happened.

The panic attack on the train just now. Flying back from the program early. Seeing Lia at the hospital. My conversations with Hunter as best as I can remember. It's almost morning by the time I'm done, and when I'm finished, I stack it under Lia's and place both under my bed.

Maybe it's stupid, like I'm gathering evidence, playing detective, but there's so little I can trust.

I definitely can't trust Hunter.

Which means I can't even trust myself.

39.

Sleep eludes me again, but it's no surprise. Tonight, I'm not tossing and turning though, just lying on my back perfectly still, staring up at my ceiling. I run through the last memory again and again. I close my eyes and try to call up the next one, remember the day after I first saw Lia at the hospital.

I must've gone back. With or without Jo. I would've gone back to see her. So how did I get there? I look up the hospital on my phone and check public transit routes. LIRR to Grand Central, then Metro-North to Westchester. I imagine taking the trip, picture myself getting on the LIRR, picture getting out at Grand Central.

"It's not going to work," Hunter says, making a sudden appearance.

"Christ," I say, rattled.

She's leaning casually against my desk, looking almost bored. At least she isn't next to me, lying in bed. I suppress a shudder.

"Go away," I tell her.

Hunter shrugs. "Do you want my help or not?"

I hesitate. "You said you wouldn't tell me what happened."

"And I'm not going to tell you."

I'm about to tell her to fuck off but then I remember earlier on the train. How Hunter managed to stop the panic attack. "Okay."

"Okay?"

"Okay, I want your help." This is as close as I'll come to asking her for it. I won't beg.

"You're focusing on the wrong things," she says, boosting herself up to sit on the desk, her legs crossed and foot resting on my chair. I hate the way it feels like she owns the whole room, the way she's invaded my space. The way she knows I can't get rid of her even if I tried.

"So tell me what I should be focusing on," I say with barely concealed frustration. She's dangling the keys in front of me but snatching them away as soon as I get close. I don't want to play this game anymore.

"Don't focus on the little things, the logistical details of getting from A to B. We almost never remember those moments. But we remember bigger things. Holidays, anniversaries, birthdays," she says.

Birthdays.

My birthday in July.

I used to hate having a summer birthday, when everyone was lost to family vacations or sleepaway camp. My parents were always crap at throwing parties for us anyway and hardly anyone ever showed up.

But then I came to love it, spending the whole day with Lia, because she'd always make it special. And Jo would bake a coconut cake just for me every year. They made me feel loved.

When I try to remember my birthday from a few months ago, I come up empty. I sit up, try to focus. Unlike the false memories I had of staying at Stanford, of coming home and seeing Lia with Hunter at school, there's just nothing. My brain hadn't filled it in.

I reach for my phone, check the flight I took home. July 8. Was Lia still at the hospital on my birthday, only six days later?

Lia would've wanted to make it special, and she would've felt frustrated to be stuck at the hospital, unable to take me to Montauk or spend the day downtown.

It comes to me suddenly, Lia's voice: "Don't come." She was on the phone with me and I immediately know it was the night before my birthday this summer. "Spend the day anywhere else."

"I just want to spend it with you."

"It's so depressing here. And it's your birthday, you should be happy, not stuck here with me. We don't both have to suffer." She laughed, but it sounded forced. I could picture her at one of the two pay phones on her hall. They weren't real pay phones with coin inserts, but they were mounted on the wall, had one of those heavy handsets that hung vertically from an old-fashioned cradle and metal buttons with scratched-up numbers you punched to dial. And for some reason, you could only call numbers with area codes in the tristate area.

"I'm coming tomorrow," I told her, and I know with certainty that's how I'd spent every day after coming back from Stanford, even if I can't remember the details now. We'd been arguing about this earlier that day, and she was calling me like she did every night before lights-out.

I heard her sigh. "Okay, it's time for group." They did this thirty-minute session with everyone on the hall before bed where a nurse would ask each patient to share something.

"I'll see you tomorrow."

"Okay," she said, giving in.

"I love you," I told her.

"Love you too." A lingering pause, then, *click*.

I stay with the memory, my eyes closed, tears escaping. The next fragment comes after a moment: the morning of my birthday the next day. We were sitting together on one of the many couches on her floor and Lia was giving me very specific instructions. "Get the coconut gelato if they don't have the cake," she told me. "And maybe the hazelnut too. Talenti. They should have it. And get a few of each." There was a Whole Foods across the street that she wanted me to go to. "Oh, and forks and spoons."

"Lia, stop," I said. "I don't need all that." She wanted to throw me a small party, here on the floor. As the memory returns, so does little bits and pieces from earlier. Things I suddenly *know* but can't tie to specific conversations. Like how I'd met all her hallmates and become friendly with some of them from being here day after day, but I didn't want them celebrating my birthday when they were there for treatment.

"But—" she began to protest.

"Let's celebrate after you get out," I told her.

She hesitated but finally nodded. "Okay."

It was so strange seeing Lia like this, giving in so easily, all the fight sucked out of her. Maybe it was the new meds they were giving her or maybe it was this place. She'd been there for a week by then.

"We'll do anything you want when you get out," I said, trying to make her feel better.

"If I ever get out," she added, tears already building in her eyes.

This wasn't the first time she'd said something like that. It's another thing I immediately just *know.* And in this moment reliving this day, her fear is palpable. Maybe that was the real reason she was so subdued, because she felt trapped here. Completely helpless.

"You will," I told her. "Jo said as soon as the doctors give the okay."

"That doctor hates me, you know that," she said. "She keeps asking me *if I've ever been so depressed that I experienced hallucinations.*"

"Really?" I asked.

"Stop looking at me like that!" she whisper-yelled. We were always being watched, and even when Lia was mad or wanted to scream, she always held back. Jo told her she was being paranoid once, but I felt it too, this oppressive air. Barred windows, drab carpet covered in stains, the nurses always patrolling. "Seriously," she said. "Stop looking at me like that."

"Like what?" I sat back in surprise.

"Like you're wondering the same thing. No, I've never experienced any fucking hallucinations." She stood up and started to pace but then stopped herself midstep and sat back down, drawing into herself. "I hate this place. I hate everything." Then she dropped her voice even lower so that only I could hear. "It makes me want to die even more, but I have to pretend I'm getting better every day so I can get the fuck out of here."

"Lia," I said, tears welling up. I reached out for her, took her hand in mine.

"Don't tell anyone," she said, suddenly panicking. "Don't tell my mom. I shouldn't have said anything. Pretend I didn't say anything." She tried to plaster on a smile but began to cry too.

It destroyed me, what she'd said about wanting to die, but what killed me more was her immediate retraction after. She didn't trust me. She felt like she didn't have anyone she could trust.

How lonely Lia must've felt.

"I won't tell anyone," I promised. "Just—just talk to me, okay? I won't tell anyone. Ever." We stared at each other through our tears and finally Lia choked out a sob before nodding. "I love you."

"Forever and ever?" Her voice was so very small.

"Forever," I swore. "Until the sun swallows up the Earth. Until the heat death of the universe."

"Okay, okay," she laughed a little. We stayed quiet for a while, her hands in mine, our eyes locked, and it was almost like we were alone. Almost. We could've been anywhere, and for a moment, we could imagine being free of that place.

"Where do you want to go?" Lia asked softly. "Once I get out."

"Anywhere," I whispered back. "You pick." I would've gone anywhere, done anything with her. It was such a relief, hearing the hope in her voice.

"No, you pick," she said. "It's for your birthday. And let's pretend it's not today. Let's pretend it's next month."

"Okay," I played along. "Maybe Montauk. We'll take the boat out."

"Mhmm." Lia closed her eyes and leaned against me, resting her head on my shoulder.

"Or maybe we'll be in Maine, stuff our faces with lobster and crab cakes and go to the beach like we always do." I wanted that future so badly my heart ached with it.

"Tell me more," she said, and as I described all the things we could do once they released her, she drifted off to sleep, snuggled against me, her breath deepening. She hadn't been sleeping well there, something about the pipes clanging in the walls, and I let her rest.

When the memory ends, I gasp as if being pulled out of a dream, my heart pounding. My hand clutches my chest, as if trying to contain my heartbreak. I think about the future I painted, the one of us in

Maine, in Montauk, anywhere. The place didn't matter. What mattered was that Lia was in it, and that's what I wanted so badly that it felt like I was being torn in two.

I didn't care where we were or what we did. All I wanted was a future with her. Any future.

40.

By the time my alarm goes off, I'm still wide awake, dizzy and nauseated. I have to check my phone to figure out what day it is. Tuesday. I'm so disoriented, so confused by all the new memories that it feels like emerging from a dream and entering another life, one that once belonged to me but now feels like a lie.

No, not *like* a lie. An actual lie.

I just want to stay in bed, try to recover more memories with Lia. But then I remember I have two tests today that I haven't studied for at all. Calc II and AP Econ. Maybe it doesn't matter, maybe nothing does.

There's no time to study, and I'm so confused by everything that's happened that I can't even remember which chapters the tests will cover. Then I remember that I've already done the Calc II test for Cole, that he also gave me a copy of the Econ test.

I slip the Econ test out of my bag and stare at it, blinking through the occasional blur of vision. Just this once, I think to myself.

It's an emergency.

Unable to concentrate without it, I pop a Focentra and work on memorizing the questions and answers. It takes me longer than it should, but by the time I need to leave, I'm ready.

Someone knocks on the door. For a second, I think it's Hunter and I flinch before I realize it's probably just Mom.

"Come in," I say.

"Hey," she says. "When'd you get in last night? You've been gone a lot lately." We have this unspoken deal, she and I. My dad too. They never question where I am or what I'm up to because of my grades, extracurriculars, and achievements. She tried to keep track at the start of high school, but then the divorce just knocked the wind out of her. It's easier this way for all of us, easiest for me most of all.

"I know," I say. "I'm exhausted."

"You're working too hard," she says, but it's not the first time she's tried to have this talk with me. "And not getting enough sleep." I don't protest because she's not wrong.

She places a warm hand at the top of my head, and it feels heavy with concern. I think about asking her for another sick note for yesterday, telling her about going out to Montauk, but I don't want to worry her any more than I already have. So all I do is nod and let her kiss my head before leaving. Then I type up a note and print it out, forging a quick signature.

In Physics, I stare at Hunter's empty seat, wonder where she is. I look for her around every corner, in every hall, but she's gone, conspicuously missing.

I'm on the lookout for her in the hall by Mr. Richter's classroom, but it's not Hunter who's waiting for me there. It's Cole.

"Shit," I say.

"You were supposed to drop off the Calc test Sunday," he says. I forgot. I solved it but completely forgot to drop it off. "I texted, I called."

"Fuck, I'm so sorry. Here," I say, reaching into my bag.

"Not here," he says, jaw tensing. "I thought I could count on you. Jesus, Chase."

Why would he say that? I've only done a handful of assignments for him. And then I think: Have I only done a handful of assignments for him?

Look who's back, he said with a broad smile directed at me.

If you want to renegotiate your cut, it's not going to happen, he said.

I never sold to Lia, even though she asked. You didn't know? he asked. *You really didn't know?*

I really thought you knew, he said.

"I had eight people counting on me for the Calc test," he says now, his frustration growing. "I had to—" He catches himself, lowers his voice. "I had to get another copy, and Lena banged it out last minute. You owe her."

"I'm so sorry," I say, but I'm in a daze.

"She says it's fine, that you covered for her when she had the flu, but I'm pretty pissed."

That confirms it. I covered for Lena. I've done this before. How long? I have no idea.

Lia wasn't part of the ring with Hunter.

Lia was part of the ring with *me*.

"Look, I was glad when you came back, but I was also worried. We all were, honestly. With everything that happened with Lia—" He sighs as the one-minute bell rings. I'm nowhere near my next class. "I just need to know I can count on you. Can I?"

This is the moment I could quit. My chance to tell him I want out. But there's a piece of my history with Lia tied up with Cole and his whole operation. Two days ago, I thought the mystery I was unraveling had to do with Lia and Hunter, but now I know the real mystery was between Lia and *me*. Now I have to trace every last step we took together. Now I have to uncover memories buried inside of my own head.

I can't leave. I don't have a choice.

"Can I?" Cole asks again. "Count on you?"

"I'm sorry," I say for the millionth time. "It won't happen again."

"Okay," he says after some hesitation and hands me the next assignment. "We'll need it by Sunday. Come over for dinner. We'll order pizza and have the whole gang back together."

"Okay," I tell him, and then remember I'm supposed to eat with the Vestianos'. "Wait, I can't do dinner. But I'll come right after."

"Sure." The bell rings and we're both late for class, but he doesn't look stressed. "Just tell them you had to go to the bathroom or something. No one ever questions us."

He's right. Being at the top has its advantages. Our grades and our status as overachievers mean we can get away with little transgressions like this. I'm just not sure what we'd do if we get caught one day, really caught.

In Calc II, I panic at the start for a moment, thinking there's no way the test Cole gave me was the real one, but then I flip it over, and it's an exact copy of the one I solved earlier. I have the same brief panic in Econ, my last period of the day, but the same thing happens.

Where does Cole get them?

41.

No matter what I try, no new memories emerge for the next four days, and Hunter is nowhere to be found. At night, I lie in bed and try to think of milestones big and small, any date that might be memorable, but nothing comes back to me.

Late Thursday night, Aidan knocks on the door. "Had to pee, saw your light on," she says with a yawn. I'm on the windowsill, eyes trained on the darkness. "Chase?" she asks. "You okay?"

"Yeah," I say, but my voice betrays me. It's been an impossible few days, my entire world turned upside down. I was treading water before, a sip of sleep here and there, but now I'm struggling just to survive. Can't sleep, can't breathe. My Altoids tin is almost empty again.

Aidan comes over, tugs at my cardigan. "Let's go look at the stars." It's then I remember that before Lia and I ever went out on the roof, Aidan and I did it first. So I grab a thick blanket, smooth it out on the shingles, pull my comforter off the bed and wrap it around the two of us. In the moonlight, our breath marks the cold November air before quickly melting into nothingness.

It's a clear sky, the stars out in full force shining down on us, and

I can't help but wonder if one of them could be Lia, if she could see us. If she could still be here with me. Aidan sees a tear escape and leans on my shoulder.

"Sorry," I tell her.

"It's okay to cry," she says. "It's okay to be sad."

It doesn't feel very okay, my life falling apart all around me, my mind crumbling inside me.

"It's okay to need people," she continues. "It's okay to need help."

I almost tell her no, that maybe it's okay for other people to need help, but it'll never be okay for me. Not when everything feels like my fault, when all I do is fuck everything up.

"That's what Lia told me once," she finishes, and it knocks the breath out of me.

"When?" I ask quietly.

"A long time ago. During the divorce, I think," she says, and when I glance down at her, I see her fiddling with her necklace, the sapphire teardrop she wore at the funeral.

"You said Lia gave you that for your birthday?" I say.

"Yeah, in September, remember?"

I shake my head softly.

"I had a sleepover and you guys took me for breakfast the morning after. You got me pancakes and French toast because I couldn't decide. And because it was my birthday."

A small laugh breaks through my crying.

"And after, we went to Long Beach and walked along the water." Aidan tilts her head up to look at me. "You really don't remember?"

"No, I do," I lie, not wanting to worry her. "Just the necklace part."

"Oh. Lia gave it to me at the diner before the food arrived."

"Right," I say, pretending to remember.

Then Aidan reaches around, releases the clasp, and gently places the sapphire pendant in my palm.

"No, no," I tell her, putting it back in her hands and closing her fingers around it. "Lia wanted you to have it. Your birthstone."

"Are you sure?" she asks, and I have to choke back a sob. The way Aidan looks at me, the way she loves me, like she doesn't want anything from me, like she only wants me to be okay—it cracks me open.

I nod, worried that speaking would break the floodgates to more tears. I always thought I was the one who had to protect her. When did she become the protector?

Later that night, Lia's words echo as I lie in bed: *It's okay to need people. It's okay to need help.* Had she meant it all those years ago? Had she meant it for herself? I think of what Dr. Quinn had said, about how she hadn't seen Lia in a long time.

She said, "As you know, it's been a while since I last saw her, but it's still a big shock."

She said, "I began working with her after her hospitalization but only saw her a few times, you know that."

As you know.

You know that.

I'd thought it so strange that Dr. Quinn thought I knew these things, but now I'm sure she was referring to memories I've locked away.

Missing time. Missing pieces of Lia. In the morning, I pick up the phone.

Dr. Quinn says she had another cancellation Friday at 8 PM, but I'm beginning to wonder if she's lying, squeezing me in at the end of her days. If she's maybe even worried about me. But she doesn't owe me anything, doesn't even know me—does she?

It's in the parking lot that Hunter finally appears with a sharp knock on the passenger-side window. It still startles me, seeing her and knowing she's not really there.

"Hey," she says softly after she gets in.

"Hey." I can't decide what she is—an ally or an enemy. To be trusted or to be feared. "Where've you been?"

"Does it matter?"

"Do you go where I go?" I hate that I sound so small, so weak.

"Something like that," she says.

"So why here, why now?" After almost an entire week's disappearance.

"Felt like it." Gone all these days only to pop up outside of Dr. Quinn's office. "Why are *you* here?" she deflects.

"I'm trying to get some answers." What I mean: Because you won't just tell me the truth.

"For yourself or for Lia?" she asks, side-eying me.

"What's that supposed to mean?"

"Never mind, forget it." And with that, she pops open the door and steps out, letting in a rush of cold, wintry air.

In the waiting room, her question tugs at me. *For yourself or for Lia?* It's all for Lia these days, everything I do. But there's an insinuation, like I'm here for myself. Like I'm here not to help Lia but to get help for myself.

I turn, almost expecting to find Hunter beside me so I can object, tell her that no, I'm here only for Lia. But she's not there, and instead, I find myself staring at one of the large canvases on the wall. It's just a combination of long, uninterrupted strokes of dull beiges and soft pinks. The kind of gentle, inoffensive abstract art that's on the walls of medical offices or corporate boardrooms. It's so suddenly familiar, and not only because I'd glanced at it the last time I was here.

I switch couches to face it fully and suddenly Lia's voice comes to me. "I don't want to go." I close my eyes and it's like she's right in front of me, like I can reach out and touch her.

"But you have to," I'm telling her. We're at her house, sequestered in her room, our voices hushed. The days after she'd been released from the hospital. It was a requirement of discharge to have appointments with a psychiatrist and a talk therapist within the first week. "Your parents aren't going to let you miss it."

"Come with me," she says, then quickly adds, "Just be outside so I know you're there."

And that was how I found myself on this exact couch, staring at that exact painting.

"Chase?" It's Dr. Quinn. The door's open, and she's ushering me inside.

This is how I knew Dr. Quinn. This is how Dr. Quinn knew me.

"I'm only here for Lia," I say before she's had a chance to pick up her pen.

"For Lia?" she asks, confused.

"Not for myself," I clarify.

"I see." She taps the point of her pen against her notebook twice as she considers what I've said. "And would it be terrible, if you were here for yourself?"

"What do you mean?"

"If you were here because you needed a little support? If you were struggling?"

The silence between us fills the room, and it feels too heavy to speak.

It's okay to need people. It's okay to need help.

Had Lia actually said those words to Aidan? Had she really believed them herself?

More important, had she turned to anyone, in the end?

"Asking for help can be an act of courage," Dr. Quinn continues. "Recognizing you can't do everything on your own—recognizing that no one can do it all on their own—and then admitting it even when it makes you feel vulnerable, I think that's strength."

"I wish Lia had asked for help," I say quietly.

"Me too," Dr. Quinn says.

"Did you ever think she'd really—" I can't bear to finish the thought as I swallow back tears and look at anywhere but in her direction.

But I don't have to complete the question. "I'm not sure, if I'm completely honest. Sometimes I think yes, and sometimes I think no, but ultimately, it doesn't matter what I think. What happened, happened. There's nothing I can do to change it, and there's nothing I could've done. I tried to help Lia the best I could. That's all we can really do—try our best."

"That can't be enough," I say.

"But it has to be," Dr. Quinn says. "It's all we have, all we can do."

"You're saying it was inevitable, what happened," I say, almost an accusation. Here I am again, circling back to this question. Of Lia and of fate.

"No, what I'm saying is that not everything is within our control. It's important to try, but it's just as important—maybe even more—to recognize that we have limits to what we can do, to let go of what's outside of our control."

There's something true in her words and it cleaves me open. Fresh tears erupt and I can barely contain myself. I'm spilling out onto this couch, in this room with pale beige walls. Everything in my life feels completely out of control. Everything is spinning, spinning away from me. Lia, gone. My mind, shattered. My future, slipping away.

It takes every last ounce of strength to keep the sobs from ripping my chest apart. It takes everything I have just to stay on the couch, heaving into tissues.

Dr. Quinn just lets me cry and cry, and after our time's up, she asks if there's someone I'd like to call and I shake my head no, do my best to dry my eyes and walk without stumbling.

In the parking lot, the air is cold and sharp. It hurts to breathe, it hurts to exist.

Dr. Quinn's words swim around in my head as I sit in the car, just trying to get warm. Maybe she's right in some ways, about recognizing that some things are out of our control. But she doesn't know me, know the ways I failed Lia, failed us. Maybe Dr. Quinn tried her best, but not me. More tears spill over and I let out a quiet whimper.

"Come with me," Lia's voice comes in, sounding nearly as desperate as I feel right now. "I don't want to do it alone."

"I don't know," I'm telling her. "It'd be weird. Can't I just wait outside, like last time?"

"It'll be easier to talk, if you're there too."

"But isn't it, I don't know, against the rules?" It hits me suddenly—she was asking me to come into the room with Dr. Quinn, into their session.

"No," Lia says firmly. "Not if it'll help."

"Okay," I hear myself tell her. There's reluctance in my voice. But I'd just gotten Lia back. Lia, my Lia. I'd do anything for her.

With this memory trickling in, I wipe my tears and focus on Lia's voice, my eyes trained on the office door. I wonder if Dr. Quinn's still inside. What she might say if I told her the truth. Hunter, Lia, these missing memories. The Focentra, the sleepless nights, the cheating ring. But she's probably gone. When I came out, mine was the only car in the lot.

I feel so alone. In the dark, I look for Hunter, almost wish she were here. Hunter, who knows everything. Hunter, who's holding Lia hostage from me. I squeeze my eyes close, try to focus on Lia's voice, tug at the memory locked away, desperate to free it.

I didn't try my best back then. I have to now.

"How are you doing?" Dr. Quinn's voice comes in. Maybe it's because I'm here at her office, or because I've just been inside, but it's like I've been transported back to the room. Lia and I are sitting beside each other facing Dr. Quinn in her stiff wingback armchair. The sun shines through her windows. It's still summer, and I'm not shivering.

At Lia's hesitation, she adds, "Whatever we say in this room stays in this room."

"I'm okay," Lia answers. "Thanks for letting me bring Chase."

"Of course. Whatever makes you more comfortable. Is there any particular reason you wanted her here?"

I look back at Lia but she just shrugs. She then launches into small talk, about the good weather we've been having, about our upcoming trip to Maine, about random funny memories from all our summers there. Meanwhile, I watch the minutes tick away on the clock over the door. Twenty, thirty minutes slip by as Dr. Quinn lets her run down the session.

"How are things with your parents?" she asks when there's a lull.

"Fine," Lia says, but I can feel her tensing beside me.

"Your mom?" she prompts.

"Jo's fine."

"Any more arguments?"

I turn to Lia in surprise. She never mentioned any arguments.

"No," Lia answers, a little too forcefully.

Dr. Quinn remains quiet, letting silence fill the room.

Lia changes the subject and I watch her waste the last minutes until it's time to go.

"You had an argument with your mom?" I ask once we're outside.

"I don't want to talk about it," she says, and when I'm about to object, she adds, "Please."

"Okay." We drive home mostly in nervous silence.

"I told you it was a waste of time," Lia tells me as I pull onto her driveway, and I just look at her helplessly, unsure of what to say.

When I open my eyes now, I feel the same sense of helplessness. If only I could've said the right thing to her. If only I knew how to help her.

42.

I spend the night in bed blinking at the ceiling, too drained to move but too wired to sleep. I think about Lia, about the new memories I've unlocked. About what I said and didn't say, about what I could've done differently, how I might've helped her.

When the sun comes up, I can tell it'll be a bright, clear day. Perfect for Montauk, but I'm too exhausted to make the trip so I head out to Long Beach just to be close to the water. I always feel closer to Lia the closer I am to the ocean.

Even though it's only twenty minutes away, we never made a habit of going there because of the crowds. It's too early and too cold for any beachgoers now, and alone, I take in the salt air and lightest spray of sea on skin. If I close my eyes and imagine the sun overhead, imagine the warmth of summer, I can almost feel Lia with me. I can almost feel human again.

"Hey." Hunter appears beside me, knocking me off-balance.

"Hi," I say but avoid meeting her eyes.

"I miss summer too," she says. "It's my favorite season." I can't help but turn toward her in surprise. It's moments like this that feel so confusing, when she seems like a living, breathing person—separate from me, unreadable.

"I want to remember everything," I say. "I just want to know what happened."

Hunter just shrugs, eyes on the dark, gray sea.

"You know. Why can't you just tell me?"

"It's better if you remember on your own," she says, not unkindly. "Just be patient."

"I'm sick of being patient. I'm sick of not knowing. I'm sick of *you*."

"Do you want me to go?" she asks, but it's not defensive like I expect.

It takes me a while to answer. "No," I eventually admit. I don't want to be alone this morning. There's something about being on the beach that's haunting. So much history between me and Lia exists by the sea, so many memories soaked in salt and weighed down by sand. All these memories—newly recovered or still lost—are ghosts that linger, both comfort and torture. I think about leaving.

"Don't go yet," she says.

"Where should I go?" I ask, hopeful for a hint, a new thread to tug at, maybe unravel this mystery.

A jogger passes us on the left, and for a second, I wonder how it must look to others, me standing alone staring as if there was someone next to me, talking to no one.

"I don't know," she says. "But don't go home yet."

So we keep walking, just me, my hallucination, and a few scattered gulls.

I think about Dr. Quinn's words, turn them over in my mind again and again. About what's in our control and what's not. About having limitations and letting go. About what it would even mean to let go—of guilt? Of the past I can never change? Of *Lia*?

At some point, I tire and sit down, pick up fistfuls of sand and watch each of them slip through my tight, tight grip. The sun's overhead now, and when I close my eyes, its rays feel warmer on my face.

Suddenly, a memory rushes in. A flood of sunshine and tenuous happiness flows through me. Maine in August. We got what we longed for—days spent eating lobster, butter dripping down our fingers, running under a glorious summer sun, the salt air sharp in our lungs, the ocean mist leaving our hair in long, frizzy waves.

I love you, we said to each other all the time. We never talked about the details, about getting back together officially, but we were together. More together than we'd ever been, and I was determined to keep it that way.

After the session with Dr. Quinn where she had me join her, Lia had begged and begged her parents to let her stop. Promised the meds were working and she was all better. But I wasn't entirely convinced.

"Tell me," I whispered to her one night when we were alone walking along the water, hands loosely linked, swinging between us. "Tell me why you did it." It'd taken me a long time to work up the courage to ask.

Lia knew immediately what I meant. She paused midstep, tugging me to a gentle stop with her inertia.

"It's over now," she said. "Can't we just leave it in the past?"

"I need to know."

"Why?" she asked. There were a million things I could've said, and it would've all been true. That I deserved an explanation. That I loved her and wanted her to talk to me. That I was scared and didn't understand. But the real reason I had to know wasn't any of them. The truth was that from the moment Jo told me what'd happened, I'd been feeling completely helpless, and I never wanted to feel like that again. If I understood why she did it, then maybe I could make sure it never happened again. If I knew, I could come up with a plan to fix it.

A way to fix her.

She didn't trust Dr. Quinn, but she trusted me. And so I wanted to make it my life's mission to keep her happy. I couldn't risk losing her, not ever again.

"So I can do something about it," I answered. "So I can make sure it never happens again."

Her silence grew uncomfortable and I looked at our feet, toes partially buried in the sand. In the moonlight, our skin looked pale and gray, a little ghostly.

"I don't know," Lia finally said. When I looked up, she was staring out at the water, at the place where the waves appeared to thin, where the sky met the sea. "A lot of things."

"Like what?"

Her hand released mine as she plopped down onto the ground, crossing her legs and burying her feet in the still-warm sand. I joined her, found her hand again.

"You wouldn't understand," she said softly. "Everything just comes so easily to you."

"What?" I could feel my defensiveness rising. "You know that's not true." I had to tread carefully. I didn't want to go down this road again, maybe the very road that had led us here in the first place. "I just mean that it doesn't *feel* like things come easily to me."

"No, you're right. I'm not saying that things are necessarily easy for you," she said, and it felt like we'd turned a corner. Like we'd left that old argument behind us. "I guess I mean that everything is *possible* for you."

"What do you mean?"

"When I said you always get what you want, I didn't mean you get everything handed to you. What I meant was that you always get what you want for yourself, because you *can*. You're smart and you work hard and you always know just what to do or what to say. You're perfect, Chase." Our eyes met—hers sincere, mine wide in surprise—and Lia leaned in, her lips soft against mine.

When she pulled back, I followed, chasing after the kiss. She kissed me back, lingering before resting her forehead against mine, our breaths mingling, our noses touching.

"It's not true, you know," I said, eyes closed, awash in the moment. "I'm not perfect. I mess up, all the time."

"Stop it," she said, really pulling back then, leaving me off-balance. "Name one thing you wanted that you didn't get. Student council. Cross-country. Stanford. Science Olympiad. Grades. Come on."

"You," I said simply. "I lost you, and I almost lost you forever."

That seemed to reach her and she softened against me. "But I'm not a project for you to fix. I'm not something you can accomplish with a to-do list."

"I can try," I said with a laugh.

She smiled. "Be serious."

"Okay," I said. "So I'm perfect. And I wouldn't understand because I'm just that perfect. This is doing wonders for my ego"—she knocked me playfully with her knee—"but let's just pretend I'm not perfect and let's pretend that I *might* understand."

She sighed. I leaned in, kissed her again.

"Please?" I asked.

Lia didn't answer right away, but I wanted to give her the room to speak so I let the silence envelop us.

Finally, she spoke. "I just didn't want to do it anymore."

"Do what?"

"Any of it. All of it. The treadmill." She was referring to the hedonic treadmill, a concept we'd discovered from a random Wikipedia article when we were in ninth grade. It represented the idea that nothing really shifts our happiness in a lasting way. That when something good happens, we adapt and then return to our baseline. Win the lottery, you feel good for a while, but soon it's your new reality and you're just as happy or miserable as you were before.

We got obsessed with the idea for a while, because it felt like everyone we knew was on it, including us. Get a good grade on a test, feel good for a minute, then back to the grind.

"It's like we're totally trapped. Hamsters on a wheel."

It reminded me of what she'd said to me when we broke up, that fight on the boat back in May, though she didn't say those words exactly. "Running in place," that's what she'd said, but I knew what she'd meant. I'd been so insulted, then, because I thought she was belittling everything I was working toward, but maybe I'd misunderstood her.

"I just wanted to get off the wheel, you know," she said. "But I didn't know how to get off. I felt trapped. So trapped. Just locked into living this life I didn't want, living this *lie.* Living this version of myself that I hated but not knowing how I could be anything else. I didn't so much as want to end my life as never exist in the first place."

"Don't say that!"

She pushed on, "I could see the rest of my life, you know. And I didn't want it. I could see it all laid out for me, everything I was supposed to do and supposed to want—grades, a top college, a fancy career—and I didn't want any of it, but I also didn't know what I *did* want. What I *do* want, even now." She took a deep breath, exhaled forcefully. "I'm really happy for you, Chase. I'm happy that you know what you want and that you've always known what you wanted and that you're going to get everything you want. And I know I'm supposed to want the same things. That we'll one day be this power couple or whatever, but I just . . . don't."

I didn't know what to say. She was clearly in so much pain, and I wanted to help, but she was right—I didn't understand. All my life I had nothing but ambition coursing through my veins. A permanent whisper of *more, more, more* in my ear. I was raised on it and I wanted everything Lia so clearly didn't want. I wanted to win the game, to play it so excellently that I could one day remake the rules.

My father was both a driver and an emblem of this dream. I didn't particularly like him, but maybe part of that was because I hoped I'd one day outgrow him. No, not hoped, *knew* deep down that I was destined to achieve more than he ever could. That there was even a part of me that felt something akin to contempt. That pitied the way he'd been consumed—*enslaved*—by work for so long with hardly anything to show for it. That thought he must've fallen short of playing the game excellently if he was still playing under someone else's rules.

It was true, everything that Lia said, about what I wanted, but if there was one thing I'd learned that summer, it was that I didn't want to do it without her. That I *couldn't* do it without her.

That even though I'd left Stanford's summer program early, I had no regrets. Risking my chances of getting into Stanford for college—something that would've once left me tortured and mired in self-doubt—was actually easy. It hadn't even felt like a decision because the choice was obvious. I loved Lia. It wasn't a sacrifice.

But that didn't mean I no longer wanted the things I wanted. What I wanted was *both*. Everything. Always everything.

To be on top and to have Lia.

Now, as the memory of that night on the beach unfurls, I begin to remember pieces surrounding that memory, though not as vividly. Like composing an e-mail to the Frontier Scholars program director apologizing again and further explaining my sudden departure in the hopes of securing a letter of recommendation for my Stanford application. Even though I didn't regret leaving, I was already planning a path forward, figuring out a way to get what I wanted. Just like Lia described.

At that point, I hadn't heard back from him yet, but even if he had declined, I'd already planned to write my personal essay on that summer, mining Lia's tragedy to not only explain my departure but provide substance and depth to my application. I already knew I'd have to invent a moral to the story, about the importance of access to mental health care perhaps. Or maybe a hard lesson learned about prioritizing what really mattered in life. It didn't matter if it was bullshit and it didn't matter if it was Lia's personal struggle and not my story to tell. I was playing a *game*. This is what you did, this was the only way to win.

As the memory unfolds step by step, I am reliving every second, every thought. And I arrive at the same conclusion I did in the past. Lia was right about the future I'd envisioned for us—both of us on top, a shiny future as a power couple. All my resentment from before the breakup was really about what I'd thought of as the advantages Lia had because of Jo, about how she never had to work hard and never would. About how her future was all but secured while I had only myself.

I never really questioned that future, or if she even wanted it. I hadn't been listening, or maybe I hadn't been able to really accept what she'd been saying until now. When we broke up, it'd felt like all or nothing, like our opposing views of our future were impossible to reconcile. But that wasn't true.

"Please tell me what you're thinking," Lia said.

"I have an idea," I said. At the skeptical look she shot me, I added, "Do you trust me?"

43.

The next time I needed to re-up on Focentra after we got back from Maine, I texted Cole like always, and he drove over. Senior year was right around the corner, and a lot of people were calling him up, he told me.

"I'm a little low, so here's half," he said when he handed over the Altoids tin.

"It's fine." I tapped one out, tucked it under my tongue and let it melt, all minty bitterness.

"Do you really need it tonight?" he asked, looking a little surprised.

"I'm knocking out all the college applications before school starts," I said, annoyed at the question.

"Oh, smart."

"Hey, wait," I said as he got back into his car. "Remember last year when you asked if I wanted in?"

He frowned, thinking, then looked up at me in realization. "Like I said before, door's always open."

I hesitated, but only for a little. "Got room for two?"

"It was me," I say out loud to Hunter. We're still on the beach, the midday sun high above us but barely offering any warmth.

She nods, sitting down next to me.

"I was the one who got her involved." I can't believe it. All this time, I'd blamed Hunter but it was me all along.

"It was you," she says, and I can hear an accusation beneath every syllable.

"I thought—" Stupid. So, so stupid. "I thought we could have it all. I thought that was what Lia wanted."

"It was what *you* wanted," she counters, her voice growing angry. "Lia never wanted those things. She *told* you. She said she didn't want that life."

"No, that's not true," I say. "She just didn't want to live like it was always finals week anymore, from one fire to the next. That's what she said."

Wasn't it?

"So I thought it would fix things," I argue. "I thought it would make it easier. That's what she wanted."

Hunter shakes her head with disgust. "That's what *you* wanted her to want. That's what *you* thought she wanted because that was what you wanted. You weren't listening."

"But she—" I feel so confused, so disoriented. My head spinning. No, the world is spinning and I need something to hold on to. I grasp at the ground to steady me but the sand is cold and loose, shifting under my palms.

What I need is Lia, the only person who can make sense of things for me. I need her to be here and tell me what happened. To tell me I didn't fuck up. Tell me that I'm not somehow the reason she's gone.

"But she was happy," I tell Hunter, half pleading, half asking.

"Maybe at first." She's completely unforgiving, her eyes stony and cold, all friendliness gone.

I want to argue, but I can't remember what really happened, not yet. I close my eyes, try to concentrate. Think back to the end of September, Lia's birthday. It's a memory I've tried to recall all week without success, but now I need to know that I tried to make things better for her, that I did everything I could to save her. That I did *something*.

Happy. Lia was happy. I can hear her laughter, the lightness in her voice in the darkness. We were on the boat, snuggling in bed. Swaying with the soft lull of the waves.

"When was the last time we did this?" she asked, voice full of wonder as she played with my hair.

"We're here all the time," I said.

"Not like this. Not studying or doing homework. But just *here*. With each other."

My heart soared. It was working.

We had time to waste because Lena was outlining the AP Euro essays, Josh was doing the AP Physics problem set, and Rebecca was in charge of AP Econ. All we had was Calc II and we were already done. Later we'd have to study for Physics and write essays from Lena's detailed outlines since we couldn't just copy written work, but that was nothing. We had access to the entire semester's Calc and Econ tests.

For now, we were free. It felt like a taste of what it meant to win the game and rewrite the rules for ourselves.

We napped and ordered soft-shell crab sandwiches from the bar by the marina and I drove us out into the sound with the keys she'd given back to me weeks ago, a gesture that put our May separation firmly in the past. It was a Saturday, a full moon lighting up the waters as we cut the motor and dropped the anchor to float, staring up at the night sky on the deck wrapped in fleecy blankets.

When it got too cold, we headed back inside, curling up on the small sectional to read, Lia's head on my lap.

"You know the ending of *Eternal Sunshine*?" Lia asked, putting down her iPad.

"Hm?"

"I'm reading the screenplay and it's completely different."

"You're reading the screenplay?" I put down my phone.

"Yeah. Found it online. It's an earlier draft. The beginning's different too." She lifted it to show me the screen.

"Different how?" I linked hands with her loosely, noticed she was wearing her favorite hoodie with the string still missing. "We should get you a new cord. Or a new hoodie," I said, picking at it with my free hand.

"It's fine. I like it this way," Lia said. "It's like a reminder."

I didn't question it but I couldn't understand why she'd want to be reminded of the weeks she spent in Westchester locked away.

"Anyway. The original ending. It's sad." Her eyes met mine. "They just keep doing it. Again and again."

"What do you mean?"

"The script begins with Clem at a book publisher's office in the future, holding this manuscript that's their story. And then you find out that they keep doing it to each other, erasing each other and falling in love."

"That's awful," I said. "Way too sad." One time was a mistake made by two soulmates. Again and again? Maybe they didn't belong to each other after all. I didn't want to think about it.

"Apparently the director agreed with you because he cut most of it. But the ending in the movie, where they're playing in the snow and it just shows them chasing each other in this weird looping way? I think it's supposed to be a sort of reference to the original ending."

"Wow, thanks, I hate it," I said, and she laughed a little. "I'm going to pretend you never told me any of this. I'm going to pretend the ending is just this playful moment of them messing around in the snow."

Lia stayed quiet, thoughtful for a moment. "I don't want to pretend. I want to see things as they are."

"But it's so sad."

"But maybe it's the truth. Maybe Clem and Joel, that's what they keep doing. Fall in love, fall out of love, erase each other and begin again. Maybe that's the moral of the story. If we can't remember, then we'll just make the same mistake over and over again."

"*Or*," I said, shifting to better face her, "we accept the movie as it is, a story about two people who made this impulsive mistake to erase each other only to fall in love again because they're *soulmates*. Like, no matter what happens, they'll always find each other again. They'll always make their way back here, to Montauk, where they first met and meet again. *That's* the moral of the story."

Lia stared up into my eyes and smiled. "Both can be true. How about that?"

"Okay," I relented, not wanting to fight about something so small.

Everything I said then was with confidence, but now, here, trapped with Hunter alone, my mind scrambled and memories missing, I think Lia was right: if I can't remember what happened, how can I stop myself from making the same mistakes?

44.

I'm tired of waiting for my memories to return on their own, and I resent Hunter for not telling me everything. It's Sunday and she hasn't disappeared yet, following me back to Meadowlark and staying by my side but not saying much.

"Why are you doing this to me?" I ask as we drive to the Vestianos' for dinner. "Why won't you just tell me what happened?"

She sighs. "Like I've said—"

"—it's better if I remember on my own," I finish for her. "Yeah, I got that. But why?"

"If I tell you before you're ready, you might not be able to handle it, and then we'll have to go back to square one."

"What?" I nearly miss a turn and slam on the brakes. After I steady the car, I glance over at Hunter, who's propped an elbow against the window, eyes faraway. "What does that mean, go back to square one?"

"You know what it means. Start this whole thing again," she says like she's exhausted by the thought, and I can't decide if I want to punch her or pull over and just cry. "So just be patient. It'll come back."

"How do you know?" I ask as we pull onto the Vestianos' driveway.

"It's been coming back, hasn't it?"

"No," I say. "How do you know I'll just forget?" It leaves me cold, the idea of losing everything I've learned again so far, the idea of losing Lia all over again. "Have I—has it happened before?"

"No. But let's just say I know your limits better than you do." *Trust me,* she's telling me again, like I have a choice.

Hunter follows me inside and I watch her warily, like she's going to do something. Like she might take over my body, say something awful.

She's not real, I repeat to myself again and again. I'm in control.

But then, halfway through dinner, halfway through pleasantries and small talk, I lose my nerve and the mask slips. Jo is asking me about what I'd like to help her make on the Christmas special when I interrupt her.

"Why Westchester?"

They're stunned for a moment.

"What do you mean, hon?" Jo asks, a tight smile on her face.

"Just, why Westchester? Why so far away?"

"They had the best care. They came highly recommended," Jo says after a long silence. "But let's not talk about that anymore."

"Why?" I ask, and they both visibly wince.

"It's all in the past now," she says firmly.

"But weren't we talking about the past just now? Lia's favorite flowers, Lia's favorite meal, Lia's favorite dessert." I can't explain what's gotten into me, why I'm suddenly so antagonistic.

Hunter smirks from the kitchen counter, swiveling on one of the barstools. "Ask them why they didn't let Lia keep the squirrels while you're at it," she calls out, but I'm the only one who hears her. "Ask them why they didn't go visit her every day."

"That's different," Jo says, her smile gone. "We're planning a tribute to Lia."

"But Lia would hate that," I say, and then clap my hand over my mouth in surprise. I'm never like this in front of the Vestianos. I'm never like this in front of anyone. Lia is the one who always says what she thinks, who isn't afraid.

"Maybe we should rethink things," Rob says, trying to make peace.

"What?" Jo asks, alarmed.

"Maybe Chase is right. Maybe what we should be asking is what Lia would want," he says. "Maybe—maybe we didn't ask that enough when Lia was here." He slumps into his chair, tears spilling over.

I try to hold it in but seeing him cry causes me to cry too, and soon the three of us are sobbing over our plates.

Then Jo slams her palm against the table, rattling all the china and startling us. "I won't allow it. I won't let you bully me into changing the special. We can't speculate what Lia wants. All we can do is honor her memory the best we can."

"No," I protest. "I *know* Lia would've hated it. She hated every show she had to do."

"How dare you?" Jo cries.

"It's true! She hated it, all of it. She told me all the time." I want to stand up for Lia, even if it's too late. "She'd hate this too. She would." I sob harder.

"Get out! Get out right now!" Jo screams. I've never, ever seen her like this. She pushes away from the table and runs up the stairs, leaving the two of us in complete shock.

"I think I should go," I finally say, and Rob doesn't object.

I sit on their driveway for a while, not moving. I'm late to Cole's but I'm too upset to drive. I open my messages, tap on Jo's name, about to type out an apology when Hunter interrupts me.

"Don't."

"Why not?"

"Because you were right and she was wrong," she says. "So why should you apologize? You heard her. She didn't care about what Lia would want. She just wanted to use her daughter's death to reboot her crappy show." It's hard to believe that Hunter is a part of me, that lurking somewhere inside is this overconfident and harsh person.

"But I did the same thing," I argue. "I used Lia for my college essays." I hadn't touched them since summer, when I submitted them, and I wouldn't have even thought of them again until I remembered that night in Maine.

"Doesn't make it right," Hunter says, like it's the final word. "What happened to Lia, what Lia went through, it's not for you or anyone else to exploit." Her words make me waver and I wonder if she's my conscience for a moment before I dismiss it. She may be right here, and she may have helped me in the past, but she's far from perfect. She's the one who's pushed me to join the ring. She's the one who's mocked or taunted me every chance she had.

I stare down at my messages, at Jo's name. I back out and tap on Lia's name, reread her last message to me. Her one and only message to me.

"Hey," I say, realization hitting me. "Where are the rest of our messages?" I'd thought I'd deleted everything after coming back from Stanford, after Lia stopped responding because she was with Hunter. But if none of that happened, then where did our messages go? "Did I delete them?" I ask her. "Why would I delete them?"

Hunter gives me a flat, impatient look and shrugs.

I clutch my phone tightly, stare at Lia's last message. I'm sick of these games. I'm sick of the growing mountain of questions. Most of all, I'm sick of missing Lia so much that I can barely breathe.

45.

It's almost nine when I get to Cole's house, but he doesn't seem angry. "Come on in," he says with the same pivot and swing of a loose arm overhead as the first time. I wonder how many times we've done this.

"Where are your parents?" I ask, following him down to the basement.

He gives me a strange look, a reminder that I have to tread carefully because I still don't have all of my memories. "They're almost never home. You know that."

"Right," I say.

"There's still some pizza left, if you're hungry," he tells me as we come off the stairs. "Hey, guys, it's Chase."

Lena Harrison and Josh Hendon are spread out on the floor, working on a coffee table. Both look up and give me a small wave, almost like they're used to seeing me. I think of the concerned looks Lena and Rebecca shared back when I first showed up. No, back when I started showing up *again*.

I hand Cole the latest assignment, a Calc problem set and an AP Chem test that was mostly unchanged from one I took last year. He pushes them back in my direction and says, "You know what to do." But the problem is that I have no idea.

"Okay, but remind me?" I say.

"Three answer keys, remember?" he says, and at my confused expression, he adds, "Do you really not remember?"

Three keys. Why? Then it comes back to me. We'd type out the answers, but none of the questions, and we'd make separate keys in case whoever used them got caught. One that was guaranteed to get a near-perfect score, one designed to get a B, and one that would get a C. Only the six of us had access to the entire key.

It was *my* idea, all to avoid suspicion. Some of the kids who used the keys wouldn't be capable of suddenly earning A's, so they'd get keys that allowed them to pass. After a few tests, they might be able to purchase the keys that got them B's, and so on.

"No, I remember," I tell him.

"Okay," he shoots me a concerned look but lets it go.

It goes pretty quickly. Even if I don't remember every aspect of the ring, some of it comes back like muscle memory. Type out the answers, change some of them, mark them down. Print them out, cut them up.

"Hey," I say to Lena when we're wrapping up. "Thanks for covering for me last week."

"It's fine," she says with a small smile. We've been competition for as long as I can remember, but she doesn't feel like competition right now. "You okay?" Lena asks, and it reminds me of the way Tad asks me if I'm all right in cross-country practices, but for once, it doesn't feel like someone is hungry for me to fail, like they're looking for a weakness to exploit. It feels like genuine concern.

I nod. "Thanks for asking."

Later when I'm home, I go for a run in the dark for the first time in a while. It's not quite raining, but there's a light enough mist to cause my shoes to squeak as I travel alone through the night. I finish six, maybe seven miles and my chest doesn't seize up like before. When an early-morning grocery truck passes on the street, I keep my eyes straight ahead and let it pass.

It's still not enough to put me to sleep, and I lie awake staring at the ceiling, just missing Lia and trying to remember everything that happened.

Then it hits me: it didn't work. My plan, it obviously didn't work.

I can still remember snuggling with Lia on the boat and talking about the script for *Eternal Sunshine*, that feeling of freedom and time, of *enough*. That hope is almost palpable. I thought I'd found the solution to all our problems. I thought we'd found a way to beat the game, permanently. I thought I was helping Lia, but it wasn't enough.

I failed.

"But why?" I ask out loud, half-expecting Hunter to appear, but she remains hidden. Sitting up, I rub my eyes and scan the room. It's empty, and I'm still alone.

I can't rely on her anymore. Can't just go out to Montauk and wait for the memories to decide if they're coming back. I have to figure it out on my own. I have to piece together what happened and why it didn't work.

On Monday, I find Cole after school. He's surprised, not expecting me.

"Hey," he says.

"I want to do everything I used to do. I want all the way back in."

He looks surprised but also relieved. "Are you sure?"

I nod. I need to retrace my steps, our steps. I need to at least know what we were doing here, with Cole and the others.

"Are you sure it's not too soon?" he asks again.

"I'm sure," I say. "But I need you to give me a rundown of everything so I don't forget anything."

"Okay," he says. "I'll come by tonight."

"I need to re-up anyway," I tell him in a whisper, and he nods.

He comes by later, when it's almost midnight and the street is mostly shuttered. We sit in his car as he catches me up.

"I'm so glad you're back, really back," he tells me. "It's been insane trying to do this whole thing alone."

"But you have Lena. Josh and Rebecca too."

"It's not the same, and you know it. I started all this but you know you took it to the next level."

"What?" I say, a little shocked.

"Yeah, you came up with most of it, remember?"

Now I'm more than just shocked.

"I thought you were crazy, but it was genius, really," he says. "I still remember when you first told me." He laughs with a small shake of his head.

"What'd I say?" I ask, hoping he wouldn't think it was strange.

"We'd found out that Mr. Wilson had admin access to Vivid." Mr. Wilson was a librarian in charge of the media center, and Vivid Classroom was our school's cloud app where teachers distributed homework and resources, among other things. It also helped track grades, store future assignments.

And tests.

Cole tells me the rest, but I could almost finish the story for him. Mr. Wilson, who was approximately a million years old, had a habit of writing *everything* down. I'd noticed a sticky note on the side of his pencil cup on the second week of school that looked suspiciously like a password.

My plan was simple, really. Cole had distracted him with a long question at the end of the day when the media center was empty. They wandered off to look for a book together, and then it was just a matter of leaning over the counter, rifling through the cup like I was borrowing a pen, and sneaking a glance: GoM3ad0wl@rk1!

We hadn't known what it'd meant initially, hadn't known that Mr. Wilson was the administrator of Meadowlark's system as the head of the media center. But once we logged in, we were stunned. It was all there, all ours for the taking. Well, almost. The few teachers who preferred paper tests, like Mr. Richter, must've kept their tests off the cloud.

What a stroke of stupid, careless luck.

But we had to be careful. The system probably logged IPs and timestamps. We couldn't just log in every day or do it from one of our homes, just in case. So every two weeks, we trekked to a library, and using a public computer, took screenshots to avoid downloading any of the tests and leaving any trace. Then at his house, we'd retype them and print before handing them out to the crew, limiting any electronic trail. Cole tells me I wanted to keep things simpler, but he was paranoid we'd slip up without all the safeguards. That someone could turn us in if we e-mailed them anything.

"Then there's the cheat sheets and distribution. Payment and split."

It sounds exhausting.

"Why'd you keep doing it?" I ask. "After I quit."

He laughs, leaning back against his Lexus. He doesn't need the money. Probably none of us do.

"I'm a masochist," he jokes.

"No, seriously."

He looks thoughtful. "Not all of us were born perfect. Some of us have had to struggle."

I stare at him in surprise. Cole Landau, struggling. Or maybe what was more notable was him admitting it.

"I'm not smart like you or my brother"—the one at Columbia—"but I have my talents. I can get a really cool group of people together. I can make myself indispensable. I'd never get anywhere if I played the game like you, but I have my own ways of gaining an upper hand."

"Should I be worried?" I ask lightly.

"No," he laughs. "I know the kind of person I am and I know the kind of person you are. We're not gunning for the same things. And besides, you're all right, Ohara. I was a little mad when you left, but I knew it wasn't personal. I'm just glad you're back. This shit's lonely."

"Sorry for leaving," I tell him, and I mean it.

"It's fine. It's like my therapist says, we're all responsible for our own shit. Well, not in those exact words."

"You have a therapist?" Tonight's full of revelations.

"When you have two guilt-prone parents who work too much, you end up in weekly therapy from the age of seven."

"Guess mine aren't guilt-prone enough," I say.

"Yeah, you gotta get those super guilt-ridden parents. The ones who fret about not spending enough time with their offspring but then proceed to do just that."

"Wow." I can't help but laugh a little and Cole joins in.

"All right," he says after a moment. "It's getting late. See you tomorrow?"

I nod and head out.

• • •

At home and exhausted, I lie down and think that maybe sleep will come for me tonight. But my mind replays the conversation with Cole from earlier and something he said keeps jumping out at me: *I'd never get anywhere if I played the game like you, but I have my own ways of gaining an upper hand.*

Maybe he was right and we weren't competing for the exact same things, but it felt like maybe we were still playing the same game with the same desire to remake the rules until we were on top. I think about how we're changing the rules now, maybe how in some ways, we were breaking the game altogether.

It was too much power. We had access to all the tests, and the system we—no, *I*—came up with picked winners and losers. Who got the A's and who got the C's. Maybe it was why Cole and I loved it so much, because for once, we were in total control. For once, we had all the power. For once, we wrote the rules.

But maybe more than that: it was proof that I could do it. That I could play the game so excellently I conquered the system—made my closest rivals part of it, made everyone else beholden to my whims. I played God with their grades. I *became* the system.

"You can't do anything without turning it into this whole enterprise!" Lia's voice comes back to me. A fragment of a fragment of a memory.

I'm startled into sitting straight up. I look around for Hunter, but she's nowhere to be found. Squeezing my eyes shut, I try to concentrate on Lia's voice, her anger.

We were at her house, in her bedroom. It was a weeknight but I don't know which one. I remember being surrounded by a mess of papers and textbooks on the floor, both of us on our stomachs.

"Should we open it to juniors?" I asked Lia.

"No," she said firmly. "It'll double the work."

"Not exactly." Since some APs could be taken in either year, there were juniors interested in buying keys. "It's more work, but maybe not that much more."

"You just want more people under your thumb," she said under her breath.

"What? That's not true."

"Whatever. You're just gonna do whatever you want anyway," she said.

"Don't say that. I always ask you."

"Yeah, but do you ever listen to me?" she complained. "You're just like Jo. Honestly, maybe she should've adopted *you*. You'd be perfect for each other."

"What's gotten into you? Where's all this coming from?" I asked, surprised. I thought she was happy. I thought I'd waved a magic wand and made all her problems disappear.

"Forget it."

"No, tell me."

Lia put down her pen and flipped her textbook shut. "Fine. It just always feels like this. Like I never get a say. It's always someone else deciding for me. I *never* get to decide."

"What do you mean? You get to decide lots of things."

"No, Chase. I don't." Her voice was flat and her eyes looked faraway. "I've literally never gotten to decide. I'm adopted. No one ever asked me if I wanted to be adopted by a famous American TV chef, okay?"

"Jo wasn't famous when—"

"Of course you're already not on my side!"

"What? No, that's not—"

"I'm just saying, I never had a choice."

"Well, me neither," I said. "It's not like I got to choose my parents. You know how shitty my dad is. You *know*."

"I knew you wouldn't understand. Just forget it," she said, but then she buried her face in her hands and began to cry.

"I'm sorry," I said quickly. "You're right, I don't understand." All I saw was this amazing family, this amazing life that she had.

"When I was eight, I was on set and it was the start of the second season, but everyone already knew she was gonna be huge, and these two people were there. Interns probably. One of them had a clipboard and stopped me. When I told her Jo was my mom, she didn't believe me, but the other one whispered that I was adopted and she said, 'Wow, I wish Jo Vestiano would adopt *me*.' Later, when I was getting my makeup done, the stylist told me to ignore them, telling me that I deserved all the luck I'd gotten.

"And I don't know, it all felt bad, okay? Like I'd taken someone else's spot or something, because I didn't feel that way. Yes, I loved my mom, but to me, she was just mom, kind of an annoying one honestly, and it was like I just didn't understand how lucky I was. Like I couldn't possibly appreciate that she'd plucked me up and saved me from some terrible fate. Like I should be endlessly grateful for this life that I've been given," Lia finished, shooting me a quick glare. She wasn't just talking about a specific memory on set when she was eight. She was talking about me too, all the spoken and unspoken times I'd been jealous of her family.

"I just feel like a fuckup most of the time, just never enough," she continued. "I mean, how can I ever repay the debt of being adopted by someone like Jo?"

"Jo's a little overbearing sometimes, but she loves you. Your dad, too. I don't think they act like they're your saviors," I said cautiously.

"I'm not saying they're shitty parents. I'm just telling you how I feel. It's like I'm living what everyone thinks is this great life but it doesn't feel great to me. I know that's how you feel," she said, eyes flickering to me before looking away.

I didn't say anything because she was right.

"I just feel kind of trapped in this life I never asked for. Like there are all these expectations I have to live up to. I never feel like I can say no to anything. To the mother-daughter specials in Korea, or the holiday shows."

"That's not true," I said. "You push back all the time. You negotiated down the number of shows you'd do."

"Sort of. I kind of just take it until I can't and then I explode. I'm always swinging between guilt and anger, and it's exhausting."

"With me too?" I asked quietly.

She took a big breath. "Sometimes. It's like you can't help it. Once you've made up your mind to do something, you can't do it halfway. It's like a compulsion. You *have* to see how far you can take it, how hard you can push yourself and everyone around you. Like this thing with Cole. It's so much worse than before."

"What do you mean?"

"You barely have time anymore. You're constantly exhausted. It's just like it always was."

"But you're not stressed anymore," I said. "You don't have to worry about grades." That was the whole point. She never had to worry again because I'd be there, because I could always fix it for her.

Lia grew quiet.

"What?" I said when I noticed, putting down my pen.

"It wasn't ever about that," she said. "This wasn't about me. This was always about you."

"No," I started to argue. "This was never about me. You were stressed about school, about all the shit we had to do for college, and I made it better."

"Are you kidding me?" she said.

"You were happy! You said you were happy," I said, thinking of the recent times we went to Montauk just to sail, just to spend time together.

"Yes, but now it's just like it always was. You and Cole, putting out fires left and right again. You can't do anything without turning it into this whole enterprise!" she said, and suddenly it felt like she was changing the terms of everything on me. I couldn't understand why she was mad. Or maybe I didn't want to understand.

"Look, let's not argue," I said, trying to keep the peace again, always trying to keep the peace. "Let's just finish this and go to sleep. We'll talk about it later, promise."

She sighed, but she said, "Fine."

When I open my eyes again, I expect Hunter to be in my room waiting for me, ready to tell me *I told you so*, but she's nowhere to be found.

I wait and wait, until it's clear she's not going to show up, and I feel almost disappointed. Ever since the revelation that she wasn't real, all I wanted was to get rid of her, but now I wish she were here, because I need someone to talk to.

Lia *was* happy, wasn't she? We were part of something together. But more than that, she could get what she wanted, and so could I.

46.

Aidan and I were supposed to spend Thanksgiving with Dad this year, but he had a last-minute work trip. It doesn't matter though, because I spend the whole time cramming for the SATs.

The day after break, Cole pulls me aside and asks if I need help. The test is next Saturday.

"Help?" I ask, not understanding.

"Yeah, *help*," he says. "It's last minute, but my brother knows a few people." His older brother, who goes to Columbia. "We'd just have to get someone who looks like you."

Suddenly, our earlier conversation comes back to me in a rush.

The test, I said. *Was that your idea, or hers?*

What did she tell you?

Nothing. She never told me.

It was my idea, not hers, he said.

All right.

She didn't want to do it, and I didn't push it. That's it.

I thought we were talking about the Physics test, but maybe Cole thought we were talking about something else entirely.

"I know you're stressed about it," Cole says. He's sympathetic, like he's looking out for a friend. Is that what we are, friends? After everything we've been through, anything's possible.

"No. Thanks, though," I tell him, and he leaves it alone.

The night before the test, I take a sleeping pill early, even though it's never worked for me before. I lie in bed, stare at the ceiling, and try to focus only on counting my breaths.

"Tomorrow's the big day, huh," Hunter says, startling me.

I sit up and see her perched on my desk again. "You disappear for over a week and *this* is the day you decide to show up?" I can't believe her. I shake my head and collapse back onto the bed.

"So this is it, the last time you'll ever have to take the SATs," she says, ignoring me. She's right, of course. It's the last time I *can* take it, the last date colleges will accept scores. It'll also be the third time I take it. "It's so unlike you," she continues. "So last minute."

"You already know why," I say. "Leave me alone." I took it for the first time last spring, before the breakup. It wasn't bad, but nowhere what I needed it to be. Then I took it again in October, and I somehow did worse even though I probably put in more hours than anyone else at Meadowlark. I signed up for the December test out of desperation, and because all the spots at Meadowlark were booked, I have to travel almost an hour to take it.

"I can't believe you pinned your scores to the wall," she says, fingers brushing against the sheet. "Lia was the one who should've pinned hers to the wall."

"What are you talking about?" I ask, suddenly wide awake. I toss the covers off and get up. "Seriously. What are you talking about?"

Hunter just shrugs, and then she's gone.

"Wait!" I shout, but she doesn't come back.

Instead, Mom knocks on my door. "Everything okay?"

"Um, fine, sorry," I say, hoping she won't open the door.

"All right, get some sleep," she says and leaves.

"Hunter," I whisper-yell. "Come back and explain."

She doesn't.

"Please," I add in desperation. But she remains hidden.

I play back her words: *Lia was the one who should've pinned hers to the wall.* But what does that actually mean? Had Lia failed too? Was that the thing that tipped her over the edge?

For the rest of the night, I can barely sleep, swinging between moments on the edge of dozing off and moments of sickening panic. What happened to Lia?

It's not until a few minutes before my alarm will go off that I remember Lia took the SATs with me in October. She skipped the one I took last spring, and when I had to retake it, she signed up with me.

We didn't take it in the same room, but we were both at Meadowlark that day. And a week later, when the scores came out, we were together too.

I get up again, go to my computer, and try to log into Lia's account to see her scores. I type in her e-mail and "nomnomnom" but it doesn't work.

Hunter clears her throat from behind me and I nearly fall out of my chair. "Try this," she says, her foot nudging Lia's laptop.

Her account info is saved in her browser. Lia used "nomnomnom" where she could but some sites required more complex passwords. It takes a second to load, but when it does, I'm shocked.

"What?"

"Told you it's wall-worthy."

It's near perfect.

It's the kind of score that's eluded me twice.

"How?" is all I manage to say.

Then my alarm goes off, and it's time to get ready.

I'm one of the earliest ones there. I sit as the classroom begins to fill up with unfamiliar faces. I had to head deep into Queens, but I'm here now.

Only, I don't want to be here. I want to be with Lia, and I want to know what happened. When the proctor gives out instructions and the test lands on my desk, I am blinking away tears just trying to hang on.

Then we're told it's time, and I flip to the first page. I'm trying to focus, but all I feel is panic.

I try counting my breaths, but my throat tightens and my chest squeezes. I feel both pinned down and untethered, unable to move and spinning away from everything I've ever known.

I try shaking my head to clear it, but it begins to pound, a familiar pressure building inside my skull.

I try closing my eyes, but the room feels unsteady and I want to throw up.

Lia's voice comes back to me: *You have to believe me.*

She was pleading with me, but about what? We were sitting together, our laptops in front of us. Suddenly, I know where we were. At my house for once. It was the Friday after we took the SATs in October, and our scores were out.

First we looked mine up, and Lia had to comfort me. "It's not that bad," she said, arm gingerly around my shoulders. She was tense because I was tense.

"It's worse than last time. How?" I cried. Then I looked over at her screen. "What?"

She glanced over too and quickly slammed it shut.

"Wait, what?" I swatted her hand away, opened it, and stared at her near-perfect scores. "Is this a joke?"

Lia looked miserable.

"I don't understand." I kept looking between our screens, thoroughly confused. "I just don't understand."

"It's just a test," she offered, but it was the exact wrong thing to say.

I pushed her off me, my tears erupting. "Just a test?" It was everything, the final piece I needed to get into Stanford, the only thing stopping me from a perfect high school career.

"No, I mean—" She didn't finish, because there was nothing to say.

"This is the second time I've taken it," I said. "You only took it once. You barely studied."

"I took a prep course over the summer. And I'm one year behind you in math," she said. "It's fresher for me."

"No," I said. "Bullshit. And what about the other sections?" I was inconsolable. I couldn't stand to be near her and I shrank further away.

"You'll take it again," she said. "December, okay?"

I barely nodded. "I just don't understand," I kept repeating.

"It's not the end of the world," she said, and all I felt was numb.

I'm still staring at the first page of the test as the memory washes over me. I soak the cuffs of my shirt with tears. That pain is still so raw, so fresh. And even now, I can feel that same resentment and anger toward Lia. I would give anything to see her again, but still, that anger is present, palpable. All consuming.

Another memory comes up, pulls me under.

"You cheated," I said to Lia. We were in Montauk, on the boat, one day later. It was her idea to go, she thought it would cheer me up.

"What?" she balked.

"You cheated, didn't you?" I repeated. "It's okay, you can tell me the truth."

"No," she said. "I didn't."

"Cole told me," I said, but it was a lie. I hadn't had a chance to ask him yet, but I knew he had the connections to pull it off because he'd offered to help me in September and I thought I didn't need it.

"*What?*" Lia said. "That's impossible. Because I didn't fucking do it."

"You did. You had someone else take it for you," I said.

"I went *with* you, Chase," she said, and for a moment I was stymied. "We were both at Meadowlark that morning. You saw me!"

"Maybe at the beginning, but then you must've gone into a bathroom, given her your ID," I said.

"And who did I give my ID to exactly?" she asked.

"I don't know! The person Cole found for you. The person who took the test for you."

"You're ridiculous," she said, getting up to go outside on the deck.

"Where are you going?" I asked.

"Just getting some air. Jesus, Chase."

I followed her out there. "Tell me the truth, and we'll never talk about it again." That was another lie because this was all I wanted to talk about.

Lia rolled her eyes. "I already told you the truth. I didn't fucking do it."

"Don't lie to me. Don't just stand there and lie to my face!"

"Why is this so important to you? You've been cheating this whole semester," she said.

"So you're admitting it." I could feel my fury rising, growing out of control.

"No, I'm not admitting anything! But I'm just saying, why do you even care? Are you mad that *you* didn't cheat on the SATs? Or are you mad that we took it at the same time and I did better?" she said, and I swore I could hear the blood pounding in my head, feel each pulse like a punch.

I was so angry I couldn't speak.

"That's it, isn't it?" she pushed on. "That's what's really bothering you."

"No," I managed to say. "It's the lying."

"It's not the lying because I didn't fucking lie!" she yelled. And maybe if I wasn't blinded by rage, maybe if I could've taken a step back, I would've been able to see she was telling the truth, but everything I was feeling overwhelmed me and I was completely pulled under.

Now, as I relive this memory, I feel the incandescent anger lighting me up, but I also feel something else, something underneath all that fury, maybe the thing fueling it. This sense of complete and utter failure. Of all my fears coming true. Of losing my dreams, everything I'd ever worked for.

Of losing control.

"This is your last chance," I said. "Tell me the truth."

And Lia, she *laughed*. "Last chance? For what? Get outta here."

"Fine," I said, and went back inside to get my bag.

"Are you serious?" she asked when I re-emerged with my things. "Are you fucking serious?"

"Yes," I said, my entire body rigid with anger, my hands forming fists at my side. "I'm leaving."

"This is so fucked up," she said. "This is so, so fucked up. Okay, okay, fine, I lied, you're right, okay?"

"I knew it," I said, glaring at her. "I fucking knew it." She flinched but dropped her head in defeat.

I couldn't possibly have seen it back then, in that moment, but here, now, in this memory, I can see the resignation on Lia's face. She was lying then, just to protect me.

Because I know now that she was telling the truth. Cole's voice echoes in my head: *She didn't want to do it, and I didn't push it. That's it.*

47.

Time is up and my entire test booklet is blank. I stare ahead in a daze as the proctor comes to collect them one by one. When we're dismissed, I go up and tell him I need to cancel my scores, and after that, I walk outside, the sunlight harsh and piercing overhead.

I don't remember how I get home, just that I manage to take the right trains, and the first thing I do is take out Lia's journal, flip to the last page.

You . . . left. You just left. I tried to explain, but you wouldn't listen. It's over, you said. It's fucking over.

No, I said. Please don't leave. You don't understand. I need you. You can't go.

Watch me, you said. Fucking watch me.

I'll die, I said. I'll die without you.

I can't live like this anymore, you said. I'm terrined. I'm always terrined of you. You have to nnd a way to live without me.

And then you were gone.

But the truth is, I know I can't. I need you.

Hunter was right all along. *I* was the one who left Lia. I read and reread her words, just trying to access that exact memory, but I can't.

When I give up, I head out for Montauk once more. On the train, I'm still in a daze when she shows up.

"I broke up with her again," I say flatly as Hunter nods beside me. "Is that when I deleted all our messages?"

"Yeah," Hunter says. She seems tense beside me, like she's waiting for something to happen. Anticipation electrifies the air around us, but I don't know why.

"You okay?" I can't believe I'm asking my hallucination if she's okay. I've officially lost my mind.

"Fine," she says, but she seems anxious. No, maybe impatient.

I pull out my phone, tap on Lia's name.

Lia: Meet me in Montauk.

It comes back to me in a rush. We were back in Meadowlark that Sunday, at her house, sitting in her room trying to work on a Calc problem set for the group.

"I already admitted it," Lia said. "What more do you want?"

"Nothing, it's fine," I said, but I was still angry. Standoffish. Pulling away whenever she touched me, avoiding eye contact, and ignoring her texts longer and longer.

At the time, I thought the reason I felt so betrayed was because she had someone else take the test for her, but the truth was I was jealous of her scores.

Would it have mattered, if I was the one who did better? Would I have even cared if she cheated, or would I have been just happy she did well?

But all my old resentments roared back to life. I was Chase Ohara, and in the story of us, I'd been the one with the grades, the brains, the work ethic. I was the student council president, captain of the best cross-country team in the state, and clear favorite of my teachers. Expected valedictorian, voted most likely to succeed. A future with my name atop skyscrapers etched in gold, multimillion dollar bonuses, Congress or the Supreme Court perhaps. A future power broker. Insider trading scandals if I went astray.

Someone destined to rewrite the rules of the game, someone not at the mercy of fate but in control.

I was the one who was going places, the one with all the potential. I was the one who got into Stanford's summer high school program. I worked harder than anyone I knew. I *deserved* it.

Didn't I?

And Lia, she had everything handed to her. She had the perfect family, the grades only because I helped her, and now the SAT scores.

Before, she had everything, but I had myself. She could rely on her mom's connections, but I knew I could rely on myself. And now I felt like I had nothing, like everything I spent my whole life building had crumbled before me. I thought of my father then, how he got into Stanford but couldn't afford to go, how I wouldn't even get into Stanford.

"You're still mad," she said, and I pretended to ignore her, staring down at the Calc problem set but not able to focus on it.

"Fine," I admitted. "I'm still mad."

"You said we could let it go. Look, just retake it in December, get Cole to hook you up. It's not the end of the world," she said, but that only angered me.

"I'm not going to cheat on the SATs," I said, like it was beneath me. Was it beneath me?

"Why not?" Lia asked. "You're already doing it now."

"This is different," I said. "This is for you."

She scoffed. "Sure, Chase. Whatever."

"What's that supposed to mean?"

"Nothing, forget it," she said.

"No, just say it." I tossed my pencil aside, giving up on Calc to fully face her.

"I never asked for this," Lia said, slumping back and running both hands through her hair in frustration. "I never, ever asked for this."

"Yes, you did," I said. "You said you didn't want to live like we were going from one emergency to another. So I fixed it for you. Now you never have to worry about school. You never have to study. You don't even have to do homework if you don't want to. I've made your life perfect."

She laughed and it was jarring, bitter. "It's like you only hear the parts you want to hear. It's like you have this reality distortion filter on. I said I didn't want any of this! Not that I wanted you to do all my homework or get me answer keys to tests. I said I didn't want to live like this anymore. I said I didn't want this *life*. The constant stress and pressure and the never-ending fucking hamster wheel we're on."

"You were happy," I said. "You were fucking happy at the beginning."

"Yes! At the beginning." She got up to pace, arms folded, eyes averted. "But that was because you had time. You had time for me, so I didn't care. You needed this thing with Cole in order to survive, so I was happy to let you do it, help you even. Be part of it. But then you had to turn it into this—this whole *operation*. It's like you can't help yourself. You just can't do anything without taking it to the next level, to its final level. Beyond anyone's imagination. It's like nothing's ever just *enough* for you! You're not happy if you're not the best, if you're not at the top, if you're not crushing everyone else to pulp."

"So what?" I said, shocking her. "So what if I'm ambitious and smart and work hard? Why can't you be *more* ambitious? Why can't you at least be happy for me instead of always trying to hold me back?"

"Are you serious?" She started crying. "Are you fucking serious?"

I was too angry to see straight. Too angry to see the truth in her words. Too angry to see *her*.

"That's it!" I said, a realization making its way through me like poison. "You're the reason. It's *you*." I needed someone to blame and that someone was Lia. I started gathering my things and shoving them into my bag.

"What are you talking about?" Lia asked, still crying.

"You're the reason I left Stanford early. You're the reason I fucked up the SATs. I'm always running around trying to make you happy, trying to fix you. Going off to Montauk because you're sad. Doing your homework and making sure you're not failing. It's *exhausting*. No wonder I flunked the SATs."

"You didn't flunk. Your scores are still in the eighty-fifth percentile!" she said, but I was on a roll.

"It's been you all along," I continued. "*It's been you all along*." I shook my head, slung my bag over one shoulder. "I can't do this anymore. I can't fucking do this anymore."

"What are you saying?" she asked, breathless.

I turned to look her in the eye. "I'm saying it's over."

"No," she whispered, her cries turning into sobs. "Please don't leave. You don't understand. I need you. You can't go."

"Watch me," I said. "Fucking watch me." I felt invincible. Like I could do anything, be anything, if only I was free. Like Lia was dead weight keeping me down. Like she was suffocating me.

"I'll die," she said, and my body went cold. I was at her door but I couldn't move. "I'll die without you."

I could feel tears welling up immediately. The panic and fear setting my heart on fire. But then the anger reared its ugly head. "I can't live like this anymore. I'm terrified." That much was true. "I'm always terrified of you." It felt like a crystalizing moment. That no matter how much I loved her, I couldn't be her one source of happiness, the one person keeping her alive. That I'd been living under this unspeakable pressure, just one more thing on top of the rest, and in my rush of anger, it was easy to blame it all on her. "I'm always terrified of you. You have to find a way to live without me."

And then I left. No dramatic slamming of the door, no screaming. I closed her door softly behind me and stepped outside into the fall chill.

It wasn't until I got home that I broke down sobbing.

The train arrives late afternoon and it's already dark. Hunter waits with me as I order a car, sits with me until we reach the marina, and walks up to the boat with me.

"Ready?" she asks, and I shake my head.

"I deleted all my messages," I repeat. "And then what happened?"

"And then you received one more message from Lia."

I stare down at my phone, at the final text.

Lia: Meet me in Montauk.

"Did I go?" I ask. "Or did our fight break me?" I want to know what happened, I do, but I'm scared too. Hunter's earlier words haunt me. *If I tell you before you're ready, you might not be able to handle it, and then we'll have to go back to square one.*

I don't want to go back to the beginning. I don't want to lose all these hard-earned memories. I don't want to lose Lia all over again.

"I think you're ready," she said, and offers her hand.

"I don't know."

"Come on." She extends it further. "I'll even help you out this one time."

I hesitate but take her hand. It sucks me under, and I'm pulled back to the moment I saw the text for the first time. The real moment I saw it.

I ignored it at first. It'd been almost a week since we broke up for the second time. She sent it Thursday night, and I scoffed. We'd been civil, avoiding each other at school. I told Cole I wanted out, then heard she'd done the same. I was running on pure anger and resentment and spite, refusing to give in to feeling anything else. Because if I did, I might've had to face what I did, the things I said, my mistakes and regrets. I might've had to face the loss of the one person I loved most in the world.

I remember the surprise but also the indignation when I first saw her message. Had she really expected me to come running, to skip school?

But then she didn't show up to classes on Friday. I called her after but she didn't answer.

Finally, I drove out there after school Friday night. I pulled into the marina, saw the light on in the boat and breathed a sigh of relief.

I take a step forward, climb onto it, Hunter right next to me.

"Ready?" Hunter asks, letting go of my hand. It's time to find out what really happened to Lia.

What really happened to us.

I unlock the door. "I'm ready."

48.

Inside, I'm alone in the dark but there's a strange energy in the air, like the past is still alive within these walls. The lights begin to flicker on and off, my memory and present reality at war until the memory wins and the lights remain on, the past superimposed over the now.

I take a step forward into the memory. Call out Lia's name. I hear sobbing and run toward it.

She's in the bathroom, huddled in the tiny shower, a knife in her hand. It's really her and I gasp.

"Lia!" I shout and rush toward her, grab her wrist. It startles her into dropping it, and I check for blood. Thank God there is none. "What are you doing? What have you done?" I'm panicking, grabbing her and checking all over. "Did you take anything? Tell me!" I yell before she's even had a chance to answer.

She shakes her head, sobbing. Then she's melting into my arms, and we're clutching at each other, both of us crying and desperate. It feels so real, the weight of her body against mine, the softness of her hair on my cheek. For a moment, for *this* moment, I have her still, and she's mine, she's safe.

"I'm sorry," I say immediately. "I'm so, so sorry."

"No, I'm the one who's sorry," she says. "I'm so sorry."

We apologize to each other over and over again, huddling and shivering and holding on to each other. Eventually, we make it out of the tiny bathroom and onto her bed. We're still shaking, still whispering apologies under the covers.

Eventually, Lia falls into a fitful sleep and I watch over her, unable to let go.

I feel sick, disoriented as the memory loosens its grip on me and returns me to the present.

"Then what happened?" I ask Hunter once I wake as if from a dream.

"You already know," she says.

I can't face it. I can't go back.

My heart's pounding. My head's throbbing. Everything hurts and I just want to escape the pain.

This is it, I think. The final memory. Lia dies at the end of it, and I have to somehow survive. To keep breathing when every breath aches. I can't face it, I can't face any of it.

"I can't," I tell her.

"What do you mean, you can't?" Hunter asks. "You wanted to know what happened, remember? You kept asking. And here we are, finally."

"I want to go," I say, staring at the door.

"Come on," she says, getting up and heading toward the cockpit of the yacht. "Let's go for a ride."

"No," I say. "We shouldn't. *I* shouldn't." Sometimes I have to remind myself that Hunter isn't real.

"It's fine. Jo and Rob won't mind."

I haven't been in touch with them since the fight. I don't know what's going on with them. If Jo's still counting on me for the Christmas special or if she's going to drop it. But I know Hunter's right. That they wouldn't care if I took the boat out.

Hunter starts the motor, goes through the motions of checking everything as I watch in surprise. Then I shake my head, hard, and look down at my hands. For a second, I can see that *I'm* the one doing everything, my hands on the wheel as we ease out of the marina before going full throttle. But then I blink and I'm back to watching Hunter operate the boat like she's been doing it her whole life.

"How is this happening?" I ask.

She shrugs. "Doesn't it feel good being out on the water again? Really out and not just using this thing for sleepovers?"

"I guess," I say, more unsure than ever.

"Look," she says. "I know it's hard, but don't you want to know what happened?"

I glance at the door, realize that I can't leave now. Was this just a trap? Now it's just me and her and my final memory on this boat. Now I have nowhere to run.

"Don't think about running," she says. "Just think about Lia."

I try to focus on her voice, on Lia, the memory of her curled up in bed, so small, so helpless, so scared and so unhappy. Maybe Hunter's right: I can't keep running away from it, and maybe Hunter is the part of me that just wants to help me remember.

"Don't you want to be with her, one last time?" she continues, her dark eyes shooting me a quick glance.

I nod, but I can't help but feel fear rushing through me. There's something about Hunter's voice. The way she's talking. It's almost menacing. Maybe she wants me to remember, but I'm no longer sure she's here to help.

"I think you're ready for the truth. I'm sorry I kept it from you this whole time," she continues, almost sweetly. Out on the open waters, there's a light mist falling against the windshield, and even in the dark, I can see a thin fog rolling toward us.

"Wait. Stop," I tell her. "It's not safe."

To my surprise, she cuts the engine. "You're right."

"I want to go back," I say.

"We can't. Not until this fog clears," she says as it engulfs the boat, submerging us into a blinding white.

"And then we'll go back?" I ask, feeling very, very small.

She nods, then moves toward me, sitting beside me. "You're in safe hands."

I don't feel very safe, but we've come this far together, so I say, "Okay."

She extends a hand again. "We'll do it together."

I stare at her palm. An open offer.

The last memory.

Finally, I take it and close my eyes.

I watched Lia sleep, held her as she whimpered, tried to soothe her nightmares away. When she woke that Saturday morning, I thought we'd maybe turned a corner. I thought maybe we were safe.

"I'm sorry," I said, the first words out of my mouth. "I'm so sorry." I spent the night replaying every moment of our fight, soaking in the guilt and shame. "You're the most important thing in my life. The only important thing. Everything else is stupid."

She laughed, but it sounded pained.

"I can't believe I did that to us. Can you ever forgive me?" I started to cry then. Lia cupped my face gently, thumbs brushing away my tears.

"I'm the one who fucked up. I shouldn't have lied to you."

"It doesn't matter," I told her.

"No, let me finish."

"Okay."

"I lied to you about cheating on the SATs—"

"I already know."

"—but I didn't cheat," she finished.

"What?" I asked, stunned.

"I was the one who took the test. Just me," she said. "Please, I need you to believe me."

Staring into her eyes, I could see the truth. She had no reason to lie now. "Yes," I said, but I was still surprised.

"I'm telling you this because I need you to know that it wasn't your fault. That it was cruel of me to put everything on you. To tell you I couldn't live without you. To try and make you stay by threatening to hurt myself. It was wrong." We were both crying now, sobbing, and still holding on to each other. "All you've ever done is tried to help. All you've ever wanted was for me to be happy." She leaned in, kissed me through our tears, and I didn't want to let go. "I'm sorry, okay?" she said.

"Okay."

"Okay," I said, not fully believing her. "Then what happened? What drove you here?" To this place, to sobbing in the bathroom with a knife in hand.

"The SAT scores. What I got," she said, sounding so sure, so definitive.

"I don't understand. Your scores were almost perfect," I said. It was impossible for me to understand how such amazing scores could possibly make her sad.

"That's the thing," she said, her voice soft. "They *were* almost perfect, but I felt nothing. I didn't feel happy. Not even for a split second.

Honestly, I haven't been able to feel anything, really, in a long time. Like there were times I would be with you, and I wouldn't feel exactly happy but I wouldn't feel as sad. You were always the brightest part of every day, and I kept holding out hope, you know? Because I just wanted to be with you and happy again. But after I saw my scores, it was like this realization. This feeling of like, oh, that's it. The thing everyone wants and it's still not enough. And I just wanted out."

Her words washed over me, but I couldn't comprehend them, couldn't understand everything she was feeling. Couldn't possibly begin to understand.

"I wake up every day and everything's just dark," she continued. "I have you, and I have my parents, and I have my grades, and now my SATs, I guess. But it's all just a little bit gray, and every day it gets a little grayer, a little darker. And I just don't—I just don't want to do this anymore, you know? This life, it's great, but I never asked for it. I never asked for any of it."

"No, Lia, don't say that. I can't live without you," I said, crying harder. Begging now.

"I used to think there was a reason I felt like this. I thought it was the stress of school, the pressure to live up to my mom, or just wanting to be taken seriously like you. I thought if I could just fix the source of my unhappiness, the clouds would lift and I'd be like everyone else. Normal. But it's not true. That source of darkness, it's *me*. No matter what I do, I just can't escape it. And it's all I want—escape. I don't want to stay here anymore," she said, sobbing too. I'd never seen her in so much pain. So desperately in pain.

"You can't just leave me here," I said. "You can't, you can't." Now I was the one who needed her. I will never stop needing her. "Please," I begged. "Please, please."

We sobbed, holding on to each other, one of us wanting to go and the other trying to make her stay.

"I just feel so trapped here," Lia said. "In this life, in this world."

"Then fuck it," I said. "I don't care about any of it anymore. Fuck school, fuck Stanford. Fuck all of it. We'll do whatever you want, okay? Live whatever life you want."

"You know we can't do that," she said. "You know this is the kind of life you want, the life that everyone else wants. A life of significance—fame, fortune, power, whatever. And I wanted to want the same thing. I *tried* to want it, I really did. All I want, all I've wanted for a long time now, is just to be done. Just to say *no*. No more. Just to feel some *relief*. It's so heavy, Chase. It's like I can't ever breathe. And it never, ever stops. Please don't make me stay here."

She was in so much pain. I didn't know what else to do. I just wanted to fix it for her. I just wanted for it to stop.

"Okay," I said finally. "Let's do it together." The words burst out of me, leaving me in shock. "I mean it," I said, my shock wearing off, and a strange, unnerving certainty replacing it.

In that moment, we were just two lost girls in need of direction. Two lost girls who felt like they had nowhere to go. Two lost girls who had only each other, alone in the entire universe.

Lia looked up in surprise at my words, crying even harder, but began to nod. "Okay."

For the rest of the day, we were subdued, quiet. A heavy sadness blanketed us as we discussed how we'd do it.

We'd always loved Montauk.

We always loved the water.

It was decided, and that night we took the boat out.

49.

It was a clear night. That's what I remember. We were out on the deck surrounded by darkness but illuminated by the stars and moon above us.

We stood on the precipice, hands linked, staring down at the inky water, the soft waves swaying like open arms.

"Ready?" she asked.

I glanced at the ladder on the other side of the deck, the one we hooked over the side to climb back up after a dip. This time, it wouldn't be there.

Once we jumped, it'd be over.

"Aidan," I said suddenly. "What about Aidan? I can't just leave her to fend for herself, all alone."

For a moment, time seemed to slow, forming around us like a clot. Aidan was the first reason that my mind latched onto. The truth was that I was scared. The truth was that as much as I wanted to give in to Lia, I wasn't sure. Not about what we were doing, not about any of it.

"Okay," Lia said, surprising me. "We don't have to." She said this almost immediately and I took it as a sign that maybe she didn't really want to do this after all. As a sign of hope.

"For Aidan," I said, even though I was barely there for her anymore. Even though she probably didn't need me anymore. In that moment, I was the one who needed her. The one who needed a reason to keep us on that boat.

"For Aidan," Lia said softly, and I was grateful she didn't question it, didn't point out what an absent big sister I'd been.

I slowly stepped back from the edge, pulling Lia with me. "Let's go home," I said, and it felt urgent all of a sudden.

If I could just get us home, everything would be fine. If I could get us home, there would be time to fix things. Get help.

Everything Lia was going through, everything she felt—it was too much for one person. For two people. She needed something I couldn't give her. But if I could just get us home, that would be enough. If I could just get her to safety *now*, then we could figure everything else out later.

I really believed that.

It quickly became the only thing I believed.

"Come on," I said. "It's getting late."

"No, let's stay," she said. "Spend the night here and head back in the morning." She yawned. "I'm tired. And it's a beautiful night."

"Okay." I wanted to give her what she wanted. I thought it could only help.

We dropped the anchor and stayed out on the deck for hours after, wrapped up in heavy blankets to protect us in the cold. Finally, we headed inside, climbed into bed. I was exhausted, practically shaking with it. I'd spent the entire night before watching over her and tried to keep vigil again.

But when the rhythm of her breathing smoothed, I felt myself taking sips of sleep here and there, until I must've dozed off.

And when I came to, Lia was gone.

50.

I am waking up again to the worst day of my life. There's no escaping it, not this time. I run around the boat screaming Lia's name as Hunter watches. I scream and scream her name, but she's nowhere to be found. She's been gone for over a month but it's like I've just lost her. Like she's only just slipped through my fingers and if I find her now, I can still save her.

I'm crying, breathless, my whole body quaking with each sob.

"Look," Hunter says, and I blink furiously, try to see where she's pointing.

Out there in the water, a figure. I step closer to the edge.

Impossible.

It can't be.

I shake my head in disbelief. But there she is, Lia, my Lia, out in the water, floundering.

"Lia!" I call, and she seems to hear me. I run and find the life preserver, toss it out toward her, but the line is too short and she's still splashing wildly.

"She needs you," Hunter says quietly.

Part of me knows this can't be happening, but panic takes over. I have to do *something*.

I kick off my boots, unzip my jacket, and the second before I dive in, I remember the ladder and hook it over the side.

Then I jump in.

Fuck.

The water is ice. December in Montauk, and my body is both freezing and burning with pain. I can barely breathe, barely manage to float as I take several gulps of icy seawater.

But there is Lia, just beyond the life preserver that's now drifting away uselessly. I swim toward her, but she seems to be swimming in the wrong direction.

"Lia!" I shout, fighting to keep my head above water. "Over here!"

She doesn't hear me, and as I struggle to reach her, she moves farther and farther away until I look around, frantic and lost. In the fog, I can't see anything.

Not Lia, not the boat, and definitely not the shore.

I stop swimming in panic, surrounded by darkness, alone in the universe.

No one knows where I am, I realize.

"You made a promise," Hunter's voice arrives from the darkness, but I don't see her. "You told Lia you'd do it with her, but then you backed out at the last second."

"Where are you?" I manage to cough out, looking for her. Looking for any sign, any direction.

"She had to do it alone. You left her to die alone!"

I'm crying, gulping seawater, barely able to keep my head up. It's so cold, so very cold, and I'm choking.

This was Hunter's plan all along, I realize. She led me to the boat, she drove it out. This is what she wanted from the beginning.

Everything she did, she did for this moment. Everything was designed to bring me here.

"I needed you to remember," she says, voice on edge, angry. "So I got you to join Cole and the others again. I got you to keep coming back to the boat. I got you to question what happened."

She got me to suspect her, I think. It was all a ploy.

"Yes!" Hunter laughs. "I got you to suspect me, and it worked, didn't it? You remembered everything! It took forever, but I did it." She sounds thrilled, triumphant.

"Why?" I choke out. "*Why?*"

She doesn't answer. She doesn't have to. Hunter isn't some villain trying to trap me. She's *not real*, but part of me.

I'm the one who wanted to come out here. *I'm* the one who wanted to remember what happened to Lia.

I'm the one who wants to join her. Who believes in my heart of hearts that I *have* to do this, fulfill a broken promise. A responsibility.

I'm so weak, so cold, so exhausted.

I'm tired of fighting. It feels like it's been seventeen years of battle, of chasing one thing after another, of wanting more, more, more. Of never being enough, of always delaying a happiness that never comes.

Of being on a treadmill, a hamster wheel. Of being scared of never being enough, never measuring up. Of putting out fire after fire. Lia was right in so many ways. And I failed her, the person I loved most in the world. She's gone now, and it's my fault.

Maybe this is what I deserve. Maybe this would fix everything.

Maybe Hunter is the truest part of me. Maybe she was right to lead me back here. Finish what I started, finish what I couldn't do on my own.

I don't know what happened after I discovered Lia was missing. Just that I couldn't find her and couldn't handle it. That my mind couldn't cope and wiped my memory clean of the last few months, inventing a new, more tolerable history. Inventing a whole new person.

But maybe what I really should've done was jump in after her.

I'm so, so tired. Would it be so bad if I let go?

We'd always loved Montauk.

We always loved the water.

"It's okay to let go," Hunter says, softly this time. I open my eyes and see her in the water before me, her clothes drenched, hair clinging to her face, the blue highlights no longer electric. "Come on," she says, hands outstretched. I reach out tentatively and she grabs me. Soon, she's sinking, dragging me under.

I kick and kick but it's no use. I try to pull away, but her grip tightens on me.

For a moment, I stop fighting and wait for the relief to flood through me. But it never comes. Instead, a sharper panic takes over.

No, I think, eyes frantically searching the dark water. No. No. *No.*

It's the same panic I felt standing at the edge of the boat with Lia, the same feeling of *wrongness*. I have every reason to just let go, to let the water and guilt take me—maybe take me back to Lia, to that other life she talked about, where we would find each other again because we were meant to be. I have every reason to give up this failure of a life, but there's still something in me that doesn't want to let go, that's fighting for survival.

Why?

I don't want to go back to the life I had. I don't want Stanford, don't want to see my name atop skyscrapers, don't want to be a future power broker. All that's waiting for me is a long life of struggle. Of clawing for control and always falling short. Of an inevitable failure to tame a wild world, to bend reality to my will. Of either being at someone's mercy or keeping others at mine.

A life of ambition and insatiable hunger for power. No, not power, but *safety*. Of being driven by fear of losing control.

There's nothing back there for me anymore.

Strangely, in burning down that life, I am finally free. I don't know what I want or what the future will look like, but suddenly, in this darkest of moments, everything is possible.

The thought of life without Lia is unbearable, the grief overwhelming. But this tiny spark of hope burns within me. I wish I could have helped her, I wish I could have lifted the weight of her pain, given her the relief she desperately needed. I wish I listened to her more, really listened. I wish I'd listened to myself, understood these things about myself, about both of us, enough to see a way out. Most of all, I wish I'd asked for help, that I hadn't believed I was the only person who could save her, that it was okay to admit I'd was out of my depth. That it was okay to admit I'd failed.

Now, Hunter and I, we're tangled together. We're both thrashing in the icy water, our heads bobbing, me gasping for breath. My lungs are on fire, and I'm blinded by the salt water, the darkness. My limbs are numb with cold. But I fight with everything I have left. I'm at war with myself, and maybe I've always been at war with myself. Hunter is the part of me that longs for self-destruction. The part of me consumed by anger and resentment, jealousy and fear. Right and wrong, guilt and punishment. Hunter is the part of me I hate, but even as I fight for my life, I can't help but see her as something else too.

Without her, I'd still be lost in a fucked-up daydream.

Without her, I'd still be in the dark about what happened to Lia.

Without her, I'd still be the old Chase Ohara, defined entirely by a list of empty achievements.

Hunter's grip on me tightens as she tugs at me, and soon, we're sinking. Maybe these two halves of me will never fully reconcile, maybe I'll never be completely whole, but maybe there's room for something like acceptance. Gratitude, even.

"I'm sorry," I tell Hunter in my mind as her grip tightens, as we're beginning to sink. "And thank you."

For a moment, we're in stasis, just two girls lost in the water. But then she lets go and there's just me, surging up toward the light, gasping desperately for air, coughing and sputtering.

Alive.

It feels so good to be *alive*. I'm thrashing to keep my head above water, but I'm here, I'm still here.

"Chase."

I turn in shock. It's Lia's voice.

"Over here," she says. I'm exhausted, desperately exhausted, but somehow, I reach out and begin to swim. "I'm here," she calls again and again whenever I waver, whenever I feel lost. Whenever I want to give up.

It takes what feels like forever in this awful fog, but finally, I see her.

I can see her.

"Here," she calls out one last time, hand outstretched.

I hesitate, afraid it's another trap, but Lia looks into my eyes, and I know I'm safe. I reach out, take her hand, but feel only cold metal.

It's the ladder. I blink in the dark and Lia has disappeared, but I'm at the boat.

I scramble up, collapse on the deck, and manage to pull a blanket over me.

In the dark, Lia returns to me. "You're safe now," she says as I shake and shiver and violently throw up seawater.

"Lia," I say. There are so many things I want to say to her. So many things I never got to say to her.

"Shhh," she says as I lose consciousness.

51.

The sound of sirens wakes me as I slip in and out. I'm blinded by the light. I'm in an ambulance, I realize, as I hear someone crying. My mom.

"Chase? Chase!" she says, but darkness pulls me under again.

When I come to, I'm in the hospital, my head pounding, my mouth and throat dry, feverish and delirious with pain.

Aidan's the first one to notice I'm awake. "Chase?" she asks and my parents turn toward me.

"Oh, thank God," Mom says as Dad rushes out, calling for a doctor.

They tell me everything and I retain almost none of it. But in the next few hours, I piece together what's happened.

When they couldn't reach me, they called Jo and Rob, who thought to call the marina. Once they found the boat missing, they called the coast guard, who were the ones that found me soaked and shivering outside on the deck. Because of the fog, they couldn't airlift me out, but rushed me back by boat. By this point, Mom had driven out to the marina and was waiting for me with an ambulance once they pulled in.

"What were you thinking?" Dad asks. "Going out there by yourself, operating the boat in fog, going into the water? Stupid, so stupid. You're smarter than that."

Mom silences him with a sharp look, and he quiets. Aidan cries by my side. I try to comfort her, but I can barely lift my hand, and this causes her to cry harder.

"I'm sorry," I whisper. "I'm so, so sorry."

I look around the room, past my family, expecting—maybe hoping—to see Lia, but we're alone.

When a doctor arrives, he reviews my chart and seems stern. He lists off a series of injuries. I've been in the hospital for almost two days. Exposure has left me with mild frostbite in various fingers and toes, painful but recoverable, and put my system in shock. Then he grows even more serious as he tells us that I tested positive for amphetamines in my system. Mom begins to cry, but Dad looks stone-faced.

"We didn't consent to that," he begins to argue. "No one asked you to run a drug test. If you release any information, we'll sue." The entire room is tense, Aidan clutching my hand. I try to squeeze back, to let her know it's going to be okay even though I don't know how it'll ever be okay.

The doctor sighs. "There's no need. We won't be reporting it to the authorities unless someone files a criminal complaint. Generally, hospitals want you to seek treatment, not punish you for it. A psychiatrist will be by tomorrow to evaluate her." And then he's gone.

"Call Jo," Dad tells Mom as soon as we're alone again. "Make sure she's not going to press charges for trespassing or grand larceny."

Mom glares at him. "They're not going to do that. And sit down. Stop barking orders at everyone."

They bicker until a nurse comes in to admonish them.

I watch them, try to say something, but nothing comes out. Even after they lower their voices, they're still fighting. Dad begins to coach me on what to say to the psychiatrist when they come to evaluate me and Mom balks. They argue some more about honesty until visiting hours are over.

After they finally leave for the night, I lie awake, unable to sleep. I run through everything that's happened, try not to cry and fail.

All I can think about is the very end, seeing Lia again. I know it wasn't real, but it doesn't matter, because even though it felt like I was going to die, I got to see her one last time.

She felt real to me, and she came back for me, to save me. And by the time the morning light shines through my window, she reappears again beside me with a small smile as a new doctor comes in.

"Good, you're alone," she says, introducing herself as Dr. Shah, a psychiatrist. "Let's talk about what happened. I hear you took a boat out and then went swimming off the coast of Montauk?" She looks down at my chart. "And you tested positive for amphetamines, hmm. Adderall?" she asks.

I shake my head.

"Focentra?"

I nod, and feel a rise in panic.

"Prescription or recreation?" she asks, eyes still scanning the chart before widening. "I'm guessing recreation?"

I nod again.

"You're not in any trouble," she says, trying to reassure me, but I feel far from safe. Then she asks a series of questions about how much I've been taking and how often.

I glance at Lia. "Tell her the truth," she says to me, so I do.

Dr. Shah watches me, notices the quick glance at the empty chair beside me. "That's a lot of Focentra," she says, but there's no judgment in her voice. "Have you ever seen anything strange, perhaps something you know isn't there?"

"I—" I look over at Lia again, and Dr. Shah definitely catches me this time.

"Are you experiencing a hallucination right now?"

I nod slowly.

"Who do you see?"

"Lia, my girlfriend," I say as an errant tear falls down my cheek. "She died a few weeks ago."

"I'm so sorry," she says, and puts the chart down. "How did it happen?"

"She drowned," I say, unable to tell her the whole story.

"Any thoughts of harming yourself?" she asks. "Particularly on the night you went swimming?"

"No." I shake my head. I think about being in the water, about Hunter pulling me under. I don't ever want to experience that again.

"Okay," she says, but I'm not sure she believes me. "Let's go back to your girlfriend. How long have you been seeing hallucinations of her?" she asks as she takes out a little flashlight and shines it into my eyes.

"Just the night I went swimming," I say, too scared to tell her about Hunter.

"I see. And how much sleep have you been getting?" she continues.

"Not much," I admit.

"And how long has that been going on?"

"Months?"

She looks surprised. "That's a long time. Psychosis is rare with amphetamine use, and usually only occurs when a patient hasn't been sleeping. We'll have to keep you for observation for seventy-two hours. I'll put in a script for a lower dose of Focentra. You've probably been experiencing some unpleasant withdrawal symptoms. I'll also add a sedative, to be given with dinner, and see how you're doing in a couple days."

Dad is furious that they're keeping me for three more days. Mom tries to ignore him as he makes calls to lawyer friends. She just looks exhausted.

"How're you doing?" she asks me when she sends Dad and Aidan off to get lunch.

"Not the best," I admit, and she squeezes my hand.

"There's just too much pressure on you," she says. "On all of you."

I glance at Lia, who's still here with me but quiet.

"What happened out there?" she asks.

I don't even know where to begin, because she's not just asking about that night. "I don't want to talk about it." She lets me get away with it this time, but I know I'll have to tell her the truth one day.

I take the prescribed sedative with dinner, and soon after, I slip away into a dreamless sleep.

When I wake, I blink in the light and search for Lia, but she's gone.

52.

Lia is gone for the next three days and I'm inconsolable. My parents think it's the withdrawal, all my crying and fresh grief, but it's not. On the third night, I stare hard at the pill that comes with my dinner tray. Would it be so awful if I missed one night of sleep just to see her again?

I hide the sedative, pretend I've taken it, and spend the entire night up, miserable, just waiting for her to appear. In the morning, as the light enters the room, she's still missing.

I'm devastated, but I have to keep it together when my parents arrive again, this time with Jo and Rob. They bring big bouquets and give me warm hugs.

"I'm sorry," I tell them. "About everything." Guilt washes over me and threatens to pull me under. "I'll come on the show, whatever you want."

"You're going on Jo's show?" Mom asks, surprised.

"No," Jo says with a sad shake of her head. "I've decided to take some time away from it. We'll be on hiatus. It was a difficult decision, but the right one."

They stay, linger. And in a quiet moment, Jo confesses, "Lia told me all the time, 'I'm not Chase. I'm not like Chase.' And I knew that. But there were times I looked at her like she was just floundering. Directionless. It wasn't that I wanted her to do what I do. I just wanted her to have something she loved as much as I loved cooking and doing the show."

Part of me understands exactly what she's saying because I've felt it too, even if I never vocalized it. I just wanted Lia to know what she wanted like I knew what I wanted.

I was desperate for her to know so I could help her get it, but I never questioned whether it was at all strange to *have* to know what you wanted out of life at seventeen. Or whether we had to take the thing we loved and turn it into a high-flying career, become the best and the brightest.

I never questioned whether there was ever room to not know, to wander, to try something and *fail*.

"I'm sorry," Jo says, but it's not to me. "I'm so, so sorry."

"Me too," I say, because it's true.

When Dr. Shah comes to see me, she asks if I've seen Lia again and I shake my head. No Lia, and no Hunter. Just me alone, for the first time since I can remember. It's terrifying, lonely.

"Any thoughts on harming yourself?" she asks.

"No," I say truthfully. I think about Lia's long stay at a psychiatric hospital, and I can't help but ask if I'll be heading there too.

"I don't think so," she answers. "I try not to refer patients to one unless I feel they're a direct threat to themselves or others. I feel comfortable discharging you as long as you have an appointment with another psychiatrist and an appointment with a therapist, both within a week of discharge. I can make some calls, try and get you appointments set up. You, your parents, and your therapist will also want to discuss rehab options. I'll write you a script for Focentra so you can continue tapering off it."

Sitting in Dr. Quinn's office two days after being discharged feels surreal after everything that's happened. It's strange to be back among the soft pink brushstrokes and neutral furniture. I was first here with Lia, then again searching for answers, and now with answers in hand but still searching.

We meet every day the first week. In our first sessions, I tell her the truth about everything. Lia. Hunter. My memories. The Focentra. The cheating ring. My parents. My grandfather. Aidan. All of it. I'm tired of living in secrets, of living in a performance of Chase Ohara instead of just *being* Chase Ohara.

Dr. Quinn listens, mostly jotting down short notes or offering words of sympathy as I talk. It comes out haltingly at first, but once I tell her about the hallucinations of Hunter, it becomes easier and easier. Since Lia's death, I've been so isolated in this world, so closed off, and the loneliness had been barely perceptible at first, but like a lobster in a pot, it quickly became unbearable, and soon nearly lethal.

"Tell me more about Hunter," Dr. Quinn says. "Why do you think it was her specifically?"

"What do you mean?" I ask.

"Why do you think it had to be Hunter van Leeuwen, European heiress, and not someone else?"

I hadn't thought about it. Or maybe I hadn't wanted to think about it. Even when I understood Hunter lived only in my mind, she had still seemed wholly apart from me, completely out of my control. Another person entirely.

I zero in on the way I felt at the beginning, the story I'd come up with when I thought Lia and Hunter were together—all that resentment, all that jealousy, not just because she had Lia, but because she came from money, because she had power I'd never had. I remember thinking if she'd gotten caught cheating, she'd still be safe. Then I think about Lia, about how before our first breakup back in May, it'd been impossible for me to see the ways she was struggling because all I could see was someone who had this powerful family behind her.

I tell all of this to Dr. Quinn, and she nods, writing a bit in her notes. "You felt unsafe, understandably. You craved stability, control over your life, your future." So my mind invented a girl I could never be: tall, White, rich, beautiful. Someone who seemed in complete control, someone whose name was already atop buildings, etched in gold. It wasn't enough that she had Lia's love—she had to have a life that was out of my reach, effortlessly.

"But now I know the truth: I don't have *any* control. None of us does," I say. Whatever control I thought I had, it was all just an illusion. I had wanted desperately to prevent Lia's death, but in the end, I failed.

Dr. Quinn pauses for a moment and taps her pen against her notepad, like she's choosing her next words carefully. "Maybe we don't often have control over what happens, but we do have a say in how we respond. We do have a choice in how we think about every situation and how we think about ourselves."

At the beginning of our sixth session, Dr. Quinn meets with me and my mom, and we discuss our options going forward. We'd set this meeting up at the very beginning so she could have a period to evaluate my situation. My dad was supposed to come too, but no one is surprised when he can't make it. Dr. Quinn isn't recommending rehab—for now. She thinks that she can work with my new psychiatrist to finish tapering me off Focentra physically, and that in addition to attending local teen AA meetings, I can work with her to address the psychological side of addiction.

I think about that word—*addiction*—and about giving up the Focentra, losing that feeling of invincibility, even if it was always short-lived. That ability to study for a million hours at a time, that sharp focus, that little extra space in my lungs. I think about all we've accomplished, me and the Focentra, even if I no longer care about achievements in the same way. About who I am now and who I'd even be without it. If I can survive on my own.

I have bad days and slightly less bad days. Sometimes I find myself reaching for an Altoids tin that's no longer there. It's worse now that I'm still out of school, that my days are almost unbearably empty. Sometimes I stare at my new prescription bottle and wonder if I can sneak a second pill before handing it back to Mom. Sometimes I make a mental list of ADHD symptoms and almost convince myself I *need* them. But mostly I lie in bed, filled with regret.

"You are not the Focentra," Dr. Quinn tells me in one of our sessions, but I can't help but feel apprehensive.

"Then who am I?" I ask.

"Well, let's see," she says. "You're someone who's been through a lot, someone who's made mistakes, and you're also someone who's acknowledged her shortcomings and who's asking for help—or you wouldn't be here. You're a survivor, and you're someone who loves with her whole heart." She pauses to let the words sink in. She means Lia, and I swipe away a tear. *I still do*, I think but don't say. *I still do love her with my whole heart*.

"As for who you could be," Dr. Quinn continues, "well, let's find out." She gives me a small smile. "I'm rooting for you. I want you to know that."

For the first time since I heard Lia's voice calling me to safety in the water, I feel a small feather of hope.

My mom stays with me that first week, but after our meeting with Dr. Quinn she begins going back to the office, telling me to call if I need anything. She sees how seriously I'm taking my sessions with Dr. Quinn, sees that there's been a shift within me, even if she doesn't completely understand it. She tells me she wants to be able to trust me, and I tell her I want to show her I can be trusted. So she takes the bottle of Focentra I've been prescribed for tapering and gives me back my phone.

I read all the well-wishes and intrusive questions. I find messages from Cole, from all the way back on the day I woke up at the hospital.

Cole: Just heard the news, I can't believe it

Cole: I hope you're okay, seriously

Cole: Call me when you see this?

Instead of calling, I send back a short text, our familiar code.

Me: Wanna hang out?

It's the middle of a school day but he responds right away, and within fifteen minutes his black Lexus is in front of my house. We go for a drive even though I'm not supposed to leave the house. No one is home and I've been going stir-crazy, so I let myself have this small breather.

"Are you okay?" Cole asks tentatively. I can tell he's been worried, and it's surprisingly touching.

"I will be," I say, and maybe I'm even starting to believe it.

"What happened?"

"How much do you want to know?"

"All of it," he tells me.

I don't tell him everything. I don't tell him about Hunter, about my missing memories. Maybe I will one day, but not today. Instead, I tell him about my parents—my dad and his obsessions—and about how hard Lia's death hit me. How much I still haven't processed. He listens as we drive aimlessly.

"Why do you think we did it?" I ask when I'm finished. "Stealing the tests."

I expect him to tell me it was all me, the way Lia had accused me of being unable to do anything without taking it too far, but he surprises me: "I've been thinking about that a lot lately. And it all just seemed so unfair, so impossible—everything we had to do *for college*. Maybe that's the bullshit we told ourselves to justify what we did, but it didn't feel that wrong, honestly."

What he's saying makes a certain sense. Yes, we cheated, and yes, it was unfair. But maybe it was in some ways a rational decision to steal those tests, to seize back that power for ourselves. It was an unfair solution to living in an unfair system. One where success was so narrowly defined, one set up so that the majority of us would inevitably fail. This sense of intense scarcity, the dramatically low admissions rates at the top schools. This life-and-death pressure of getting it right at the age of seventeen or else your entire life was nothing but an immense failure. No second chances, no room for mistakes, doubts, exploration. That was the message we got our whole lives.

"I don't want to do it anymore," I say, but I mean more than the cheating.

"You don't want to pass it on, give it to a junior?" Cole asks.

"No," I shake my head. "I'm done. And I think we should all quit."

Cole laughs nervously. "With finals around the corner?"

"Just tell them we're locked out of the system. What are they going to do?"

Cole looks like he's about to object, but then he smiles. "Honestly? It'll be a relief."

I try to talk him into anonymously e-mailing Mr. Wilson, the librarian whose password we stole, to change his password, but Cole hesitates. He still wants the tests for himself. He may hate the system, but he's not ready to leave it yet. I don't press him.

"When will you come back?" he asks.

Dr. Quinn and I have talked about missing the rest of the semester, but Dad wants me back as soon as possible. I think about what's ahead: homework, projects, papers, finals. The Stanford Early Action decision coming out in a few days. It's too exhausting to think about, so I answer honestly: "I don't know."

Cole seems worried, and part of me is too. Still scared about what might happen to me if I slip up, if I lose control even once.

But I've already lost control, I'm beyond a simple slipup.

I almost died.

Maybe part of me will always be that scared girl watching the grandfather she loves completely at the mercy of her powerful father. But I feel something new emerging too, something that broke free within me as I fought Hunter—myself—in the cold waters off Montauk: a sense of freedom, of wonder, even. Of knowing my old life was over and a new one awaited me if I was brave enough to seize it. Of understanding deep in my bones that everything was *possible* and I only had to reach. And even now, as terrifying as it is not knowing what my future will look like, it's also liberating. I don't want to give up that taste of freedom, not for anything. And especially not for the illusion of safety and security.

When he drops me off back home, he pulls out a fresh Altoids tin and offers it like a question. I did text him our code after all.

I hesitate for a moment. "No, thanks," I tell him.

"You don't need it?" He seems genuinely puzzled.

"I think I just need a friend." It's new for me, this admission. The old Chase never needed anyone, at least that's what she believed.

Cole smiles. "You're all right, Ohara."

For a while, we idle in my driveway. It's cold out but the sky's clear, a crisp blue. "Do you think you'll miss it here?" I ask him when we say our goodbyes. Meadowlark: it's all I've ever really known, this town, this life. It's where I found Lia, where we fell in love.

He thinks for a moment before answering. "No. You?"

I shake my head. "I want to see what else is out there."

53.

Most nights, I climb out onto the roof from my window, wrap a big blanket around myself, and nurse a hot cocoa that always cools too quickly. Often Aidan joins me and we sit quietly, stare at the sky. There's a rhythm to our breathing that's kind of meditative to watch, the way our exhales burst forth against the moonlight and dissolve into the cold air.

She stays out as long as she can stand it, then tells me she loves me before heading back inside. One night, she stays out a little longer than usual.

"I'm scared," she says without looking at me. "Every day I go to school and I'm scared I'll come home and you won't be here. And every night, I go to sleep and I'm scared I'll wake up and you'll just be gone. Forever."

For a while, I don't answer because I don't have the words. "I'm sorry," I say, because that's all I can say. "I'm sorry I make you worry."

"I didn't want to tell you before, but—" She doesn't finish. Maybe she can't bottle it in any longer. Maybe she thinks I'm starting to get better, that I'm strong enough to hear it now. "I'm just scared," she finally says. "I don't want to lose you."

I think about the last time we really talked, when I told her I'd always be here. When I promised her she wouldn't lose me even though we both knew there were no guarantees in this life, no promises that couldn't be broken.

I can't help but feel responsible, like I've been the worst sister in the history of sisters. Dr. Quinn and I have been talking about that word, *responsibility*, about guilt and shame and grief. "Responsibility is simply the ability to respond," she's told me. It's understanding our lack of control and then choosing to act anyway, choosing how we want to act.

I take a deep breath and choose my next words carefully. "I can't promise I'll always be here," I tell her, and she starts to cry. "There are no guarantees, but you will always have me—my love for you, our memories together, this moment. You'll still have me, no matter what." By the time I finish, I'm crying too.

It takes both of us a long time to recover. Finally, Aidan hugs me tight before heading back inside. "Love you," she says.

"Love you too," I tell her.

Alone on the roof, I finish the cold cocoa and wrap the blanket tighter around me. It's only in these moments when I'm out here by myself, empty mug in hand, that I feel closest to Lia. I think about seeing Cole earlier, the Altoids tin he offered, my hesitation. For a second, I thought if I had the Focentra, I could stay up every night until I could see Lia again. For a second, I thought it'd all be worth it if I could just talk to her one more time.

But then there's what I said to Aidan tonight, about how she'd still have me if I were gone. Is that something I really believe? That even without Lia here, I still have her love for me, our memories together, the last time we were out here on the roof, just the two of us? That I'll always have her, no matter what?

I close my eyes, shut out the moon and stars, search for Lia across the universe until fresh tears fall down my face. That's when I find her, feel the love we shared flood through me, a little bit at first and then all at once. I find it through the guilt, through the grief. Through the memories, good and bad. I was terrified that I'd find nothing, but it's still there underneath everything, stronger than ever.

"I miss you," I say.

She doesn't answer, but I feel a surge of emotion and suddenly I'm not cold anymore. There are so many things I want to tell her, so many things I want her to know. But finally, I tell her, "I hope it's better where you are."

We stay out there for a little longer, until I feel her presence wane and I'm alone again. In my room, I lie awake unable to sleep, but it's different this time. There's no frustration, and the sadness I feel is bittersweet. Finally, around 2 AM, I get out of bed, pull on my warmest gear, and lace up. Outside it's just me and the night, the streetlights alone guiding me under the black sky. For once I'm not running from anything, not running toward anything.

For once I'm just Chase Ohara, and there's enough air in the world for someone like me.

RESOURCES

ADDICTION

Alateen

https://al-anon.org/for-members/group-resources/alateen/

Al-Anon

https://al-anon.org/

Narcotics Anonymous

https://na.org/

DEPRESSION

Teenline

https://www.teenline.org/youth

800-852-8336

Depression and Bipolar Support Alliance Local Groups

https://www.dbsalliance.org/support/chapters-and-support-groups/find-a-support-group/

SUICIDE

US National Suicide Prevention Lifeline

988 or 1-800-273-TALK (8255)

Outside the US

UK: 116 123

Australia: 13 11 14

IASP.info or Suicide.org

SURVIVORS OF SUICIDE LOSS

Alliance of Hope

https://allianceofhope.org/

Friends for Survival

https://friendsforsurvival.org/

Parents of Suicides and Friends & Families of Suicides

http://www.pos-ffos.com

ACKNOWLEDGMENTS

TK